I0713202

the
SISTERS
of the
SORROWS COVE

The Goddess Trilogy

Published by Rowan Moon

BOOK ONE: MEGGE OF BURY DOWN

BOOK TWO: THE LADY OF THE CLIFFS

BOOK THREE: THE SISTERS OF THE SORROWS COVE

the SISTERS *of the* SORROWS COVE

The Bury Down Chronicles, Book Three

REBECCA KIGHTLINGER

ROWAN MOON

© 2026

THE SISTERS OF THE SORROWS COVE:
Book Three of The Bury Down Chronicles
Copyright © 2026 by Rebecca Kightlinger

This is a work of fiction. Names, characters, places, and incidents are the product of the author's imagination or are used fictitiously. Any resemblance to actual persons, living or dead, or actual events is purely coincidental.

Published in the United States by Rowan Moon LLC
Meadville, Pennsylvania
Address inquiries to rsk@rowanmoonpress.com

ISBN: 978-1-7343168-8-9 (Soft Cover)
ISBN: 978-1-7343168-9-6 (EPUB)
ISBN: 979-8-9935915-0-6 (Audiobook)
Audiobook Narrator: Jan Cramer
Cover art and book design: Tamian Wood, Beyond Design Books

Library of Congress Control Number: 2025922856
First Edition

Printed in the United States of America

Permission:
"147 [someone will remember us]" from IF NOT, WINTER: FRAGMENTS OF SAPPHO by Sappho, translated by Anne Carson, translation copyright © 2002 by Anne Carson. Used by permission of Alfred A. Knopf, an imprint of the Knopf Doubleday Publishing Group, a division of Penguin Random House LLC. All rights reserved

For David

Μνάσεσθαί τινά φαμι καὶ ὕστερον ἄμμεων

someone will remember us
I say
even in another time

Sappho, *Fragment 147*
Translation by Anne Carson

PROLOGUE

"Amice!" Alf called into the rising wind. He bent his back into another swell as he rowed us toward the waiting ship. "How do you like the sea?"

Amice looked to Ffion and then to me, still wrestling with the demons that had taken her voice.

Barely breathing, I awaited her response as we labored against the tide, leaving in our wake the ancient cliffs that haunted this silent child, the sacred cave that whispered of death and rebirth, and the standing stones atop Cairn Hill, where our past lay in ashes—lost to time, but no longer forgotten.

PART ONE

ANNA

CHAPTER 1

My mother struggled onto her side on her narrow pallet, bits of dust and straw escaping in puffs from a small hole in the seam. She drew a whistling breath through a nose so flat, its wings lay on her cheeks like brittle bark on an aging tree.

Her thin voice rasped, "There should be dancing, my little Anna. The women should bring their best breads and pies, the alewives their finest caudles and mead." She drew a husky breath. "Everywhere else, May Day is a time of sunshine and music. Of rejoicing in the promise of new life. But here . . . here it is something else. Something dark. Something wicked."

She inclined her head toward the cup of poppyseed draught that Eleanor, the healer, had made for her. Never would her numb, shortened fingers have been able to hold the cup, so I put it to her lips. She took a sip, sighed in relief, and lay back. Her voice went low.

"It's time you knew."

A shiver swept through me.

"The fete has been outlawed, but always it comes back. Always a horror. For always, a girl goes missing."

She coughed hard and needed to spit, so I handed her one of the squares I had cut from soft, clean cloth.

"Here, Mother. Spit here."

She spat yellow matter into the cloth, then handed it back to me, took a breath, and continued, her voice strengthening.

"Now, mothers take their girls away—to Aldestowe or Bodmin—where you should have been taken, days ago, to be safe." Anger hardened her voice. She seemed to draw strength from it. She pushed herself up on one elbow and looked toward the door of our tiny cottage. "I begged your father to take you away. But he said you are all we have and that he needs you here to tend to me. That my fears are for naught. That he would protect you should those demons come for you."

"Demons, Mother?"

"Those *Sisters*. That coven of demons. Long ago, they claimed May Day as their own. Like heathens, they called it Beltane. And every May Day morn, amid flowers and feasts, they would crown a 'Sister' Queen of the May. Six months later, on Samhain morn—" her eyes went wide and filled with tears.

I could not take my eyes off hers. "What, Mother? What happened to the girl on Samhain morn?"

"I know only this—that the Sisters called out to the Lady of the Cliffs to summon her back from the dead—and after that rite, the girl they had crowned Queen of the May was never again seen.

"The men issued decrees meant to end that madness, and even now, they believe the Sisterhood is done. But though they have banned those blasphemous rites, I—and all the mothers I know—believe that the Sisters still hold them—in shadow.

"I, especially, fear their rites, for I know—here—" she raised a gnarled hand to her brow and lowered it slowly to her breast, as if drawing knowledge from her consciousness, from her very spirit, into her heart, "that you shall one day face them. So, Anna, there is something you must know." She fell silent.

"Tell me, Mother. What is it I must know?"

"Close the shutters, Anna."

I went to the window and pulled them shut. Soon, I knew, without the breeze to dispel it, the miasma rising from my mother's leprous sores and dying flesh would fill the room.

I sat quietly at her bedside, pushing those bits of straw back into her pallet while I waited for her to speak.

"I felt a stirring the moment you were born," she said. "A knowing." She pursed her lips. The silence grew weighty.

"Mother?"

"The birth pains seized me long before you were due. Eleanor said you would be so small, you would not live. She believed she was comforting me when she said the goddess had blessed you with an early birth. 'For the child will not live to see what will befall you.'"

Mother wiped her lips with a clean cloth, frowned at the streak of blood, and set it aside. "But you did live. And you have seen what no child should see. *Lepra.* This curse. It has taken my life. And caring for me has taken your childhood." A smile tried to come. "If ever you were a child." She reached for the cup. I put it to her lips, and she took another sip. "Why, what Eleanor has taught you has made you a healer yourself."

"It was not only Eleanor—"

How could I explain that a woman's voice came to me each night as I slept and taught me the arts of healing the sick and easing pain at the time of death—arts which Eleanor, though a master of wortcraft, had never known?

I took Mother's wasted hand and held it, careful not to touch her weeping sores or blunted fingers, though I knew that even were I to put a flame to them, she would feel no pain.

"You came into the world so swiftly that Eleanor had no time to make ready. She ordered her apprentice, 'Run to the window and throw open the shutters, that this child's spirit might come.' The moon was full that night, and for a moment, light flooded this room.

But a cloud sailed across the face of the moon, plunging us into darkness." She sat up straight, taking short, rough breaths. "'Quickly!' Eleanor ordered me. 'Ere the child draws first breath. Name her for the one who watches from the ether.'"

My mother was nearly breathless with emotion as she relived the moment.

"I heard a voice," she said. "Not here," she touched her ear, "but somewhere inside me. Somewhere that has no name. A woman's voice. Bold. Assured. 'Name her for me,' she said, 'for she is born with a charge. And should she fall into peril, you need never fear, for I shall be ever at her side.'"

Mother clutched my hand. "And so, I named you for her, that you might call upon her if ever you are in peril."

"Saint Anne?" I asked. "Saint Anne spoke to you?"

She shook her head. "You were baptized *Anna*, and to the world, that is your name. The Church fears the old ways and our powerful women, so we name our girls for their saints. But our true names the priests never hear, for we hold them close and whisper them only in shadow, only when it is just we women."

"What is my true name, Mother?" I whispered.

Her lips moved, but I heard nothing, for my spirit was in another place—and before me was a young woman in white. Standing at a tree stump, she ground seeds under the pestle, like a healer's apprentice, to make ready the salves and draughts a healer might use to cure the folk of this far-flung land.

Turning from the stump, she walked silently along the edge of a cliff beside a many-plaited, black-haired woman, listening as the woman bemoaned her fate. "My very spirit wars with the healer I have become, for I was born to bring not life but death."

The two descended a path to the sands at the foot of the cliff, and the apprentice and five girls gowned in white stood before a shallow stone font deep in a cave at the edge of the sea. Beside the apprentice stood the healer. She held out her hand.

The image of the cave, the women, and the font went dark, and as if a breeze were fanning the pages of a book, images came to me of that young woman in life after life: an archer, a healer, a soldier, a scribe, a woman, a man, a mother, a priest.

"Close your eyes, Anna," said the voice that had long taught me in my dreams.

In my mind's eye, the woman came before me, a huntress with a bow held loosely in one hand and an arrow in the other. A thick leather strap crossed her chest from shoulder to hip, binding her quiver of arrows to her back. A short tunic revealed long, muscular legs above well-worn boots.

"When the goddess returned to the ether that day, I vowed to protect her and make ready a place in the living world where she might return, a healer finally able to wield the terrible power laid upon the goddess at her birth."

I had no reply. What had this to do with me?

"That time has come, Anna, and the place is ready to receive her. Unaware of her true nature, the goddess walks in the living world. After a thousand lives, a thousand false starts, she has but one task to complete before she regains her power. But an obstacle stands in her way.

"It—*he*—has thwarted her in each new life by distracting her from her course, hindering her work, or ending her life. Long ago, in her life as a seer, she made him her apprentice—and he cast her as a witch, burned her at the stake, and stole the writings that held her power. I saved those pages—and put an arrow through his heart.

"In this life, he intends to rob her once more—this time, of the two great books that hold her power."

"Why are you telling me this?" Even in my thoughts, my voice had risen.

"Because he must fail. You must stop him."

"Anna," my mother mused, drowsing under the poppyseeds' spell. "Such a tiny child to shoulder so great a burden, my little Anna..."

Not *Anna*, I thought as slumber claimed her.

"What is my true name?" I asked the woman.

"Your mother named you for me—for Anwen, the Huntress of Tintagel, the archer who avenged a seer's death and guarded her power for a thousand years. Though you do not yet remember, we have walked together many times in the living world. And though I warned you to stay in the ether this time, you defied me. You took the place meant for another, stronger Mentor and are now burdened with her dread charge."

"*Mentor?*"

"A spirit who has vowed to return to the living world when given a charge—a duty to fulfill for the good of another."

Her dread charge.

"But I am so . . ." Wretched, I thought, for I was losing my mother. And innocent, for I knew naught of the world.

But more, I was small. So very small.

"Yes, Anna, you are small. You will always be so—but your small size and sweet countenance will always be your greatest blessings, for the final task the goddess must perform will require the aid of a girl."

The creak of door hinges startled me, but did not awaken my mother. My father entered, waving a hand before his face as he went to the window. When he touched the shutters, my mother stirred.

"Not yet. Not yet."

Silently, he went to the table and lit the candle. The room soon filled with the scent of lavender and rose. Mother thanked him with her eyes and, taking my hand, fell back to sleep.

"Is she near the end, Anna?" my father whispered.

Tears sprang to my eyes, and I nodded.

"I shall go for the priest," he said.

Dusk fell, and through the night, I dripped poppyseed draught onto my mother's lips, and she rested, each rough breath fainter than the last. Soon, I could scarcely hear them, and the silence between them lengthened. Unable to give her anything now but comfort, I dipped a clean cloth into cool water and touched it to her lips, her brow, her neck, her hands.

Dawn came, and with it the priest. My father knelt beside her pallet as the black-robed man shook drops of holy water over Mother and laid a cross upon her bed. He spoke to her in a voice so low that I could hear not a word.

He blessed her with the sign of the cross, listened to her whispered sins, and granted her forgiveness. He gave her communion, then anointed her brow, her hands, her lips, and her feet, while saying his final prayers. When he had finished, he spoke quietly to my father, then blessed us both and was gone.

Mother opened her eyes for a moment and held my father's gaze. "You swore an oath—"

Father nodded and covered her hand with his. As he grieved for his dying wife, I wept for the wise, courageous mother who had given her daughter a loving home—and a valiant protector—before setting her on her path in life.

Mother's lips parted, but no breath came. I pressed my hand to her chest and neck, searching, as the midnight voice had taught me, for the signs of life—a movement, a pulse, a breath, a sound—but there was only stillness and silence. And for Mother, blessed peace.

I blew out the candle and eased open the shutters, that her spirit might finally take flight.

CHAPTER 2

ay Day came, and there was no mead. No pie. No rejoicing. Alone in the cottage that dreary morn, I was strewing fresh rushes over the floor when snatches of talk came through the open door.

"She has no mother," a woman's voice chided. "No woman to raise her as a girl should be raised."

My father grunted.

"And you—you are at your work all day."

My father still made no reply.

The accusing voice then softened, pleading, "Who cares for the child? Who tends to her needs?"

I peeked out the door at the stranger, a woman standing with her back to me in a white robe with a wide hood. She stepped closer to my father, who was sawing a plank, and I drew back into the cottage, my back to the wall, and listened.

"It is a good man who puts the needs of his child above his own wants," she said.

"And it's an evil woman who disturbs his work."

"Anna needs a mother. She needs women about her."

She knew my name! I dared to peek out the door again.

"She's got plenty of women." Father did not look up from the plank. "And you've no business here. Be gone."

"I see no women." Her voice grew fierce. "Let her grow up amongst us. The Sisterhood is a sacred calling."

The Sisterhood—

You shall one day face them.

I dropped the rushes.

"I know naught of your *calling*." My father bent forward so his face was close to hers. "But my wife did. She feared and loathed your coven of demons. That is what she called you—'That coven of demons.'

"'Never the Sisterhood for our Anna,' she ordered. I took that oath and shall keep it until the day I die."

He put down his saw and walked to the door. Before he reached it, he stopped and looked back at her. "She was born for a purpose, our Anna. Not for a sacrifice. Now, be gone."

He came inside and closed the door, but I went to the window and watched the woman retreat from the house. She crossed the field and vanished into the woods.

"Come, Anna. Eat," my father said. Not even he knew my shadow name.

I carried two bowls to the hearth and filled them with a hearty stew made with rabbit meat, turnips, onions, carrots, tarragon, salt, and sage. Savoring the aroma, I set the bowls on the table, and Father closed his eyes, saying a silent prayer.

"Heathen woman," he muttered as he dipped his spoon in his bowl.

Mother had used that word. "What is a heathen, Father?"

"A godless creature. And these *Sisters* are not merely heathens, they are demons. They should be damned to the fires of hell." He blew on his stew and ate.

"She wore a lovely robe."

He laid down his spoon. "Robes are for priests, Anna. For monks. What she wore was the garb of a godless woman." He spat the words. "Who knows those women do to restore to life that . . . goddess."

"Godless . . . goddess . . ." I repeated the words. I had never before heard him speak with such venom.

He laughed, one hard *Hah!* "Godless goddesses! That's right, girl!"

We finished our meal in silence, but I weighed his words. *Godless goddesses . . . fires of hell.*

What did the Sisters want of me?

While Father toiled in the field the following day, I tended the cottage and weeded the herbs. As I dug out a long-rooted weed, my trowel broke. I took it to my father and watched as he fitted a new handle to it, marveling at how, with but a single tap, he could make the nail vanish into the wood.

He handed me the trowel, left the workshop, and mounted his horse. I watched them go, the mare's anvil-sized hooves plodding back to the field, then went to his worktable and studied his tools. They were arrayed on his workbench as neatly as a healer's. Those pliers, I thought, could extract a tooth, and the short, pointed rod—an awl, my father had called it—could be heated to staunch a wound.

From the direction of the field, I heard the mare scream—and my father bellow. Then . . . silence.

"Father!"

I ran to the field just as the mare, head high, nostrils flaring, bolted for the barn. My heart pounding, I searched among the rows of wheat, calling out for my father. Finally, I found him—lying on his back in the dirt, his eyes staring dully into the sky.

Frantic, I cast about in search of someone to help me, but no one lived nearby.

Something moved at the far end of the field. I shaded my eyes to look. A woman appeared to stroll out of the afternoon sun toward me, her robe the soft gold of summer wheat, her hair covered by a veil that fell to her waist. As she approached, she looked down at my father and then at me, and my eyes filled with tears.

In a moment, she was at my side, and I was weeping into the folds of her robe. Her soft voice, her gentle hands, and her very scent—honeysuckle and rose—comforted me. Everything about her soothed.

"Such a dreadful mishap," she said. "Come with me. Let us seek help."

"My father—" I clung to her. I desperately wished I could help him. But I knew—those staring eyes—

"There is nothing you can do for him now but pray."

I had no words, and no prayers came—only more tears.

"What is your name, child?"

"Anna."

"Can you say a prayer to Saint Anne?"

We were walking now, my face wet with tears. She handed me a cloth, and I wiped my face and blew my nose. I looked up at her, and only then did I notice her milk-white skin, her pale brows, and her gentle eyes, the blue of the summer sky.

"Let us find your mother," she said.

The tears came afresh.

"You are an orphan?" She knelt before me and took my hands. "Who will care for you?"

My breath caught. I had just heard those words. From that godless woman. That *Sister.* The shiver up the back of my neck warned me not to tell her the truth. "My family will."

I drew away, pulling my hands from hers. I had not seen the Sister's face or hair the day she had angered my father, but I heard something of her voice in this woman's.

She stood and looked all around. I followed her gaze. There was naught but wheat. In the distance were tiny cottages and huts, but no one to help me.

"Such a small settlement," the woman mused. "No one to take in an orphaned girl. No one to put food in her empty stomach." She took my hand again, and her blue eyes held mine. "I am called Magdalene, and I have a home and food for orphaned children. For forsaken girls like you."

Before I could insist that I was not forsaken, she led me through the field and away from my home.

"I, too, lost my father," she said. "And like many children, I was forced to wander alone. But one day, a kind lady claimed me as her own and gave me a home."

As we walked, she told me of the many girls she and the lady had helped. When finally she went silent, I looked over my shoulder, wanting to run back home, but I could not see my cottage. I turned in a circle, looking all around. We had walked a long way and were alone at the edge of a wood.

She clutched my arm and moved me swiftly through the trees until we neared a high, rounded hill. Just beyond the hill was a cliff, and beyond that, the sea.

"Do you know what this place is called, Anna?"

I shook my head. Never had I been this far from home.

"They call this cove *The Sorrows*," she said. "Do you know how it got that name?"

Again, I shook my head.

"As the tale goes, a sailing ship was lost at sea, and the cove was named for the grieving wives of the men who had lost their lives. But much longer ago, the women of the cliffs lost even greater a treasure—and it was that loss for which the cove was named. You have much to learn, Anna. I shall teach you."

The setting sun colored the sea blood-red. I had to look away—and saw just beyond us an ancient church with a high stone tower. The woman pulled me toward it.

The path to the tower, nearly hidden in deep grass, was so narrow it might have been made by feet stepping heel to toe in order to leave only the merest mark. As we walked, the grass seemed to spring up behind us, so we left no sign of our steps.

A wooden bar crossed the great tower door, held in place by brackets on the wall on either side of the door. A hinged iron plate affixed to the top of the bar had a hole near the end that fit over an iron ring bolted to the center of the door. From the ring hung a lock nearly the size of my hand. Magdalene put a key in the lock and turned it. She freed the lock from the ring and pulled the plate down. With a grunt, she pushed the bar out of the brackets, letting it fall to the ground with a thud.

Why was this door barred from the outside? Goose flesh rose on my arms. I wanted to run.

Magdalene knelt before me and studied my face. She ran a fingertip over my cheek, just below my left eye, and nodded.

CHAPTER 3

ake off those boots, Anna. They are caked with mud."
Magdalene's silken voice had gone harsh and cold, her soft
eyes hard as flint.

She held out her hand, and I gave them over.

"The stockings, too. You'll not need them."

Before I could ask why the door was barred—and locked—from
the outside, she heaved it open and shoved me inside. The stench of
filth and excrement made me retch.

Magdalene put her shoulder to the door. Groaning with the
effort, she pushed with all her might and shut it. She drew a wooden
bar from a hole in the right side of the door's stone frame, pulled it
across the door, and fed it into a slot on the left. Like the bar on the
outside of the door, this one also had a hinged metal plate with a hole
near the end. She lifted the plate, slapped it over an iron ring bolted
to the door, and hung a lock from the ring. When she slammed the
lock shut, the clash of iron locking iron stopped my heart.

"Sisters," Magdalene said with a clap of her hands. "Meet Sister
Seven."

Six girls clad in thin, grey tunics crouched against the wall on
the far side of the tower. Silent, with their knees drawn up to their

chests, they clasped stick-like arms around skeletal legs. The biggest girl looked up and caught my stare. Tears welled in green eyes much too large for her face. With her eyes on mine, she nodded her head, a slight movement, then looked back down. None of the other girls had even looked up.

Though it had been spring outside, it was winter in that tower, and the stone floor was icy against my bare feet.

"There is power in the earth, child," Magdalene said. "Power that seeps in from the soles of our feet."

Hers, I noticed, were shod in leather boots.

"Come, girls." She clapped her hands. "It is time for the evening meal."

The girls got up slowly, shivering, their threadbare tunics no match for the sea winds whistling in through a window high above the tower door.

In the wool tunic I feared would be taken from me, I fell into line behind them. A long, narrow table along the far wall was set with wooden cups and bowls.

Magdalene went out through a small door opposite the big tower door and returned a moment later with a pot of broth, a loaf of bread, and a jug. She ladled broth into the bowls, filled the cups with pale liquid, and dropped a sliver of bread in front of each girl. There was no fruit, no wine, no cheese.

She pulled out the stool between the two tallest girls. How had she known, I wondered, that she would need a seventh?

"Sit, Sister Seven." She pushed me onto the stool and lifted her chin toward the food before me. "Eat. Be filled."

I pulled on her sleeve. "I want to go home now."

"This is your new home."

"But I—"

She narrowed her eyes. "Are you a willful girl, Seven?"

I shook my head. But I did not want a new home. In my home, I had hot meals, a soft bed, and a warm embrace before sleep.

"We are your family now," Magdalene said. "These are your Sisters."

This pale creature was not my kin. And these haunted girls with their bony hands and dead eyes—they were not my sisters.

Some squirmed in their seats, but none spoke. I looked from face to face, all gaunt, all with pale skin marred by boils and scabs. Their heads were bare, and five wore their sparse, dirty hair in lank plaits. The youngest's hair, coarse and tangled, might have been hacked off with a knife.

Magdalene left us through that same small door. As she opened it to leave, I looked through the doorway. It opened into the church. Magdalene slammed the door and threw a bolt, locking us inside.

The girls fell on their food, the youngest ones cramming their bread into their mouths, and the eldest, the two beside me, soaking theirs in their broth before chewing it slowly and with great care. How long had it been, I wondered, since they had last eaten?

But for the sound of chewing and swallowing, silence reigned.

I picked up my bowl. It was cold. I looked inside—broth. I sniffed—no scent. I sipped—no taste.

I leaned closer to the girl on my left, the second eldest, hoping she might speak to me. Though her bowl was empty, she put her arms around it and bent over it, breathing fast, her breath stinking of decay. She turned her head and looked at me, suspicion in her deep blue eyes.

"No, Miss, I don't want your food."

I cannot stay here. I cannot become one of . . . them.

Magdalene returned to the tower and began picking up the bowls. When she took mine, I tugged once more on her sleeve.

"I would go home now," I insisted. "I pray you, Lady—take me back."

Without replying, she crossed her arms and studied me for a very long time. Finally, she pursed her lips and nodded.

"Tinker will come for you." She turned and went out through the church door.

She's fetching someone to take me home!

Joy and relief buoyed me. I was going home!

CHAPTER 4

It was still dark when Magdalene opened the lock, drew back the bar, and pulled open the tower door. A gust of wind blew leaves and dirt inside. But neither the sound nor the breeze awakened me, for I had not slept. I had no blanket, and neither the thin pallet nor the threadbare shift Magdalene had given me when she took my tunic had protected me from the cold hovering over that stone floor.

Heavy boots thudded as someone entered the tower.

"Where is she, then?" a man demanded.

"Here." Magdalene pulled me to my feet, and I swayed from hunger.

He bent close enough for me to see a smooth face even fairer than Magdalene's—pale skin without blemish; wide, full lips; eyes the green of new grass.

His lips tightened into a thin, straight line, and he held out a hand to Magdalene.

She untied a small leather pouch from the belt at her waist and opened the top. The man looked inside, and when he nodded, she gave it over.

"That will be all, Tinker."

He hefted the purse, making it jingle, then secured the drawstrings to his belt.

"Walk, girl." He pushed me toward the tower door.

The rough stones scraped my tender feet, and the jagged ones cut my toes.

"My shoes," I pleaded.

"There'll be no more shoes."

He tugged me outside, and Magdalene, with one last look at me, closed the door. The lock inside the tower rang shut, and dread seized me.

As much as I wished for a warm cloak, I desperately needed my boots, for stones bruised and sliced my feet as this *Tinker* pulled me behind him along the path until we had reached the edge of the cliff.

Are you a willful child, Seven?

Magdalene had paid this man to throw me over the cliff!

My breath came so fast I could not even scream.

I looked over the brink. Far below was a vast, sandy beach scattered with purple and black rocks. No one was in sight—only the far-off sea, its angry waves thundering in the weak, near-dawn light.

He pulled me down a rock-strewn path covered in briars. I stumbled, then cried out as he dragged me down the hill, the stones cutting my knees, and his hand crushing mine.

"Stop that wailing." He lifted me roughly into his arms and carried me to the beach, then dropped me onto the cold, damp sand and stalked into a cave that seemed to go deep into the sea wall.

I was too frightened to scream and too bruised to run. Where would I have gone? The beach stretched for miles with no huts or cottages in sight, only a hill in the distance with a trail that wound up the side, and black clouds were rolling in over the sea.

I could hear the man moving about in the cave. Metal clanked against metal, much as it did when the blacksmith was assembling his anvil and tools to shoe Father's mare.

Was this man a blacksmith?

Why would a smith drag a girl to a cave?

I had to escape.

My settlement was near a cliff—perhaps this was it. Mother had never allowed me near it, so I could not be sure. Perhaps if I crept toward the path on the hill, I could find my way home. The hill was steep, and the trail wound back and forth up it. It would be a long, hard climb, and the storm was nearing.

I edged away from the cave's gaping mouth. Sharp rocks cut into my feet, leaving blood in my tracks. Despite the pain, once I reached the sand, I ran.

The path was much farther away than it had first appeared, and the gathering storm clouds thundered. The wind rose, lashing my face and arms, and the rains let loose, drenching my shift so it clung to my legs. I lifted my hem and continued to run.

Footsteps pounded behind me. Breath huffed.

A powerful arm came around my waist and pulled so hard it stopped my breath. I thrashed. I tried to scream, but the man, cursing and shaking his long, golden hair out of his face, caught me up under one arm and strode back toward the cave. My head bobbed so hard, I feared my neck would break.

I kicked and bit—to no avail.

The sandy beach passed beneath his thick leather boots. Then those sharp, black rocks. And there it was.

The cave.

Deep inside, a fire leapt in a grate, illuminating small metal tools laid out on a low bench as precisely as Father's or Eleanor's.

What is he going to do with those tools?

He hauled me past a tall stone font and into the belly of the cave, where the fire, the bench, and all those tools lay. I shut my eyes. Afraid that if I screamed he would hurt me, I forced myself to be silent.

He flung me to the ground and held me there, his knee crushing my chest. I opened my eyes to see him reach for a cloth and a blade. I sucked in a breath. My chest nearly burst as I held it. Bending over me, he thrust his face into mine, his lovely features now contorted into a mask of hatred and rage. His eyes mere slits, he looked as if he might spit in my face. Instead, he thrust the cloth into my mouth, grabbed my tongue, and pulled.

He is tearing it out!

Animal sounds clawed from my gut to my throat and filled the cave. I shrieked like a rabbit being killed.

He swept his blade across my tongue, setting my mouth afire.

Blood sluiced down my throat, gagging me. And still he held my tongue. Something burned my chin. I opened my eyes to see a poker glowing red.

Through my screams, I heard a girl shout, "Stop! Oh, Father—stop!"

A small figure lashed by the rain stood at the mouth of the cave.

"Britlen!" His hand still clamped on my tongue, the man lowered the poker. "Get out of here. Go. Now!"

The girl stood as still as that stone font.

"Leave." He brandished the poker. "Now."

"You've hurt that girl!" She turned to flee. "I shall tell Mother," she warned. "I am telling her!"

He let go of my tongue and lunged for her.

Blood gushed from my mouth, so I clutched what remained of the bleeding stump and held it as tightly as I could. I wanted to run, but could not move for the fear that gripped me.

But I saw.

Just as he had done to me, he grabbed the girl, dropped her to the ground, and planted a knee in her chest. With two fingers, he prised open her eye. As she begged him to stop, he touched the poker to it. She screamed and fell silent, and then he blinded the other.

"Tell your mother," he warned the nearly lifeless girl, "and I will carve out your tongue and slit her throat."

He left her lying still and silent in the pouring rain. I crawled backward to escape, but in three long strides, he was upon me.

He clutched my tongue, pulled it hard, and pressed the glowing poker to it.

"Tell one person—*Sister*—and my blade will sing over your throat."

I awoke in the tower, my mouth afire. I tried to cry out, but my tongue was so thick it would not form words. And the pain was a wild thing. I would have thrashed, but my arms were bound to my sides.

"Magdalene," I tried to cry out. "Magdalene—" The name I could not utter tasted of blood.

"Hush, Sister." She bent over me. Looking at her face, I believed I was seeing one of the angels painted on the wall of the great church in Aldestowe.

Then I looked into those cold blue eyes.

She lifted a cup to my parched lips. "Drink."

I drank, and Magdalene's face faded away. But Tinker's followed me into the dark.

CHAPTER 5

Over time, I became nothing more than Sister Seven, and I grew accustomed to the silence. My name was never uttered, though I heard it in my dreams, for no one could silence those.

Words pushed against my throat, but my tongue, that block of char, could not give them voice—nor would I have spoken. Who knew what that horrid Tinker would do to me if Magdalene told him I could speak?

I dreamed each night of rescue, of my father bursting through the tower door.

"Anna!" he would shout. Then he would lift me into his arms and carry me home.

Even now, I can recall the solace that blanketed me in those dreams—and the despair that swamped me when I awoke.

During the waning days of summer, we Sisters hoed, planted, and weeded the garden inside the walled courtyard. Sister One, the eldest of the girls, worked alongside me. The high stone wall enclosed the crumbling church, which had but one lovely feature—a stained-glass window that reached from my waist to a height far above my head.

Sister Two, the feral girl who guarded her food, weeded alongside Sister Six. Her watchful blue eyes were ever upon me, but her stare was never more wary than when we were at table.

Did she still fear I would snatch a morsel from her plate or a sip from her cup? Even had I wanted to, I never could have, for the moment Magdalene set her bowl before her, she grabbed it, brought it to her lips, and drank.

Every night was the same. When we finished our meal, we would pile our dishes beside the small church door. The bolt would rattle, and Magdalene would come inside, pick up the dishes, and leave, bolting the door behind her. We would pull our pallets to the center of the floor so we could lie close to the cold grate in which Magdalene would light a small fire before eating her soup. As we warmed ourselves, she would tell us the tales of the goddess and healer she claimed we would one day call back to the cliffs.

One night, as she set down the tray that held her bread, soup, cup, knife, and spoon and lit the fire, it occurred to me that while she was in the tower, the church door remained unlocked. As the fire's warmth spread over me, I looked with longing at that door. But, knowing I could not escape, I ordered myself to be satisfied that the small fire had dispelled the cold.

My hunger gnawed as I watched Magdalene spoon her glorious, meaty soup into her mouth, but it lessened as I lost myself in her story.

"Did you know, Sisters, that the Lady of the Cliffs cured the lame, the weak, and even the lazar?"

The Lady could have cured Mother? Why had Eleanor never told me?

I moved closer to Magdalene and watched her face as she recited the remedies I knew by heart for the sores and the wasting and the loss of breath that had taken my mother from me.

"No potions or poultices healed those marred by lepra," she said. "Only the Lady held the cure."

If the Lady of the Cliffs could have cured Mother, I thought, why had she so loathed the Sisters? It was their calling to return the Lady to the living world. I looked around the circle at all those girls, and I remembered. *Always, a girl goes missing.*

"Sister Seven." Magdalene motioned for me to sit beside her. "I see how you regard the other Sisters." She lifted her chin toward Sister Two. "Do you distrust them?"

Five pairs of hollow eyes looked dully at me, but Sister Two's stare pierced me. I looked at each girl and shook my head hard.

No! I said with my eyes and a shake of my head. *I don't distrust you! I pity you! I pity all of us!*

"You girls are called Sisters because you are joined in spirit. You are as close as if you had the same mother—for you do. The goddess. Did you know, Sister Seven, that the goddess had two sisters of her own? They were called Clotho and Lachesis."

I had never heard of them. Frowning, I tilted my head.

Sisters Five and Six drew in their breath.

Magdalene exhaled hard. "No one remembers the goddess's sisters! Clotho and Lachesis. The Sisterhood was named in their honor. One day, you too will be a true Sister—one of the Circle of Six, the mortal daughters of the goddess."

How can there be seven Sisters in a Circle of Six?

But even more perplexing was how the goddess could have been my mother. I knew who my mother was, and she had not been a goddess. I shook my head. *No.*

"Yes, Sister Seven." Magdalene turned and spoke to the others. "In the living world, we all come from mortals." She doused the fire. "But our spirit comes from the goddess herself."

Lying in the dark after Magdalene had left the tower, I wondered if that were true. The priest had taught us that God had created us and that God was a man. That God was our protector.

But my mother had told me that women had power. Did she mean we had the power to protect ourselves? And if she knew where

I was, would she tell me that no man—not even Father, not even God—could rescue me? That I had to save myself?

I struggled to breathe.

And so, I named you for her, that you might call upon her if ever you are in peril.

Anwen! How had I forgotten?

Had Anwen known I would one day be imprisoned in this tower? Had she seen Sister Two's slitted blue eyes stalking me? Had she seen Magdalene and Tinker and known I would need to escape?

Was the Huntress with me even now?

From across the tower came low, throaty sounds. The meager light from the high, narrow window revealed Sister Two hunkered with Sisters Three and Four.

As one, they lifted their heads.

Three pairs of Sister-eyes seized my gaze, driving me under my sheet.

I shut my eyes tightly and silently called upon the one who had promised to protect me.

"Anwen."

CHAPTER 6

"You are no Sister, Anna."

There she was, behind my closed eyes—Anwen the Huntress.

I could breathe again.

"Nor will you ever be. But Magdalene will speak to you as if you were, and you must allow her to do so. She will call you *Sister Seven,* and you must never object. You must be silent. Silent and obedient." She let me think about that for a moment. *"Obedient,* Anna."

"Yes, Anwen."

"But you will speak to me in your thoughts, in this silent tongue, lest you forget your words. And we shall converse as adults so that you may speak as a woman when the moment comes. You are a child no more. You are strong. You are whole. And when I give you leave, you may speak."

"I haven't uttered a sound since Tinker took my tongue. I cannot speak, Anwen."

"You can—and one day you shall."

"Never! Not while Tinker lives."

"I may ask you to remain silent even longer than that, for the goddess's spirit is at grave risk. I cannot tell you my reasons for this, only that you must trust me and obey. Tell me you understand."

"I do not, Lady, but I trust that you will make me understand."

"Very well, Anna. I am ever with you. Whatever befalls you, be strong. Never cry. Never speak. Nod and obey. And be kind to Sister Two, for she is consumed with fear."

As the days grew shorter, the girls' sidelong glances at Sister One made me ever more aware of words unspoken. Of fears unexpressed.

Why are we here? I wanted to ask them. *Are we to be kept in this tower forever?*

Through an averted gaze or a shake of the head, the Sisters warned me to stop questioning them with my eyes.

But their empty eyes spoke the words I asked Anwen each night as sleep eluded me—*What did I do to deserve this?*

"You did nothing, Anna—nothing to deserve this."

Eyes closed, I rode the gentle waves between slumber and wakefulness, and Anwen came to me in spirit, tall and strong, her quiver at her back and her bow in her hand.

"Why, then, does no one search for me? Why has no one sought the other girls?"

"Do you remember what Magdalene said the day she found you? That she had . . ." Anwen coaxed.

What had Magdalene said? That she . . .

"That she had a home and food for orphaned children . . . for forsaken girls like me. But I was not forsaken, Anwen."

"Nor were the others. Five were orphans, but Sister Two yet had a father."

"Why has he not sought her?"

"He has, Anna. He searches without cease. But Sister Two lived far from here. Never would her father think to come to the cliffs, and to this desolate place—after so long a time—in the hope of finding her."

"My mother knew of the Sisterhood. Other mothers did, too. And Eleanor must have known. Why have none of the women come for me?"

"Though your mother had distant memories of the Samhain rite, this church is believed forsaken and the tower accursed, so no one, not even Eleanor, would think to seek a lost child here."

"If that is so, then I will never be found. I am well and truly alone."

"You are not alone, Anna. We are talking, are we not? Are these moments in spirit not as real as any in your waking day?

"One day, you will find the ones to whom you belong. One will take you in, and another will call you *friend*. When this happens, you will know you have found your home. But first, there will be hardship. Fearful times. Times that will demand courage, which you have always possessed. And restraint, which you have so often lacked. It was your rash will that tore you from the ether's calm to take up this perilous charge."

"The ether?"

"Yes, the ether, where we abide between lives. In each new life, your ancient spirit has been reborn. One day, you shall be reminded of who you once were and all you once knew. And until then, I shall always be at your side, whispering in your ear, guiding you, and keeping alive the speech you will one day need."

"Must I one day speak?"

"When the time comes, you will want to. But I will tell you when you may do so. On that day, though you appear a child, you will speak clearly, as one much older, for you and I shall have conversed like this every day."

Sleep began to take me under.

"But, Anna," she warned, "until I allow you—"

"Yes, Anwen, I shall hold my silence till you bid me speak."

CHAPTER 7

When the leaves had turned the color of flame, Sister One went very still. And when those leaves began to fall, her fading green eyes cast shifting glances about the tower as if gauging the thickness of its walls, the weight of its massive door, and the height of that narrow window.

When the branches went bare, she stopped searching. She also stopped eating. Not a sliver of bread or a sip of soup passed her lips. Her cheeks were sunken, her skin ashen, her lips pallid.

"We've but three days," Magdalene announced as she opened the tower door. It was not yet dawn.

She clapped her hands once. "It is time to rehearse for the Samhain Rite."

I got into line behind Sister Six.

Magdalene held me back. "You are not yet one of the Circle of Six. *I* shall teach you your vital role."

She led the Sisters out of the tower and later returned carrying a large, silver ewer filled with water.

"On your feet, Sister Seven. And watch." She walked across the tower while carrying the ewer, then turned to me. "Now, you."

I carried the water between the doors, wanting only to run through them to freedom.

"During the Samhain rite," she instructed, "the ewer will at first be empty. You shall carry it to the font, fill it with water, and present it to the woman garbed in white."

Carrying water was so simple a thing. How could my part be *vital*? How could carrying water matter when the other Sisters were summoning a goddess back from the dead?

Magdalene left me alone the next day while the others rehearsed. As I shook out the pallets and swept the floor, I moved my tongue inside my mouth as I did when I "spoke" to Anwen.

She had said I could speak. Could I?

I listened at the door for approaching footsteps. Hearing none, I blew a puff of air between my tongue and the roof of my mouth to see if I could sound the letter *t*.

It sounded as loud as a thunderclap! I slapped my hands over my mouth. Anyone might have heard!

I saw the glint of Tinker's blade. Felt its bite. Heard that sizzle. Tasted the char.

As long as Tinker lives, I vowed, I will not utter another sound.

Two nights before Samhain, Sister One trembled beneath her thin blanket, her hands clasping each other tightly over her breast-bone. I got up and went to her. Her dull green eyes searched my face as I covered her with my blanket. Under Sister Two's ice-blue stare, Sister One touched my hand in thanks, then closed her eyes and pulled the blankets up to her chin.

I returned to my pallet and saw through the window the waning moon. A girl would need only the merest light to escape, I thought.

I wrapped my arms around my chest, pretending those arms were my mother's. The tears came, and my nose ran.

A rustle came from across the tower. Heart thudding, I opened my eyes.

Sister One was dragging her pallet across the floor.

She laid it next to mine and covered us both with those two ratty blankets. She wiped my eyes and nose with a corner of her blanket, and we turned on our sides, her chest to my back, and slept.

Magdalene tore away our blankets and kicked Sister Two awake long before dawn. She led us into the church and down the long aisle to a door that was even taller and wider than the tower door. Something else was different. I studied it.

The drawbar had no lock.

Magdalene pulled the drawbar from its slot on the left and pushed it into the hole on the right, then gripped the handhold and pulled with all her might. It slowly opened with a long, low moan. I looked on the ground outside the door for the other bar. There was none. Nor were there brackets on the door frame.

This is the only bar! And it is on the inside!

But what did that matter since the door between the tower and the church was always bolted?

"Sister Seven!" Magdalene pointed with her foot to a pile of dirty white robes lying on the ground near three barrels of water and two long poles.

"You and Sister Two shall launder my robes for the Samhain rite."

Sister Two dropped the robes into a barrel of soapy water and sloshed them up and down with a pole. I joined her, and though the strong lye burned my hands and arms, I plunged those robes with all my might.

"The hems, girls," Magdalene called. "They must be pristine."

She dropped a heavy, long-sleeved black tunic on the ground.

"This is the priestess's," she called as she walked back to the church. "Wash it quickly and hang it in the sun. It must be dry by dusk."

Sister Two picked up the garment with the thumb and first finger of each hand and held it up by the shoulders. Both of us could have fit inside. She dropped it on the ground and kicked it away.

I lifted my hands and tilted my head to ask, "Who is the priestess?"

Sister Two's mouth twisted in revulsion, and she shuddered.

Glancing into the barrel of white robes, she took out the pole and used it to push the filthy, stinking garment closer to me. I looked up from it, and Sister Two lifted her chin toward the other barrel. I dropped it in and watched the water go dark. I plunged it until my shoulders ached, then rinsed it, wrung it, and hung it to dry, all the while wondering about the priestess who wore this huge, black tunic and why Sister Two detested her so.

CHAPTER 8

t dawn on Samhain Eve, clad only in our dirty, tattered shifts—and starving, for we were fasting for the ceremony at hand—we followed Magdalene, in her freshly laundered white robe, to the courtyard. An old woman wearing that awful black tunic and leaning on a knotted stick shambled in through a gate in the high stone wall. I watched the other Sisters and, like them, bowed my head as the priestess came before us. Though I kept my gaze from meeting hers, I could not look away from the nightmarish crone with the grizzled hair, pewter eyes, and downturned mouth.

She pointed her stick at Sister One. "Are you a virgin, Sister One?"

Sister One only trembled.

"Are you?" the priestess demanded. "Are you a virgin?"

Prodded in the back by Magdalene, Sister One nodded.

A rough hum of satisfaction sounded in the priestess's throat.

"Sister One," she said, raising her chin, "eldest Sister and Queen of the May. Yours is the honor of returning to the cliffs the goddess and healer Atropos, that her touch may cleanse us of dread disease and restore the spirit of the afflicted. Tell me you accept, Sister One."

The girl did not move.

Tapping her foot, the old witch forced a falsely sweet, gap-toothed grin on the terrified girl.

"Do you, Virgin One? Do you accept this charge? Or shall I send you off with Tinker and let Sister Two take your place?"

Sister Two gasped.

Sister One only stared.

As did I. Never had I seen anything as sinister as this old gargoyle. She bent forward, bringing her face close to Sister One's and breathing so hard that the girl turned away, wincing.

"Do you, Sister One?" she barked again.

Sister One shrank from her. Bringing her hand to her breastbone, she gripped something beneath the neck of her shift, then took a long, slow breath—and nodded her head.

"All is ready for the Samhain rite," the priestess declared and lumbered away.

Magdalene turned Sister One and nudged her. "Walk."

We followed in a grave procession back to the tower, starving for the bowl of cold broth that Magdalene would serve and eager for the fire she would light.

After we had eaten, Magdalene took away our bowls and returned with her own bowl of steaming soup and a tall, pewter cup. She savored the soup, then picked up the cup. Surrounded by seven shivering, starving girls, she lifted a jug and filled the cup with hot amber liquid. She took a sip, smacked her lips, and looked at each girl, stopping when she came to me.

"Do you know where the goddess dwelt, Sister Seven?"

Dwelt? I shook my head, wondering when she would light the fire.

"The great healer once lived in the sea cave you saw when you first arrived."

The cave where that vicious butcher cut my tongue? Where he blinded his daughter and left her for dead?

Horror gripped me. I could not swallow.

"It is said that all who descended to the goddess's cave would be cured. And they were." Magdalene sipped and tilted her head. "Alas, the goddess died. She took her own life—there, in that very cave."

She took her own life? That accursed cave—that place of blood and fear—once claimed a healer?

"Every Samhain, in the goddess's cave, the Sisters perform the sacred rite in which the Lady of the Cliffs was lost to us." She smiled now as if in bliss. "Come the morrow, she will return, and never again shall the people of these cliffs suffer sickness, pain, and untimely death, for the Lady, now at her rest in the ether, shall dwell forever amongst us. Forever in the living world."

CHAPTER 9

"On the morrow, Anna, you shall see Magdalene blaspheme a hallowed rite," Anwen said. "For no plea from this *priestess* will bring the goddess back."

"Why did she take her own life?"

"Because she carried within her the seed of death."

"Did it kill her? This seed?"

"It killed something within her. The best part of her, she believed. Something she could not live without."

So she ended her life, I thought. There, in that cove. That is why they call it *The Sorrows*.

"Magdalene said the goddess is taking her rest in the ether," I said. "But you said she walks amongst us, unaware of her true nature."

"You hold fast to what you hear, Anna!"

"If the goddess walks amongst us in the living world, how can Sister One restore her to life?"

"She cannot. Magdalene has not told you the truth, for she does not know the truth. Atropos has walked in the living world many times, but never again as a healer and never at the summons of a false priestess.

"In each of the goddess's lives, her mother and I have tried to awaken her to her true spirit, but either she shuns her duty, or the 'obstacle' I spoke of hinders her. Awakening her will be a mighty task, and it must be done in this life. It must be done while she abides at Bury Down. Sometimes, Anna, terrible steps must be taken to fulfill such a charge. This is such a time. This is why you are here."

"Berry . . . Down?"

"Not *Berry* Down, Anna. *Bury* Down. A place of timeless hope, of sacred healing. I have been called to Bury Down many times—to instruct, to guide, and to serve."

I pondered that as she held my gaze, her eyes urging me to understand.

"But now, you are here. Have you come to teach and guide me?"

"Yes, Anna. And to serve you. As you shall one day serve—"

Something lurched inside me. "Not Magdalene."

"No."

A tremor shot through me. "Not the priestess in the awful black tunic."

"No, Anna. You do not yet know this woman. You shall. But first, you must endure this place."

This tower. That cave.

The butcher.

"Why did he hurt me, Anwen? That terrible knife-man they call *Tinker*. Why?"

A shadow fell over Anwen's face. "Someone hurt Tinker in a long-ago life—so badly that the pain damaged his very spirit. And each time his spirit returns to the living world, it is more enraged and seeks ever more wrathful vengeance against women."

"Why women?"

Anwen's face clouded, so I gently asked, "Who hurt him, Anwen?"

"A woman he loved." The clouds darkened. "He was a warrior. A swordsman. He returned home after years of battle and found his wife with another . . . woman." Her voice went low. "He slew his wife. Then he drew his blade on her lover." Her eyes glittered. "But she nocked an arrow—and pierced his heart."

Anwen nodded to herself. "In this life," she went on, the cloud now lifting, "his rage was kindled by a shame not his to bear—though he felt the pain of it all the same."

"Whose shame was it, Anwen, and why did Tinker feel the pain?"

"When Tinker was a boy, his father—a widower—fell under the spell of a lovely young woman named Jenifer. They married, and soon after, she bore him a child. But the child was not his, for she had loved another man, and he had cast her off. Desperate to find a husband before her child was born, she cast her eye on Tinker's father—an older man grateful for her love.

"Tinker was still a child when he learned that his father had been deceived, but the shame of being a cuckold's son awakened his rage, and he began to kill. Animals at first, and then women. With the help of another damaged soul, he burned his stepmother and his half-sisters at the stake. But vengeance did not slake his lust for slaughter—it stoked it. Now he vents his fury on helpless girls."

"The Sisters."

"Yes, the Sisters. The black-garbed *priestess* needs your silence—and something more—and she pays Tinker well to provide her with both."

CHAPTER 10

amhain had yet to dawn when Magdalene entered the tower carrying a bundle of garments the color of spring leaves. As she passed each pallet, she dropped one upon it.

I reached out to touch my pristine, light-green robe.

"Do not—" she warned, pointing a finger at each of us. "You will bathe—with soap—before you touch these robes."

I felt I would faint from hunger and prayed that Magdalene would return with bread. But she walked to the door, apparently finished with us.

"This is a sacred rite," she said over her shoulder, her hand on the door, "so you shall fast until it is done."

She returned carrying a bucket of frothy water and a few small towels. Without a word, she left the tower, and the Sisters looked to Sister One.

With her hands at her throat, she stared at the water, and wept.

Sister Two went to her and eased her hands from whatever it was she gripped beneath the neck of her shift. She untied the strings at the neck of Sister One's tattered shift and pulled it over her head, revealing a cord of braided thread around her neck. From it hung a piece of stone—rough and grey, like the stones that had cut my feet on the trail to the cave. Wrapped in thread, it was tied to the cord. I stared at it. Had I seen it before? No—I never had. But I wanted to touch it.

She stroked it as the Sisters washed her face, her neck, and her arms. There was no clean water with which to rinse her, and I feared the harsh soap would burn the sores dotting her skin. But her dead eyes and slack mouth never moved even as the Sisters held her new robe high and lowered it over her head. It fell from her knobby shoulders to her poor, plank of a chest, to her nettle-scarred ankles, but its sleeves did not reach her wrists.

While the other Sisters bathed and dressed, I loosened Sister One's braid and raked my fingers through her thin, greasy hair, easing the snarls and plaiting it once more.

As I moved toward the bucket of water to wash, she touched my arm, halting me. Reaching up, she lifted the string over her head. Her gaze held mine as she lowered it over my head, dropping the stone beneath the neck of my shift. I put my hand over it and covered that hand with the other.

I will keep it safe, I told her with my eyes.

I washed and hurriedly donned my new robe just as the church door opened and Magdalene entered, long sashes draped over her arm. She handed each Sister a crimson sash, and they tied them around their waists. She handed me a yellow sash and gave a long tallow taper to Sisters Two through Six.

"You know what is expected of you." She looked at each of us in turn. "You will obey in that cave and fulfill your duty."

Had the Sisters paled because of their fast, or had fear of this *duty* blanched their skin? Several trembled. Sister One went very still.

"Go now." Magdalene ushered the six outside.

"Not you." She held me back. "Not yet."

Grey clouds in the distance crept over the sea as the girls filed around the base of the high, round hill and stopped at the edge of the cliff.

As Magdalene and I walked behind them, buffeted by the wind, she swept her arm out over the sea.

"This cove was named *The Sorrows* on the day the goddess took her life. And when Clotho and Lachesis followed her into the ether, the women of the cliffs, desperate for aid, sought to lure her back by playing the parts of those she had loved best—and the Sisterhood was born.

"Today, the Sisters shall call to her once more."

Standing at the edge of the cliff, Sister Six, her posture rigid, her eyes wide, looked to Magdalene for her cue. Magdalene nodded, and she began to descend the path, followed by Sisters Five, Four, and Three. Sister Two, however, stopped and looked at me. Her intense blue eyes held my gaze. She closed them for a long moment, slowly opened them, and was gone.

Sister One now stood at the brink. She looked over her shoulder at me, her green eyes gentle, her countenance calm. Bowing her head, she followed the others down the path to the cave.

"We shall go this way." Magdalene pointed to the rock-strewn trail that Tinker had dragged me down.

Brambles tugged at my robe, and nettles scratched my ankles and stung my bare feet as I picked my way down the steep trail. I bit back screams as my heels skidded down a patch of sharp rocks. The tide was out, so the sand was dry, but the storm clouds were upon us. Swirling winds flattened our robes against our backs as we entered the Lady's cave, not through its mouth but through a tall, narrow fissure that opened into a passage leading to the rear of the cave.

I followed Magdalene through its depths, lost in the shadows. Far ahead, near the cave's yawning mouth, was the font I remembered and the fire grate I could not forget. Guided by the fire's light, Magdalene led me to the spot from which we would watch the Sisters perform their rite.

Led by Sister Six, all the girls except Sister One filed into the cave, heads bowed, candles at their waists. One by one, they approached the fire and lit their tapers. Golden light danced over five somber faces that turned as one when a tall, slender woman gowned in white, her hair and face obscured by her hood, glided from a passage across the cave and halted next to the font.

The priestess?

No—this was not the old woman in the dirty black tunic. Were there two priestesses? I looked at Magdalene, the question in my eyes.

"She is called 'the disciple.' She serves in the priestess's stead. The priestess could not make the treacherous descent, so she waits in the church for Sister One's gift."

CHAPTER 11

hunder rolled in the distance, and all eyes turned to the mouth of the cave as Sister One entered, eyes blank, hands empty. Her breath came fast, and her lips moved silently.

The disciple glided to the font, raised her arms, and one long, golden lock escaped from her hood and fell over her shoulder. She nodded to Sister One, then lowered her arms, and Sister One approached, gaze flat, shoulders bowed.

She wiped her palms on her robe and knelt before the font. The other Sisters formed a half-circle behind her.

Rain drummed as Sister One stretched her arms over the font, holding her trembling hands palms up.

The disciple turned to look into the dark recess where I stood trembling. She extended her arm and summoned me.

Magdalene laid in my palm a slim silver rod tipped with a gleaming blade. "Go."

There had been no knife in our rehearsal. There had been a ewer—only a silver ewer. What was that woman going to do with that knife?

"Go to her." Magdalene nudged me. "Go!"

On rigid legs, I took step after step until I stood before the disciple. I held out the knife.

She took it from me and dipped the blade in the font, just as Eleanor had always dipped hers in water before pricking my finger for my mother's cure.

Magdalene beckoned me with a wave of her arm, and I returned to her, wondering when I would be summoned to carry that ewer.

Sister One's hands now trembled over the font. I wished I had known about this part of the rite. I could somehow have made her understand that it would not hurt. It would just be a prick—

The disciple swiped the blade over Sister One's wrists, and twin bursts of red pulsed from her arms and flowed into the font. I bent forward, hands on knees, and tried to calm myself.

"Sister Seven," Magdalene hissed.

I could not look up.

"Sister Seven!"

I lifted my head. Magdalene held out the ewer. "Take it."

Holding it in my trembling hands, I stood dazed. The disciple stretched out her arm to me. I could not move.

Magdalene nudged me, and I looked up to see the Sisters lower Sister One to the ground.

"Go!"

Somehow, I took step after step toward the disciple and dipped the ewer in the font, filling it with water the color of those crimson sashes. The disciple snatched it from me and strode out of the cave and into the blinding rain.

Unsure what to do, I looked to Magdalene. She held up one hand.

"Stay," she hissed.

Trembling, I beseeched Anwen, "Let Sister One live—and let her blood be strong."

The Sisters surrounding Sister One wore expressions of desperate hope, while I looked down with sorrow and dread at Sister One, so pale, so still.

Something scuttled from the passage through which Magdalene and I had entered the cave. *A rat.* I saw only its tail as it disappeared into the blackness. I wished I could follow it into the shadows.

As one, the Sisters drew a sharp breath.

The goddess!

I turned to look.

It was the disciple, her pounding footsteps scattering the pebbles at the mouth of the cave. Her wet robe clung to her as she strode to the font. She lifted a dripping arm and beckoned me. In her hand was that knife. I feared my bowels would loosen.

"Go," Magdalene urged.

She had not mentioned this part, either. I searched the cave. There was nowhere to run, and hiding in the shadows would not save me. One careful step at a time, I approached the disciple.

Head bowed, hands clasped at my sash, I stood before her. Not knowing what to do, I waited. She said nothing and remained still.

What is she waiting for?

I had to look.

I raised my head, and the tip of that blade bit into my cheek just below my left eye. I gasped, but dared not scream. The disciple wiped the blade on her robe and, without a glance at me or the other Sisters, turned and walked out of the cave.

Sister Two came to me and pressed a cloth to my cheek. I closed my right eye, exhaling in relief that I could still see out of my left. She took my hand and put it on the cloth. I held it tightly against the wound and struggled to slow my breathing.

Sister Two knelt beside Sister One, untied her sash, and drew it from beneath her. She gently removed my yellow sash and tied the crimson one in its place.

Weeping now, I followed her to the row of Sisters and took my place beside Sister Six.

"Look at me, Anna," Anwen said.

I looked into the distance, trying to find her, but saw instead the eyes of another woman—golden-brown eyes, like mine. I could not look away. My hand dropped from my face, and Sister Six pressed the cloth firmly to my cheek.

The stinging pain returned my attention to the cave. That awful woman in white had gone, and the rain had stopped. Magdalene came out from the shadows and led the procession out of the cave and up the path, leaving Sister One behind.

At the top of the cliff, Magdalene pointed to the high, round hill. "Do you know the name of this mount?" she asked.

I shook my head.

"It is called Cairn Hill. Do you see the standing stones at the summit?"

I looked to the top of the hill and nodded.

"The goddess's ancient cairn. There lie her ashes—and those of her forgotten sisters."

CHAPTER 12

even girls had gone into the cave—but only six had come out. Would Sister One soon join the goddess and her forgotten sisters atop Cairn Hill?

We six stood side by side in the tower, awaiting our orders from Magdalene.

She looked at Sister One's pallet.

"Sister One lacked the blood strength to restore the Lady, so she has gone home." Magdalene looked now at Sister Two. "And you, Sister Two, are now Sister One."

Sister Two covered her face with her hands and wept. I wanted to go to her, but Magdalene's voice halted me.

"Sister Seven—" Magdalene looked hard at me. "You are now Sister Six."

Six Samhain rites away from the summit of Cairn Hill, I thought.

That afternoon, I opened a small hole in the seam of my pallet. That night, after we had supped, I tore a piece of cloth from my shift, wrapped bits of bread crust and turnip in it, and slipped it through the hole.

I was lying next to the girl I had known as Sister Six—now Sister Five—when Anwen came to me.

"Magdalene told us that Sister One had gone home," I said. "Is she truly alive and in the arms of her family?"

I hoped Magdalene had spoken the truth. And if so, I hoped I, too, would lack blood strength when called upon to restore to life the Lady of the Cliffs. I cared nothing for cures. I wanted only to go home.

"Another lie. The girl you knew as Sister One perished." Anwen held up a hand when I began to weep. "But she did, in another sense, go home."

I struggled to understand.

"She is one of us, Anna. Her charge fulfilled, her spirit returned to the ether."

"Her charge?" I brushed away my tears and wiped my nose on my arm. "She had a charge, Anwen? What was it?"

"To pass you the stone."

I touched the stone hanging from the braided string.

"What does that mean?"

"When Mentors return to the living world, we do not at first know those with whom we once walked. So when two Mentors must find each other in the living world, another is sent ahead to mark them."

"Sister One was sent to mark me?"

"Yes."

"With this stone?"

"Yes, Anna."

"Who will know me by this stone?"

"The woman you seek. She will not know you at first, but you will know her by the stone, much like yours, that she wears."

"If I know her, why will she not know me?"

"Much has been kept from her, Anna, for her own good."

"What are you keeping from her about my stone?"

"That it marks you as kin."

CHAPTER 13

fter a very long winter, spring finally arrived, and in a somber Beltane rite in the walled courtyard, we crowned the blue-eyed Sister Two—now Sister One—Queen of the May.

Always a horror, I heard Mother say. *For always, a girl goes missing . . .*

Just as she had feared, I had gone missing the day after May Day.

This must stop, I decided, before Magdalene brings us another Sister Seven.

As our gaoler led us back to the tower, we passed some flowers that had just opened in big, yellow blooms. I looked closely at one.

Horned poppy.

"What part of the horned poppy do we use?" Eleanor would ask me as we made ready to tend my mother.

"The seeds," I would reply.

"How are they prepared?"

"Soaked and steeped."

"For what purpose?"

"To bring forth sleep."

"But?"

"But the seed of the horned poppy is more potent than any other poppy seed and can bring forth a sleep from which the dreamer never awakens."

Magdalene walked at the head of the line, and I at the tail. Feigning pain, I knelt and pretended to pick a thorn from the sole of my foot. But I was snapping off poppy seed pods and picking up rocks—one flat and one round and heavy—and sliding them up my sleeve.

"Sister Six," Magdalene scolded. "Come along."

Sister Six.

I clasped my hands at my waist, bowed my head, and rejoined the line behind Sister Five.

That evening, along with the new Sister One, I looked all around the tower, searching for a way out. The doors were locked, the window impossibly high, and not a single gap between the stones would allow even a mouse to slip through.

No girl, I was certain, had ever escaped.

But I had seeds of the horned poppy—and I was skilled in their use.

When darkness fell, I laid my flat stone on the floor, then shook seeds from each pod onto it and crushed them with the big, round rock. The crunch of the seeds was lost in the sobs of Sister One crying herself to sleep.

CHAPTER 14

Throughout that spring and summer, Magdalene had no time for her garden, so we Sisters hoed, planted, and weeded from dawn until dusk. Now and then, though, we had periods of rest when Magdalene would leave the tower, wearing either her white or her pale-yellow robe, and lock us inside for the day.

She's hunting a girl.

High summer came, and still there was no new Sister. Magdalene had become anxious and angry—and as her time at the font drew near, Sister One had withered. Her skin had gone pallid, her vivid blue eyes nearly grey.

She will not last until Samhain.

One afternoon, when our gaoler had gone out hunting, I opened the hole in the seam of my pallet and took out several of the crusts I had hoarded. I was about to pass them to Sister One when I heard Magdalene's voice outside the church door.

Someone was with her.

The back of my neck prickled.

Not a new Sister, I prayed.

A man's hoarse voice barked, "The Samhain fete? She and Kaatje ended it years ago, and now *she* is performing that blasphemous rite?"

It was not a girl! I went weak with relief. But who was this man? I listened.

Heavy footsteps sounded again, and I could almost see him stalking away from the door, turning, and approaching again with an outstretched arm, an accusatory finger aimed at Magdalene.

"I've heard talk, Magda. Tales, I believed. So I've come to see for myself that they were lies. But you tell me they are true?"

"One girl, Michael. The priestess takes some blood from the arm of a girl. It causes her no pain, and the girl gives it willingly." Magdalene's voice was higher than I had ever heard it. There was silence for a moment. "She does it for you. It is *all* for you," she spat, "as it has always been."

"How does she get this girl?" he demanded. "Does she set a trap? Or do you seize her from the market road as she makes her way home? And how does your *priestess* take the blood? Does she bleed her like a surgeon?" he shouted. "And afterward, does she send the girl home to a mother who says nothing?"

Magdalene did not reply.

"Why does the sheriff not come to this place and haul you both off to the gallows?"

"It is no crime to perform the Samhain rite. And for the Sisters—the starving orphans whose lives we save—it is an honor to give up their lifeblood for the Lady."

"Their *life*blood? You just said, 'some blood.' Are you as mad as your *priestess*?" he scoffed. "Are you telling me that young girls willingly give up their *lifeblood*, as you call it—their lives—so that an old conjurer can resurrect a goddess long dead? Is this how she intends to cure me?"

"No!" Magdalene's voice shuddered. "Or no longer." Her footsteps moved to and fro across the doorway. "Restoring the goddess's life was our intent. But in the next Samhain rite, she shall use the maiden's blood not to return the goddess to us, but to create a new cure that will heal you."

"So." He exhaled hard, and his tone went dark. "She will take a life—an innocent life—to concoct a potion no more likely to cure this damnable disease than her spells and potions and poultices have been? Look upon the result of her *cures.*"

A gasp. A gag. A moment later, retching.

"Every village healer uses blood cures, Magda. They fail. Do you think I have not used countless such cures? If she has nothing more to offer, I'll go, and this will be the last you'll see of me."

Shuffling footsteps and sharp taps sounded in the church and grew louder until they halted outside the door.

"Yes," came the rasping voice of the priestess herself. "Until now, Michael, blood cures *have* failed you. We both know why."

The man did not reply.

"What have I told you I require?"

"That damned incantation." The man sounded defeated. "From those damned books."

Books?

"No potion alone will cure you now," said the priestess. "Nor will a goddess who spurns our call. Magda soon will bring me a maiden, so gather your men and do what you must to bring me those books— and the blood of the whore."

"I will not."

"The priest told you true—if you are to be cured, you must be absolved of your sin of fornication. And I am telling you that to do so, you must drink a potion I shall prepare with the blood of the whore and that of a maiden. The maiden's blood will cleanse the whore's, so it may absolve without further staining you. But I must have the incantation in those books at Bury Down."

Bury Down? I struggled to slow my breathing. *What has the priestess to do with Bury Down?*

"Bring them to me by Samhain Eve, and I shall cure you."

The man did not speak, and I could not glean what his long silence meant. Was he going to refuse? To barter? To curse her?

To thank her?

Let him refuse, I prayed. Let him open this door and see us. Let him take us away from this place.

"Claris is no whore." He spoke each word calmly, coldly—and then thundered, "Her blood needs no cleansing. And I will have naught to do with the blood of maidens. I will not accept the blood of a girl."

The priestess's voice went sly. "Tell me, Michael," she taunted, "How many innocent women—*and girls*—have gone to their deaths at your hands?"

He did not reply.

"Do not play the saint with me, Michael. Bring me the books and the blood."

"You will not take another child in my name."

"Or what?" she snapped. "You will refuse your cure? Look at yourself. Why, you are nearly a corpse now. No, you *are* a corpse—a corpse that wants naught but the grave. And only I have the cure you need."

Another long silence.

"I shall bring you the books."

No!

The priestess snorted. I could hear her shuffling steps and her stick striking the floor as she moved down the church aisle, followed by the man's ringing ones, the sounds growing softer until the door to the courtyard groaned shut.

I held my breath.

"Make him change his mind, Anwen. Make him open that door, storm back down that aisle, and demand to search the tower."

Silence.

My slow exhalation deflated me.

That man, so sick that the priestess had him called a corpse, was going to take blood from a whore—whatever that was—and steal the seer's books from Bury Down.

These, I thought, must be the books Anwen spoke of. What was it she said?

That they held the goddess's power. That he would rob her of them.

That I must stop him.

He sounded like a big man.

Sister One sat up on her pallet, her upraised hands and the tilt of her head asking what she had just heard.

I knew what *I* had heard, but questions assailed me—the most compelling, *Who was that man?*

Only Tinker had ever come to this place, but the priestess had sought—for years, it seemed—to restore life to the goddess just to heal this one. And now that his disease had worsened—so terribly that seeing his face had made Magdalene retch—she was about to resort to blood cures.

"Hold out your finger, Anna," Eleanor would say as she prepared one for my mother. "A drop of your pure maiden's blood will help your ailing mother."

I would feel the quick prick of the knife's tip and watch my blood flow into her shallow bowl.

"You're a good girl, Anna," my mother would say as Eleanor mixed my blood with arsenic and hellebore, then rubbed it over Mother's weeping sores, her sunken nose, and the stumps that had once been her fingers.

My blood had never helped her.

As I recalled my mother's soft, rasping voice, I heard once more the shout of that outraged man. "... so an old conjurer ..."

Not "a priestess," but "an old conjurer."

He did not worship the priestess as Magdalene did. Rather, he held her in contempt. He knew that the potions she would brew from our blood would never cure him.

Magdalene knew this, too. Now that she had seen that the man was dying, did she understand that our blood would be spilled for naught? Or had seeing his suffering strengthened her resolve to rid him of the scourge that was taking his life?

CHAPTER 15

The trees flamed, the leaves fell, and the light coming through the tower window went dark earlier each night. Sister One, now naught but bone and sinew, wept ceaselessly. One night, as we waited until dark for Magdalene to return from her hunt, the tower was still but for Sister One's sobs and the distant roll of thunder.

Magdalene threw open the church door and slammed six bowls and a pot of cold broth on the table. She left without a word, flinging the door shut and throwing the bolt.

We Sisters all looked at one another. Magdalene was frequently vexed, but never had I seen her enraged. Samhain was nearing, and as each day had passed with no Sister Seven to witness the rite and become the new Sister Six, she had become ever more desperate.

Sister One filled the bowls, her hands trembling. She ladled a little more broth into my bowl than she had into the others, and as she handed it to me, she smiled. I had never seen a Sister smile before. Sister One was missing several teeth, and those she had were black.

She had suffered enough, I decided. We all had. And soon, if Magdalene had her way, another child would be brought in to suffer alongside us.

I have poppy seeds, and I have rocks. One or the other will allow me to do what I must this night.

"Anna," Anwen's low voice warned, "what are you about to do?"

"I need not see another Samhain rite to know what must be done here."

"You are not to harm Sister One." Never before had Anwen appeared daunted. "She has a charge."

"Sister One?" Baffled, I shook my head. "Sister One has a charge? What is it?"

Anwen seemed not to have heard me, for she looked away for a moment, thinking, and I saw understanding dawn. She looked me in the eye. "I shall distract Magdalene. Do what you must."

While the other girls sipped their broth, I drank mine to draw from it what strength I could. Then, with all stealth, I reached into the hole in my pallet and drew out my rocks, my hoarded food, and the tiny cloth bundle that held the poppyseed dust. I hid them all beneath my hip.

Magdalene took away our dishes and returned with her evening meal arranged on her tray.

Wind whistled in, and just as Magdalene glared up at the window, a bolt of lightning lit the tower, and thunder cracked. She shrieked, spilling hot soup down her tunic. Gasping, she tried to pull the hot, sodden cloth away from her skin, but thunder crashed and she jolted again, spilling yet more soup on herself. Cursing, she set the tray holding her bread, soup, knife, and spoon beside her pallet and left the tower, bolting the door behind her.

With five pairs of Sister-eyes fixed on me, I poured the crushed seeds into her soup and stirred, praying there would be enough time for the seeds to steep.

Magdalene returned only moments later, wearing a clean tunic. She tore off chunks of her bread, dropped them into her soup, and ate with deliberate slowness, her smug gaze sweeping over us with each spoonful she savored. She wiped the empty bowl clean with the heel of her bread, then finally lit the fire and settled in to tell her tales.

"Shall I tell you about the goddess's shish-tersh?" Magdalene rubbed her eyes with the heels of her hands, then shook her head as if to clear it. "Clotho sh-pun thread." Her speech slowed. She swayed. "Lache-shish measured it, and Atroposh, with her . . ."

The Sisters stared at her, frowning. But their brows lifted and their eyes lit when she fell back on her pallet, the story still on her lips. Moments later, when she had not moved and did not appear to breathe, the Sisters turned to me as one, their enormous eyes asking, "Did you kill her?"

I did not care if I had.

I gathered my blanket and rocks and snatched Magdalene's knife. I glanced into the church. Empty.

I took hold of Sister One's hand and pulled her through the doorway. The other girls followed, and we fled.

Sister One and I pushed back the drawbar, then pulled on the handhold with all our might. When the door did not budge, I hefted my heavy rock and threw it through the stained glass window. I wrapped my blanket around my hand and began breaking off shards of the thick glass.

A growl drew my attention. Sister One, her face dark with fury, gripped the handhold and pulled. To no avail. She grasped it again, leaned back, and, bellowing, pulled again. The door flew open. On the other side stood a broad-shouldered man in a hooded black cloak, his arm still outstretched from pushing on the door. I could not see his face, but I knew the voice that cursed, "Jesus Christ!"

We girls gaped at him.

"How many—" He did not stop to count. "Run!" he shouted. "Go to your homes. Tell your fathers what has befallen you here."

The girls fled into the gale as the man charged into the church, his boots ringing with each stride down the aisle. I stood at the door, watching the man's back—so grateful to him, I could neither think nor move.

Sister One, having nearly arrived at the courtyard wall, halted, turned, and ran back to me.

"H'ank you," she said, her voice mostly wind. Then, her pale blue eyes tight on mine, she kissed me—hard—and vanished into the night.

CHAPTER 16

ehind me is the church. Ahead of me, the sea. To my left, more sea. To my right, Cairn Hill. Which way—

"Around the hill," Anwen ordered. "Run! Beyond it is a small settlement."

Thankful that the rain had stopped, I ran through the punishing wind around the base of Cairn Hill toward the cottages and huts I could see in the distance.

When I reached the first cottage, I was freezing, weary, and nearly broken. But—for the moment—free.

Hanging on the drying line outside a hut was a tunic with no sleeves or hem. Beside it hung a pouch made of the same cloth, the drawstrings so long they could wrap around me.

"Take the tunic, Anna," Anwen urged. "Put it on!"

Shaking, my arms covered with hen-flesh, I grabbed the tunic from the line and pulled it over my head. It was so large, it nearly swallowed me. I pulled the pouch from the line, dropped my food, knife, and rock into it, and tied the drawstrings around my waist so it hung at my hip. A moment later, I took out the knife. I hoped I would not need to use it.

"Ahead is a willow grove and a spring," Anwen directed. "Go!"

I flung my blanket over my shoulders and fled the tiny settlement, running so hard I feared my heart would burst. I took shelter among the trees, shivering beneath my blanket, my knife clutched to my breast.

"Tinker must live nearby," I said to Anwen. "Magdalene will send him searching for us when she awakens."

If she awakens.

"Tinker is nowhere near, so you may rest. Sleep here, Anna," came Anwen's soothing voice. "You have done good work this night. When you awaken, walk toward the rising sun. That way lies the River Camel. Follow it to the moors, a great distance from here. Speak to no one, and do not stray from your course until you reach the market road just beyond the moors. I will tell you then where you must go. It will be a long journey, but my voice and your dreams shall guide you. Do not fear. Sleep now, and when you wake, walk."

I walked for hours each day, sleeping in glades along the River Camel and hiding from those who might have offered me succor.

Eating garden vegetables, roots, mushrooms, and fallen fruit, I was better fed than ever I had been in that tower. My arms and legs gained muscle and fat, and my skin, soothed by the late autumn sun, went brown as I made my way to the moors.

CHAPTER 17

picked my way through a vast wilderness of brambles and scrub, finally coming to a rutted road. From around a bend came the creak and rumble of a cart.

I took cover in a thicket.

The cart stopped, and an old woman got down. She put a hand to her brow and searched the woods, calling, "Lass! You, girl! Come out."

I hid behind a tree and watched as a much younger woman descended from the cart, her sheer veil failing to cover the brilliant, gold-touched red of her hair, which tumbled in waves over the shoulders of her bright blue tunic. Holding the hand of a flaxen-haired girl who swept a stick over the ground before her, the younger woman shaded her own eyes and, like the older woman, searched the woods for me. The girl stood quietly beside them until the driver, a clean-shaven man, jumped down from the driver's bench and spoke to her.

She raised her head to speak to him, and I saw her eyes—white. And I knew. This was the girl from the cave—the one Tinker had blinded and left for dead.

My heart leapt to see her alive, and I wondered if these people had rescued her. If they had, might they rescue me?

"You are nearly there, Anna," Anwen said softly. "Let this cart pass and continue on your way. You are tired and ready to be done with this journey, yet you must go on. Alone."

Tears stung my eyes as I watched the younger woman tenderly help the blind girl—her daughter, I supposed—into the back of the cart. How I wished I were still protected and cherished like that girl.

The old woman stood in the road, still searching the woods. All at once, she stopped, gazed steadily my way, and closed her eyes. She stood very still, her hands clasped at her waist. Finally, she opened her eyes. Still looking my way, she nodded.

The cart rumbled off, and I followed the road until the afternoon light was nearly spent and I had reached the foot of a slope dotted with grazing sheep.

"Where do I go, Anwen?"

"At the summit of this hill is a grove. See the oaks? They will give you cover. At their roots you will find truffles. Rest there. The woman you seek has already seen you, for a Mentor has sent her a vision. She will come for you."

My breath came fast. "How will I know her?"

"Surely, you have not forgotten." Anwen spoke lightly, her voice no longer laden with warning.

I absently fingered the stone at my throat.

"This?"

"She wears one as well. And you will see that she looks a bit like you, with your golden-brown hair and eyes. With her, you will feel a kinship you have felt only with your mother. And she will take you in."

Winds tore across the summit, but stilled in the grove. I sat at the foot of an oak and dug in the earth with Magdalene's knife, searching for truffles. Twilight gave way to night, and I slept.

The sound of footsteps moving over the soft forest floor woke me.

A frisson of warning shot from my gut to my throat.

A woman with long, flaxen hair stepped into a patch of moonlight. *Magdalene!* Brandishing my knife, I ran from her.

The woman followed me, shouting, "She has a knife!"

Before me, at the edge of the grove, stood another woman, her hair blowing in the wind, one hand held up to halt me. "You are safe, little one."

I looked from her to the willowy woman.

"Anwen," I called, "Help me! I'm trapped!"

"Look closer, Anna."

The wind dropped, and the second woman brushed long, brown hair back from her face so it fell in wild curls over her shoulders and down her back.

The clouds parted, and moonlight glinted off a silver ball at her throat.

She wears one as well . . . golden-brown hair and eyes . . . she will take you in.

Relief surged through me, purging my fear and strengthening my legs. I ran until I collided with her, knocking her to the ground. She wrapped me in her cloak and held me fast.

Warm for the first time in such a long time, I lay safe in her arms with Anwen's voice at my ear. "Your journey to Bury Down is over, Anna, but you have yet to fulfill your charge."

. . . he intends to rob her once more—of the two great books that hold her power.

. . . I must have the incantation in those books at Bury Down.

He must fail. You must stop him.

Anwen spoke with compassion—and finality. "The same charge binds both you and the goddess, and you must not fail."

Sleep was overtaking me.

"Do as Megge asks," Anwen said. "Watch and listen. Heed your dreams. And hold your silence until I bid you speak."

I awoke warm and dry—and swaddled like a corpse.

Thrashing, I fought my way out of what I came to find were two heavy cloaks. I stood and looked all around. The crimson dawn heralded a storm, so I searched the hill and pastureland for refuge. At the foot of the hill was a cottage, its door cut in half, with only the top half open. Firelight glowed in the kitchen, and fragrant smoke rose from a stone chimney.

This was the woman's cottage. Megge's.

She will take you in.

She was watching my every move, her gaze puzzled and tender by turns. That silver stone—the stone that marked this *Megge* as my kin—hung at her throat.

Unaware of her true nature, the goddess walks in the living world.

Megge . . . I stared at her. The woman who was once the goddess.

She looked nothing like a goddess. I had imagined golden robes, perhaps a halo or a crown. But her head was bare, and she wore an old brown cloak and leather boots as heavy as mine had been.

I reached into the neck of my tunic and brought out the stone Sister One had given me.

As Anwen had foreseen, Megge did not know it as our mark of kinship, for she only touched her own stone.

"My mother gave me this," she said. "Did someone give you yours?"

Unable to turn my eyes from her stone, and still bound by my vow of silence—and Anwen's order—I kissed my stone and dropped it back into its hiding place.

Megge held out her hand. I took it, and we walked down the hill to her cottage, where a rooster and a flock of hens pecked in the dirt with their chicks. The aroma of hot food wafted from the kitchen. I wanted to burst into the cottage and eat my fill, but a young herder with shining dark hair caught my eye—and my heart.

My gaze clung to him as he opened the gate to a pen and released the sheep. Carrying two rattling buckets in one hand, he put his other hand to his mouth and whistled, then swept the sheep before him. I tried to whistle as he had, but merely blew out spittle.

Clouds rolled in, pelting us with raindrops the size of pebbles, so he herded the sheep back into the pen. I watched him, waiting to see what he would do. Would he come to us? Would he speak to me?

Megge tried to entice me into the house, but though thunder cracked and lightning tore the sky, I was unable to move. Megge sheltered us both beneath her cloak, but soon it began to leak. Still, I stayed, watching that herder and waiting for him to find me.

Once the sheep were safe in their pen, he ran to the cottage, and I followed him inside.

"This is Alf," Megge said as we dried ourselves with soft, clean towels. But somehow, I already knew—and loved—this sweet, gentle soul with the crooked smile.

Days later, when Megge could not persuade me to speak of my family or tell her my name, Alf decided I should be called Amice— "for *friend*," he said—and I knew I had found my home.

PART TWO

CHAPTER 18

Nestled between Ffion and Megge on our bobbing little boat, I watched the sea creep toward the shore, bit by bit devouring The Sorrows Cove.

"Amice!" Alf's shout startled me from my reverie. "How do you like the sea?"

How did I like it? I had hoped never to return to the waters that would forever call to mind the cave in which Magdalene had forced Sister One to die. I had just begun to feel at home and safe at Bury Down, with Megge, when Anwen awakened me with the words I had hoped never to hear: "It is time for you to fulfill your charge, Anna, and for Megge to complete her final task."

And the very next day, Megge and Ffion had taken me back to the cliffs, where I—and Megge, in another life—had so badly suffered. Now, at the end of that treacherous journey—a pilgrimage for us both—Megge watched me intently. Was she hoping I would shout a reply to Alf?

Tinker was locked away in the earl's gaol, so perhaps I should have felt safe enough to speak. But he was still alive, so I did not—for if the priestess's tower could not hold me, then no gaol would hold Tinker for long.

CHAPTER 19

MEGGE

I would honor my promise never to ask Amice to speak, never to demand that she tell me what had befallen her in that tower. But every morning since the day she entered our lives, I had asked myself, *Will this be the day she breaks her silence?*

Lips tight, eyes grave, she glanced at Ffion and then studied my face. *Perhaps today?*

CHAPTER 20

I smiled at Alf and waved, knowing he expected no more from me, then settled back between Megge and Ffion, and slept.

I awoke when our boat gently nudged the side of *The Navigator*. Neville, the stonemason who had subdued Tinker in the village and then forced him to reveal all he knew, waved to us. He and the earl's man, Hugh, leaned over the side of the ship and lowered a rope ladder.

With a broad smile lighting his face, Neville extended his arms in welcome. I smiled at him, and he laughed, pointing to his own front teeth. I knew he never would have laughed had he known how I had lost mine.

"Come aboard, Amice," he shouted.

Does he believe I can climb that wall?

"Martyn," Megge said quietly, seeming to have had the same thought, "I don't think—"

But Martyn was already tying the ends of the ropes to the rowboat's seats while assuring me that it would not be hard to climb.

I tipped my head back and looked all the way up to the top of the ship's side. It looked as high as the tower.

Ffion asked, "Are you afraid of a ladder, Amice?" The elderly woman with the black, black hair picked up both the sack she had brought from her hut and the bulky, heavy sack that held Megge's books and set one foot upon the lowest rung. "You simply climb."

"I'll carry those sacks, Ffion," Alf offered and reached for the heavy one.

"No, Alf." Megge reached for it. "I'll take it up."

I wondered how either Ffion or Megge could manage that climb while carrying such a heavy sack.

Alf looked at Megge. So did Ffion. Finally, Megge nodded.

"I'll keep it safe," Alf promised, and he held out his hand to Ffion.

"Hold it tight, Alf." Ffion handed over both sacks and gripped the ropes.

I gaped as she climbed the swaying ladder. Once at the top, she raised a hand to Hugh. He and Neville pulled her aboard. Leaning over the rail, she called, "You see, Amice? It's nothing!"

I stood on the seat, steadying one side of the rope ladder with my injured hand. I grasped the other side with my good hand and stepped onto the lowest rung. Megge stood behind me. As I climbed, she followed me up. When I reached the top, I held out my good hand to Neville. He gripped me beneath my arms with his strong, gentle hands and lifted me off the ladder.

"You're a brave girl!" he told me as he set me on my feet.

But I had never been brave. I had merely trusted Anwen. Now, I knew I could trust Neville, too.

CHAPTER 21

MEGGE

No sooner had Neville taken Amice aboard than the wind picked up and waves began to toss the boat. Though Alf and Martyn steadied the ropes, the ladder swung back and forth. My palms began to sweat, but I kept climbing.

Upon reaching the top, I held out a hand to Hugh, but Neville moved in front of him and took it. He helped me over the side, and I fell against him. He put his arms around me, steadying me, and I clung to him for a moment, relishing his warmth and strength before slipping out of his embrace.

Martyn and Alf scaled the ladder, Alf with my books, and Martyn carrying a coil of rope over each shoulder. They heaved themselves over the side, and Ffion took the sack from Alf.

"Megge?" Frowning, Martyn touched my brow. "You're sweating. And your face is red."

"I felt faint, is all—that swinging ladder," I said, my face still aflame.

"Give us a hand here, Neville." Martyn slung his rope over a hanging pulley. I looked down at the bobbing boat. His rope was tied to the front, Alf's to the back.

Alf threw his rope over a second pulley. He and Neville pulled that rope while Martyn and Hugh pulled the other, and they hauled the rowboat onto the ship. Neville turned and grinned at me, sweat staining the front of his tunic in a long V that reached from his tanned neck to the middle of his broad chest. I struggled to catch my breath.

Amice stood at his side, regarding me calmly, no longer as a child under my care, but after all we had been through, as more of an equal.

"Megge!" Hugh motioned me over. "How did Amice hurt her hand?"

"Agnes cut her wrist."

"She *what*?"

"She cut Amice's wrist and tried to bleed her."

"Bleed her?" He lifted Amice's wrist and gently touched the dried blood on the cloth. His expression went dark. "We shall speak of Agnes later."

I walked with Hugh toward the front of the ship, Amice silently trailing us.

"Where is the prisoner?" I asked.

Hugh pointed. I saw only coiled ropes and fastenings for those immense sails. I lifted my hands. "Where?"

"Beneath that hatch." He pointed with his chin to a square cut into the floor, a large iron ring recessed in the wood. "In the hold. Bound and under guard."

The *hatch*, I thought. Beneath it is the *hold*.

"Does everything on this ship have a special name?"

"Aye." He pointed. "The front's the *bow*, the rear's the *stern*, these poles are *masts*, and the floor's not *the floor*, it's *the deck*."

I nodded with each new word and started toward the hatch.

"Wait." Hugh caught my arm. "Does his mother, too, carry the disease?"

"I don't believe so. Where is she?"

He pointed toward the bow. "There."

Amice's breath caught, and she stared.

CHAPTER 22

AMICE

The priestess, tightly wrapped in a heavy black cloak, looked nothing like she had in the church or in the courtyard on Samhain Eve. Gone was the glint in those silvery eyes. Gone, too, was that downturned mouth. Her gaze was dull, her lips slack.

Somehow, I no longer feared her.

Somehow, I almost pitied her.

Perhaps I had, indeed, become brave.

CHAPTER 23

MEGGE

Agnes Gough lay swaddled on a pallet made of sacks of grain. Her face was slack, her eyes closed.

"Is she dead?" I called back to Hugh as I ran to her. "What have you done to her?"

"Nothing you wouldn't have done yourself to keep her from biting and kicking you." He came to stand by me. "She's mad, Megge. Before we wrapped her up, she fought like a demon. Like nothing I had ever seen. Neville had to help me bind her hands and get her into the boat—and even then, she tried to throw herself over. It was done for her good as much as for ours."

"Did the swaddling quiet her?"

"Oh, aye. It took the fighting spirit right out of her."

Fighting spirit . . .

"This 'fighting spirit.' When did it leave her?"

He scrubbed his knuckles over his beard. "Not long after we started rowing out to the ship. I didn't know where you were." He cocked his head. "Where were you?"

"I had a task to complete in the cave." My hand went to the mulberry spot below my left eye—the mark of the goddess.

"Release her, Hugh," I said. "Remove the swaddling and untie her hands. She's but a tired old woman."

"What have you brought aboard this ship, Megge?"

Before I could reply, he held up a hand. "A lazar below decks. And this . . . devil-woman above. And *you*. You sent me . . ." He floundered. "A dream. But I was awake."

"You saw it, then. The vision I sent you of the cliff, the cave."

"Not only did I see the cave—I heard your voice." He looked at me, bewildered.

"I heard it here." He tapped his finger against his temple. "'He is here,' you said. And I saw that cave. I saw Gough lying on the ground at your feet, you standing over him, the point of your stick at his throat, like a warrior." He stared at me. "What have you become, Megge?"

Though I knew what I had become, I did not know how to reply.

He brushed a finger over the mark on my cheek, "Alf says you've the goddess in you."

I had more than that in me, but I could not explain it to him. He was frightened. This man I had known for years, this behemoth who could best any man, who was taking the blacksmith to the earl to be tried and hanged, looked upon me warily.

"You needn't fear me, Hugh. I'm still Megge. And you know all about the women of Bury Down. What we are, what we do."

"Oh, aye, the mystical women who cure the sick, birth the bairns, read the skies, and counsel an earl. But what I've seen of late—of you—"

"What, Hugh?"

"You're no longer the Megge I knew." His voice was wistful. "The herder. The little girl who would follow an old woman around the pasture and sit atop the slope, reciting tales of seers and ship captains. Who would—"

I stopped him. "Something has changed, Hugh. I cannot yet explain it, not even to myself." I touched his huge, furry arm. "*I* have changed. Until the night Aunt Claris died, I was that little girl you knew who recited Morwen's tales of Gytha the Seer and Adaem, once the captain of this very ship. But in the hours before Claris's death, I became a woman of Bury Down. Since that night, I scarcely know myself."

His countenance softened.

"Today, I became something more. And though I would not have chosen it, a new path has opened to me. Where it will lead, I cannot say. I tell you this knowing that you might not understand, but trusting you'll believe that I'm still Megge."

"Alf calls you *Meg.*" For the first time that day, the frown left him, and he chuckled.

"Yes, he told me. 'A woman's name.'"

Neville approached with Amice trotting after him. She stood beside him, waiting, I supposed, to see what we were going to do.

"Neville," I said, "Unwrap Mistress Gough. She poses no risk."

Neville looked to Hugh.

"Go on."

"She gave me a fine kick to the shin." He grinned as he rubbed it. "It'll heal. And I see she's stilled over there."

Slapping Martyn on the back as he passed, Neville motioned with his head toward the subdued Agnes Gough. Martyn followed him.

Hugh turned back to me. "Now, what of the blacksmith?"

"He's suffering," I said. "Take me to him. I may be able to do nothing more than enrage him, but let me see what might be done."

CHAPTER 24

I followed Hugh and Megge to the little door someone had cut into the deck of the ship—the *hatch*, Hugh had called it. He picked up the brass ring in the center and pulled it open. A moan rose, carried on hot, fetid air.

Megge composed her face. I breathed through my mouth. Hugh rubbed his hands over his forest of beard, not even trying to disguise his disgust.

Megge followed him down a ladder, into the hold. I strained to see, but it was too dark, so I followed her.

"Where is he?" she asked.

"This way," Hugh said.

As the smell of sickness grew stronger, I knew we were nearing him.

The dim light from a hanging lantern revealed a big man lying on the floor, slumped against a beam, his arms behind his back, his hooded head bent, his chin resting on his chest. Long legs stuck out before him, his ankles bound with rope.

I knew that heavy black cloak. I remembered that hood. I could still see those long legs stride into the priestess's church and hear the ring of those boots on the floor.

Whatever else you have done, Sir, you saved my life. I will help Megge save yours.

"Who's done this to him?" Megge demanded of Hugh. "This rope is slicing his wrists." As she struggled with the knots, she pointed with her chin to his feet. "Loosen these ropes, Hugh."

"He is my prisoner, Megge."

Megge got to her feet, and I could see in her the powerful goddess as she rose to meet Hugh, her gaze steady on his.

She will help this kind, brave man, I thought, and woe be to anyone who would stop her.

"I may not be a sheriff, Hugh, but I know that even the vilest prisoner cannot be bound like this."

Vile?

"Not even a healthy man could breathe tied to a post, with his head falling forward like this." She lowered her voice to a whisper. "And this man . . . look at him."

Hugh nudged Megge aside, moved to the sick man's back, and freed his hands. "You look. I've seen enough."

The man slid sideways to the floor. Megge helped him sit with his back against the post and looked up at Hugh. "A dipper of ale, if you would, Hugh."

Hugh folded his arms over his chest.

How can a man as fair and solid as Hugh be so cold, so harsh?

But then I looked into his face, and I read fear.

CHAPTER 25

MEGGE

I gave Hugh my mother's stony look that said, "Not one word."

The ladder creaked as he climbed out of the hold.

I bent to the blacksmith's destroyed face. "He's fetching ale."

"Witch," he croaked.

Something dark roiled in my gut and rose into my throat. I tamped it down.

"Take care, Blacksmith. You have no idea what I am."

I looked down at the suffering lazar whose disease would soon claim him, and I chided myself.

You have taken your vow as a healer and protector. You must banish this rage so you can be both to this man.

Even Mother had set ill will aside when healing was needed. If I could not tend this man, then I was not worthy to tend anyone.

"Let me help you."

"Leave me. Give me a quick death and cast my carcass overboard."

I'll give you death. The vile words came to me in the deathbringer's growl—why, then, did I taste their bitterness on my tongue?

"Death is not for me to give you," I said. "Be still."

He needed that ale. Where was Hugh?

I looked up at the open hatch just as Alf walked past.

"Alf!" I shouted up to him. "Ale!"

I turned back to the blacksmith and spoke in a low voice, my jaw tight. "You have crimes to answer for, Blacksmith. You'll die when the judge says you will."

He coughed, and something deep inside his chest rattled. Each breath brought a gurgle, each exhalation a wheeze. He was suffering more than anyone I had ever seen. Why could I find no pity for him?

My mind's eye showed me Brighida's burned legs and the stump of her left arm. This, I thought, was why.

Alf touched my shoulder. "Meg?"

I shook myself and took the cup he held out to me. I put it to the blacksmith's lips.

"Drink."

He turned his face away.

Amice stood behind me, watching.

"Amice, help me here. Hold this."

Instead of taking the cup, she knelt behind the blacksmith and lifted his head so I could put the cup to his lips. She was so at ease, and her touch so gentle, I could only stare. Had she once tended someone ill?

"Drink." Pulling up the blacksmith's hood so Amice could not see his face, I dribbled the ale onto his cracked lips. Much of it ran down his chin, but when he tasted it, he grasped the cup between his palms and brought it to his lips. I steadied it for him as he drank.

Though he wanted his suffering to end, his body wanted to live. I, too, wanted it to live— long enough for him to be tried.

Tried and condemned and—

I braced for the deathbringer to growl *hanged,* but my healer's spirit hailed me from afar.

A draught for pain is what he needs. Poppyseed and birch bark, poultices and heat—

And in my mind's eye, I watched myself, the healer Atropos, garbed in white, kneel and pick poppies from a seaside cliff. The vision came to me in a rush, nearly overwhelming me.

Was this to be my new life? A battle between deathbringer and healer?

No, I decided. This conflict ends today.

"Meg?" Alf cocked his head.

I struggled to see him clearly. "Yes, Alf?"

"You said something. I didn't hear it all."

Did I say something?

My vision cleared. "It was nothing, Alf. A thought is all."

The blacksmith held out the empty cup. I took it, and he leaned back on the post. Amice tried to look inside his hood, but I glanced at her, and she sat back.

Alf winced. "Should Amice be here with him?"

"Alf—" I was losing patience with men doubting me. "Yes, she should."

"If you're certain . . ."

"I am."

For the first time in my life, I was certain. And not only about Amice. The knowledge I had gleaned at the foot of that cliff was returning, and I knew what the blacksmith needed.

"Hugh's men needn't stand guard," I told Alf. "But have them fetch something we might use as a pallet. And some gruel, soup, or other soft food."

Alf just smiled.

"What?"

"We're on a ship, Meg. It'll be salted fish or salted meat. Perhaps a biscuit."

"Fine. And more ale. No one need come near. I shall go up for the food if you call out to me. Tell Hugh he needn't worry about the blacksmith—he can't climb the ladder, and he is too weak now to harm anyone."

"Except you," Alf insisted. "Gough is a lazar. Look at him, Meg. Do you want to become one as well?"

I did not want to become a lazar. I just wanted to keep this one alive.

"A pallet, Alf—and food."

CHAPTER 26

AMICE

lf returned to the hold, a sack of fleece slung over one shoulder.

"A pallet," he said as he laid it on the floor.

Megge helped him move the man—*Gough*, the others called him—onto the sack, but the hot air was so foul and hard to breathe, I knew no mere pallet would bring him ease.

"Is there a window, Alf?" Megge waved a hand before her face.

Alf looked all around. "Not a one, Meg," he said. "There's only the hatch, and it must remain closed lest someone fall down here."

I tried to take a deep breath, but the air was stagnant. If I could not breathe, how could a man this ill?

"Keeping him below decks is cruel," Megge said. "He needs fresh air."

Hugh descended the ladder carrying a bucket and a dipper.

"We must move him, Hugh," Megge said.

"This is better than the gaol that's waiting for him," Hugh mumbled.

Gaol.

"Even a prisoner is entitled to breathe," Megge insisted.

Hugh motioned with his head toward the hatch. Megge and I followed him up. The moment my head rose above the deck, I tasted sea air, a breeze fresh and clean.

Megge would get Mister Gough up there, I knew, but I thought of the sea winds that had blown in through the tower window at night, chilling us. How would he fare when those night winds blew?

CHAPTER 27

MEGGE

mice and I followed Hugh to the bow. His long, slow strides—head bowed, hands clasped behind his back—told me he was brooding. I suspected I knew why.

"You told me earlier," I said, "that the earl would not thank us for bringing a lazar into his gaol."

He whirled around, frustration twisting his features, his words bristling in defense. "How could we have known he was a lazar?" He rubbed a hand over his beard as he stared out to sea. "Forgive me, Megge. I always believed he covered his face with that hood so no one would know him. Not to hide that face . . . that nose. Those lips."

I waited for him to recover.

"You said he was suffering," he finally said. "How bad is he?"

"He can barely breathe. His skin is covered with boils and leprous sores. He took off those gloves in the cave and showed me his fingers. Some are missing the nails—others, the tips. I have not yet seen his feet. But you've seen his face."

"Aye. How does he breathe through that sunken nose? And that cough—"

Is that pity I see?

"And how could he have ridden across Cornwall on that great stallion?" I asked. "He was sick when he stole my books. Sick and weak. Surely, it cost him what strength he had to ride to the cliffs. And he must have taken that treacherous path down to the cave only today, when the tide was out, for he was dry when I found him, as were the books."

"It may be he's not as weak as he looks."

"I believe he is," I said. "His hatred for me gives him whatever strength he possesses."

"How strong must he be to hang by the neck?"

Amice stiffened.

I knelt and put an arm around her shoulders. "Perhaps you should go to Ffion."

She shook her head, drew away from me, and stood solidly beside Hugh.

I spoke quietly to him. "You said it would be months before he could be tried. In the gaol, he'll die in a week, so there will be no trial. He will never see justice. And how many prisoners will suffer his fate?"

"Aye." He rubbed his beard as he thought. "The gaol will become naught but another lazar house." He looked out to sea, then back at me. "I've come to a decision. We're taking him to one."

"One what?" I asked, grateful that he had come upon the solution himself.

"A lazar house. I know of several."

"Brother James tends one just outside the village," I offered.

"Aye, your mother's."

"You know about my mother's work?"

"Oh, aye. The house is on the way to Lostwithiel, nearly at the river's edge. There'll be carts at the wharf. If my father is there, I'll ask him to take Gough, the murdering—"

I twitched my head toward Amice, and he cut off the curse.

"A monster," I agreed.

Hugh thought for a moment, then took a breath and spoke in a low voice. "Not long ago, the earl appointed me sheriff."

"Sheriff? Did Sheriff Haskins die?"

"No, but he's not well. He's finishing the matters he began, and the earl turned over to me the deaths of your mother and Claris. We know who committed them, but we need to know why. We need testimony. Proof. I've been talking with people ahead of the trial—because aside from those murders, I'm also looking into the ones Agnes committed—all those girls—and what Gough had to do with them."

Hugh paced. I waited.

"I spoke to Brother James," he finally said. "He told me Gough had gone to him for a cure. When the good brother told Gough that he had to confess and be absolved of the sin that had made him a lazar, Gough refused.

"Then I spoke to Brighida, who told me that just this summer, Agnes had convinced Gough that absolution could come only through a potion containing the blood of a virgin and the blood of the woman he—" He lowered his voice. "Forgive me—the woman he fornicated with." He swallowed hard. "And before summer was done, Gough had cut Claris's throat and taken a vial of her blood. But Megge—"

"Brighida was there," I interrupted. "She saw him kill her mother and take her blood. And you and Martyn saw Aunt Claris's body, so do not tell me you doubt Brighida's word that the blacksmith killed her."

"I told you—I've no doubt that Gough killed Claris. But it's hard to see him saying all this to Brighida while he was killing her mother. So how could she have known what Agnes had promised him—and when?"

She must have summoned a vision.

"I can't say how Brighida knew," I said, "but Gough himself told me much the same thing when we were down in the cave. He even gave me the vial of Claris's blood—"

"Leave it with me, Megge. I'll uncover the truth. We know he has murdered—you and Brighida will testify to his killing your mother and aunt, and Alf will testify to seeing him burn his own sister and nieces—Tinker's stepmother and half-sisters—at the stake." Hugh's face had gone ruddy. "One way or another, he'll hang."

"You must wonder how I can let you take this man to a lazar house and put him under the care of Brother James rather than demand that you shackle him below decks and drag him to the gaol, where he can die in the torment he surely deserves."

"Perhaps you share Brother James's opinion." Hugh shrugged. "'Let the judges—and God—decide his guilt.'"

"No. Let them decide his sentence. I know he is guilty. I only want him to live long enough to be tried."

Looking out over the waves, Hugh nodded. "And how do you propose we do that?"

How *do* we do that? I wondered.

You are a woman of Bury Down. Your spirit is that of Atropos, the Lady of the Cliffs, the greatest healer Cornwall has ever known. You have work to do.

"I shall tend him," I said.

"You?" Hugh gaped at me. "You would tend the murderer who left you and Brighida orphans?"

"Orphans are children," I said. "We are women."

I paced as I considered the blacksmith's sores, his pain, and that cough, and the names of a dozen herbs that could ease his suffering came to mind. But of all the remedies I knew he needed, fresh air was the only one I could give him—but I could not give him even that below decks.

"I shall see to him up here." I swept an arm over the deck. "He cannot climb that ladder, but he can be carried up. You've plenty of strong men."

Hugh held up his hands. "Oh, aye, I've strong men, all right. But they'll not be carrying that lazar anywhere. If you must tend him up

here, he'll come up the same way he got down there—on his feet."
He turned toward the stern and called, "Martyn! Neville! Alf!"

"I'll fetch his pallet," I said, "but he will also need a cup and a pot."

"A pot?"

"To make water."

"Megge—" Hugh stared at me, aghast.

"Or a bucket. Whatever the shipmen use. I'll not have him soil himself." I patted Hugh's arm. "You needn't look at me that way, Hugh. I shall keep all the others away so they needn't look upon him."

"Or smell him? Or breathe the air he poisons with that breath?"

"Perhaps we can hang something to block the wind and keep him and his breath away from the others."

"Have you ever been on a ship, Megge? Do you even know what you're asking?"

"I am asking for a barrier—a cloth, perhaps. You have arrested a diseased murderer, Hugh. If we can get him to the lazar house alive, without the shipmen becoming lazars as well, the earl will thank you for having kept him apart."

"But what of you? How will you keep yourself from becoming . . . unclean?"

I was wearing a long tunic, and I had my hooded cloak. I would go near him only to give him food and drink. And to cleanse those sores. And—

"Megge?"

"Have no fear for me, Hugh. You can leave food and ale at a distance, and I shall take it to him."

"Do you mean to tend to a man this ill out here, on this deck, with only a sheet to keep out the wind and the spray? He'll freeze."

Hugh was right. The day was warm, but the sea breeze had picked up. Come nightfall, a cold wind would likely blow over the deck.

"It'll take something sturdier than a cloth," he said.

I looked all around. "A sail, perhaps? Surely there's sailcloth about."

He nodded a grudging assent. "Martyn can see to that."

Martyn, Neville, and Alf crossed the deck toward us.

"Neville, come with me. We're getting Gough out of the hold. Alf, Martyn, rig some sailcloth to block the wind. A tent of sorts."

"How about I rig up a plank?" muttered one of the passing shipmen. He looked out over the water and spat. "That'll solve it."

I turned to follow Hugh and Neville to the hatch and noticed Amice sitting on the deck just behind me. I had forgotten all about her. How much had she overheard?

CHAPTER 28

AMICE

Claris . . .

Claris, I remembered, was the name of the woman the priestess had ordered Mister Gough to take blood from. And he was so desperate, he had done it—he had killed Megge's aunt Claris and taken her blood. *Before summer was done*, Hugh had said. But he returned to the church in the fall, likely to bring his mother the blood, and he discovered us. He set us free even before he entered the church—so the priestess could not have made her cure since she would have had no maidens to give her their blood. Why, then, did he go back to Bury Down, steal Megge's books, and take them and the vial of blood back to the cliffs?

I noticed movement. Megge and Hugh were walking away, now talking about bringing Mister Gough up to the deck. I leapt to my feet and followed them to the hatch. As Hugh and Neville descended into the hold, Ffion joined Megge and me and took my hand.

"Look, Amice. There!" Ffion pointed to a wiry boy scaling the mast near the stern. When he reached the very top, he wrapped the tip of a big sail around it and secured it high overhead. Martyn, Alf, and half a dozen other men affixed the bottom of the sail to the deck, so it formed a wide cone. Never before had I seen anything take shape so quickly.

The hatch thumped open. Muttering complaints and curses, Hugh helped Neville push Mister Gough up through the hole. He rose like a great tree from the earth and stood swaying until Megge and Ffion took his elbows to steady him. I could not look away.

"Let me help you, Megge," Neville said as he took Ffion's place and helped Megge guide Mister Gough to the great cone while Martyn stitched a heavy bolt to the outside of it. I wondered what he meant to do with that bolt.

Hugh descended again and rose from the hold carrying the sack of fleece that Alf had taken down just a short time before. He strode ahead of Megge and Neville, the sack slung over one shoulder, and placed it inside the tent. When Megge and Neville arrived at the tent, Mister Gough stumbling between them, Martyn folded back the edge of the sail to form a flap, then nimbly sewed a loop of string to the edge and passed the bolt through the loop. Now the tent had a door. Megge touched his arm in thanks as she and Neville helped Mister Gough inside.

Spellbound, Ffion also watched. She was paying me no mind, so I peered through the tent opening as Mister Gough slid down the ship's great mast until he was sitting on the sack—now his pallet—and gasping for breath. His cloak had fallen open at the neck, and through his nearly palpable stench now wafted the stinging odor of the pitch-and-sulfur salve that called to mind one word: *Mother.*

All at once, I was back in my cottage, dabbing that pungent black unguent onto my mother's weeping sores and covering them with cloths.

I swayed, bumping into Ffion.

"Amice!" She took my arm and led me to the bow, and there we huddled, wrapped in her cloak and a heavy blanket, while she fed me little lumps of cheese. I breathed deeply the clean sea air.

"Don't do that near him," Ffion warned. "We must not breathe

the air the sick man exhales. They say . . ."

I knew what *they* said. *They*—even the people of my own settlement—said that this curse was brought on by sin, but that it could be spread through the breath. Father once told me that the priests often sent lazars away so that others need not even look upon them. I cried, and he vowed that my mother would never be sent off, for we would tend to her.

Ffion continued talking about "the sick man" without saying the word *lazar*, but she did not have to speak it, for I knew lepra. And in that tent, I had smelled it.

CHAPTER 29

MEGGE

"Ale," croaked the blacksmith.

I stepped outside the tent and saw that someone had left a bucket of ale and a cup just outside the tent while I was tending to the blacksmith. I filled the cup and was about to carry it inside when Neville came to me, holding out a pair of leather gloves so long that they would have reached past my elbows.

"For you, Megge."

Though I had no need of gloves, Neville's thoughtfulness moved me. "I daresay you won't want to wear them after they have touched anything inside this tent."

"We've plenty more at home." His gaze softened. "Besides, even had I no other pair, I would want you to have these."

I had to look away from the earnest expression on that broad, handsome face and the warmth in those soft, green eyes. I looked instead at the gloves.

"You are very kind, Neville." I pulled them on, tucking my sleeves inside the high cuffs.

A rasping shout came from inside the tent. "Ale!"

I stiffened. *Who are you to command me?*

I forced my fists to relax and my breathing to slow, so my heart would stop pounding.

Moving aside the heavy cloth, I stepped into what I was beginning to see not just as a tent but as a healer's chamber. *My* healer's chamber—just as the sea cave had been mine when those I tended called me *Lady.* There was no place in this sacred chamber for hatred or spite.

I held out the cup to the blacksmith. He took it between his palms, put it to his lips, and drank greedily.

"You should have let me die in that cave." He belched, his breath so rancid, I had to turn away. "These shipmen would have thanked you."

Though his voice was still rough, his breathing had become quieter.

"How long has it been since you last supped, Blacksmith?"

He shrugged.

"Can you eat?" I asked, pulling off the gloves.

He looked away.

"Try though you might to have done with this life, Blacksmith, it may be that life's not done with you."

"That's right. Feed me so I'll live to see the gallows. Hang by the neck."

Struggle and gasp at the end of a rope.

Be silent, I ordered the deathbringer.

But had those poisonous words truly come from the deathbringer? I had not spoken them aloud, but I had felt them rise from my gut and scrape over my throat. I could still taste their venom.

Could such unspeakable thoughts have been mine?

Never, I told myself. They came from the unstill spirit. I would close my mind to the rage that feeds the deathbringer, and I would behave as a healer.

"Your self-pity will not sway me, Blacksmith. I'll see justice done."

I heard heavy footsteps outside the tent and called, "Can you help me?"

A man's voice responded with a wary, "Aye, Lady?"

"Is there food?"

No reply.

"Hello?" I called.

"I'll see what can be spared." He hurried away, his footsteps slowing only when he was well past us.

"You would feed me?"

"Certainly. I won't let you starve."

He pulled the edges of his hood forward so his face was hidden in shadow. Bending forward, he coughed hard and spat.

"Not on the floor, Blacksmith." I cast about in search of something for him to cough into, but there was nothing.

I flung back the tent flap and stood outside, breathing slowly to quiet my roiling stomach. I soon calmed and looked again at the diseased man sitting on the pallet, his head bowed over his cup as he sipped between bouts of coughing.

"Down in the cave," I said, "you told me you had gone to the priory for a cure."

He stared at his hands.

"Why did you really go?"

"I told you. For a cure." He finally looked up, and I did not shrink from him as I gazed upon that face.

"Did you believe that a man of God could cure you?"

He set down the cup and scowled at me.

"Or did you believe that only your mother could? Did you ask her to kill those girls and use their blood for a cure?"

Something like pain—or sorrow—flickered over his face.

"*Did you*?" I had not meant to speak so harshly, but the words had forced their way out. And once out, they could not be taken back.

He turned away, but I heard him moan.

"If you did not believe that Brother James could cure you, then why did you seek absolution from him? To avoid damnation? The Church teaches that unless you repent, the punishment for a life such as the one you've lived is eternal flames. Flames, Blacksmith—like the flames that consumed my mother. Alive." My heart was pounding. "Did you want to avoid an eternity of such suffering?"

"I wanted only an end to *this* suffering. Eternity be damned."

"It is folly to curse eternity, Blacksmith, for eternity may hand you another span of days in the living world so you might finally glean some truth."

Silence.

I softened my voice. "Already, you have lived a good many years. What have you gleaned?"

"That I'd rather drown in a sea cave than be forced to listen to a herding wench prattle on about eternity. Be gone."

The slur might have pained me had Mother's sharp words not cut deeper. *Herding wench*, though crude, scarcely touched me.

"Be *gone*?" I laughed. "Hear this, Blacksmith—this *herding wench* is all that stands between you and the sea. Do you believe these shipmen want to carry a *corpse,* as you have called yourself, all the way around Cornwall to a lazar house so that you might be tended in comfort? Were it not for me, they would throw you overboard and tell the earl you'd died in that cave."

"It's the gaol they are taking me to. The *gaol.* Where I'll *rot.*"

"The earl would not want you in his gaol. And his men and the other prisoners would not want to breathe the poisonous air you exhale." I waited for him to look at me. "So we are taking you to a lazar house, where I shall use your diseased body to hone my skills as a healer."

He scoffed, "What healer's skills could a herding wench possess?"

The skill to gut you.

I drew in a breath. Never before had I even imagined such vulgar words. But there was no denying that I had thought these—and had wanted to say them—for they rang in my ears, and their bitterness clung to my tongue.

This was not a fight with the deathbringer—this was a battle between compassion for a sufferer and loathing for a murderer.

Somehow, I thought, compassion must prevail.

I would force it to prevail.

"The skill to ease your pain." My eyes held his. "And the skill, if you persuade me you want—and deserve—it, to give you the peace you so desperately crave at the end of your life."

He grunted.

A hand pulled aside the tent flap.

"Meg," Alf said. "Charles said you asked him for food. For . . . for *him*." He tipped his head toward the blacksmith. "Better you come to me and not ask the men. They fear for their lives but dare not tell you nay."

He handed me a piece of salted meat and something that looked like a round, flat rock. Assuming it was food, I tried to break it in half, but couldn't. Then I tried to bite into it, but feared I would break my teeth.

"What is this, Alf?"

"A biscuit. It's too hard to eat like that. Dip it in ale to soften it."

I was so hungry, I thought I might eat even this rock, but I was not sure I could live on this food for long.

As if he knew my thoughts, Alf smiled. "It'll be a short voyage, Meg. I'll leave Gough's food and ale outside your chamber. You can come out for them when you will."

"Give it over," the blacksmith snarled when I entered with his food. "Likely, you've poisoned that biscuit with nightshade. So be it. Let us end this now."

"I told you, Blacksmith. I will not end your days." I tore the meat into small pieces and dropped the biscuit into a cup of ale. "So do not deceive yourself that you will so easily escape what lies ahead."

"The slaughter."

"Believe what you will." I stepped outside the chamber. I needed to wash.

"Alf," I called to him as he strode away. "Might you fetch me a bucket of water?"

"Surely, you don't mean to drink seawater?"

"I mean to wash."

Alf found a bucket and filled it for me. I carried it to my chamber, and as I dipped my hands into the water, I thought of the font over which I had just spoken my vow. How many times had I dipped my hands into it before and after a healing?

"Lady," Ffion beckoned from the bow. I lifted my hands from the water and joined her on the bench. Amice sat next to her, cutting a large piece of cloth into hand-sized squares.

"What is this?" I picked up one of the raw-edged pieces.

"That," Ffion said, pointing to the cloth Amice was cutting, "was once a blanket. And this," she held up a square, "is a spit-cloth for the blacksmith." She handed it to me. "Amice heard that man hacking and spitting—on the deck, I'd wager—and she took my shears and started cutting. When I asked why she was ruining my blanket, she picked up a square, coughed into it, and tipped her head toward him."

Ffion passed me a small sack.

I pawed through it. "There must be a dozen in here. And Amice thought of this?" I looked down at Amice as she dropped another square into the bag.

Ffion chuckled. "She's clever. Better he spit into one of these than on the deck. Throw them overboard when he's used them. No telling what he's coughing up."

"Amice, how did you know to make these?"

Before she could respond, a growl came from the ship's bow.

"What was that?" I stood and looked around.

A small tent encircled the base of a mast near the bow. From it came a long, low moan. It called to mind the howl I had heard just before a pack of wolves descended on my flock.

"What is in there?"

"Not *what*, but *who*?" And there was the dimple that called to mind her sister, my beloved confidante, Morwen. "The priestess herself."

CHAPTER 30

That was not the priestess I knew. I wished I could tell Megge and Ffion about the cruelty that silver-eyed crone had inflicted on Sister One on Samhain Eve. I could still hear the scrape of that voice.

Are you a virgin, Sister One?

I touched the stone at my throat.

Are you?

"The sheriff will search for the truth of her crimes," Anwen said softly. "When he asks you what she, Magdalene, and Tinker did to you and the other girls, you must tell him. But not until I bid you speak."

So be it. I would remain mute.

But I was not deaf. Nor was I blind.

I picked up my cloth and resumed cutting out squares while I listened to Megge and Ffion discuss the wicked old woman I had persuaded the others to enclose in a tent because, though I pitied her, looking at her made me shudder.

CHAPTER 31

MEGGE

The priestess? Agnes Gough? Why is she in a tent? She's not a lazar. When last I saw her, she was sitting quietly out in the open."

"Amice thought it best to keep her out of the wind."

I looked at Amice and then back at Ffion. "After the suffering she endured at the hands of that woman, Amice did not want her to get *cold*? How did she tell you that? Did she speak?"

Ffion wrapped her arms around herself, shivered, and pointed at Agnes. "That's how. The girl needn't speak to make herself understood."

I walked to the tent and opened the flap just far enough to peer inside. Agnes sat on a sack of grain, muttering to herself and scraping dried blood from the hand that had sliced Amice's wrist.

I closed the flap and sat next to Ffion. "Should she be so near Amice? Mightn't she frighten her?"

"Agnes has not so much as peeked out."

"Are you certain Amice does not fear her?"

"Amice pays her no mind. Now that Agnes is inside that tent, it is as though, to Amice, the old woman's not even there."

"Has Agnes spoken?"

"Confused muttering." Ffion shrugged. "And, as you have heard, she growls. Sometimes she moans. I can't say why. She does not appear ill or injured. She appears bewildered. Lost."

Sitting at the end of the bench with her back to us, Amice cut out another square of cloth and put it in the sack. Absorbed in her work, she ignored Agnes's garbled questions and long, muttered speeches.

I got up. I wanted to speak to Agnes, but did not know how. What, I wondered, would Aunt Claris have done?

I walked to Agnes's tent, opened the flap, and looked inside. She was picking her nose. I closed the flap.

Aunt Claris, who soothed, comforted, and assuaged fears, would have seen the old woman as I did now—not as the conjuror who had ordered Claris killed, but as a lost soul. Claris, though, would have known how to approach her and what to say. I remembered my gentle aunt coming to me on my rock after I had argued with Mother, bringing me a bowl of cooked eggs and a cup of ale—and I knew. Aunt Claris would have fed her.

I walked to my chamber and ladled ale into a cup.

"Alf," I touched his arm as he passed, "would you fetch me some meat or fish?"

"Aye, Meg, high time you ate."

I carried the dried fish to the bow and opened the tent flap just enough to see the woman sitting inside, rocking to and fro, singing to herself and sniffing her fingers.

"Mistress Gough." I reached in and touched her shoulder. "Will you have some ale? Some meat?"

She looked up. Her silvery eyes had lost their gleam. Now grey, they roamed dully over me. She did not know me.

But no mother would ever forget her son.

"Michael's had some." I held out the fish to tempt her. "He's here, you know, on the ship. And he's eaten. He wants you to have a meal. It's been a long, distressing day." Indeed, it was nearly night, and a cold sea wind was blowing into the tent. I went inside and pulled the flap closed.

"Michael is here?" Suddenly lucid, she looked around. "Where is he?"

"He's there." I opened the flap and pointed to the stern. "In a tent just like yours. He is safe and being tended. Now you must eat."

She reached out and took the ale.

"What have you put in it?" She took the merest sip, rolled it over her tongue, and licked her lips. "Tastes like poison."

"It's ale, Agnes, nothing more." I turned to go.

She tasted the fish. "Needs salt."

"*More* salt?" The fish fairly glittered with salt. I opened the tent flap.

"You." She pointed at me. "I know you."

"Megge. I'm called Megge." I watched for a sign that she knew me and waited for her to curse me.

"No . . ." She wagged her finger at me. "I know who you and your sister are."

"Sister? I have no—"

"Girls, naught but girls," she mused. "One already a healer and the other a seer. Granddaughters of the all-powerful Gytha. My son would take your sister, Claris, the seer, to wife. But *Megge*, you say? I never knew you had a name."

Seeming to have forgotten her fear of being poisoned, she ate heartily. When she picked up the ale, I left her to her meal and sat beside Ffion.

"She is mad, Ffion. She believes I am my mother, that Mother and Claris are still girls, and that Claris is still betrothed to her son."

CHAPTER 32

AMICE

Though madness had rendered the priestess docile, I could still hear her taunting voice demand that Sister One accept her own death.

Do you, Virgin One? Do you accept this charge?

I put down my cloth and stood by Megge's side, listening, grateful now for my small size, which Anwen had told me would be one of my greatest blessings.

"Meg?" Alf touched Megge's shoulder, then smiled at me. "Biscuit?"

He held out a flat piece of coarse bread to Megge, Ffion, and me. Ffion and I took one, but Megge, lost in thought, seemed not to have heard.

Alf sat with us on the long bench, dipping his bread in his ale while I studied mine. I tapped it on the bench. It was so hard, it did not break. I set it aside, and Ffion picked it up and put it in her small sack along with the one Alf had given her.

"The sea is so quiet," Alf said, "we might well be sitting at table in the cottage."

"Yes, quiet," Megge said softly, looking over the still water. After a moment, she came to herself and looked at Alf. "Yet we seem to have traveled a great distance."

"Aye, the sails are a marvel. They catch the merest breath of wind and move us swiftly along. We'll reach the Fowey in no time." He pulled his biscuit from his cup and took a bite. "You were far away, Meg. What troubles you?"

"I wasn't so much troubled as confused. But now, I'm beginning to see."

"I saw you with Agnes. I feared she might lash out at you as she did at me when I helped Hugh and Neville put her into the rowboat. She was hard to master even for them."

"When did she calm?" Megge asked.

Alf shrugged. "You'd have to ask Hugh or Neville. By the time I boarded our rowboat, she was already quiet."

Neville, passing by as Alf and Megge spoke, absently touched the top of my head. He must have overheard their conversation, for he stopped and asked, "Are you speaking of Mistress Gough?"

Megge looked up at him.

He laughed. "She was like a wild animal. Fought, bit, spat, kicked, and cursed us all to hell. We had to bind her hands and wrap her in Hugh's cloak to protect ourselves." He shrugged. "All at once, she went still. She stopped fighting, dropped her head, and heaved out a breath so long, I feared she would have none left inside her. She was sitting beside Hugh. I was rowing. He had to hold her up, for it looked like she had fallen asleep. Or died." He raised his hands, palms up, and shrugged.

His gaze found Megge's and held it. "I feared for you, Megge, all alone in that cave. I kept watching for you to come out. Finally, just after Agnes collapsed, you came out and looked around. I waved, but you didn't see me." He looked toward Agnes's tent. "She's been calm ever since. Even as we helped her up the ladder, she made no protest."

The priestess's hand reached out of her tent, set the empty cup gently on the deck, and retreated. The flap fell closed.

"Little Amice, too, has been calm." Neville bent close to Megge, but I heard him add, "Too calm, it seems to me. How can she sit so near the woman who imprisoned her and show no fear?"

I wished I could tell him that I knew the danger had passed.

CHAPTER 33

MEGGE

"I see you've fed her," Neville said to me, tipping his head toward Agnes's tent.

"Even a prisoner must eat."

"That's what Hugh said." He knelt and spoke to Amice. "Shall we get some food for you and Megge?"

Amice got to her feet and reached for his hand. She waited for a moment, but when she saw I was staying, she sat back down on the deck.

"I shall go for it, Megge," Neville said.

When he had gone, Alf tightened his lips in an effort to keep from smiling. "He's not stopped saying your name."

"Who?"

"Neville!"

"My name?"

"Megge," he said in a dream-like voice. "It is ever on his lips."

I watched Neville walk away and imagined him swinging a stone mason's hammer with those strong arms and muscular shoulders, and splitting a granite block in two.

"Alf, did he say Agnes had stilled just before I came out of the cave?"

"Aye."

Hugh beckoned Alf from across the ship, and Alf got to his feet. "I must go, Meg."

Agnes had gone still just before I came out of the cave—the moment I took my vow as Lady of the Cliffs and bound the death-bringer's unstill spirit to my own.

Amice and I walked to the side of the ship. No one was near, so as she pulled a short length of rope apart fiber by fiber, paying me no mind, I spoke my thoughts aloud.

I raised a finger. "Agnes believed that when Michael married Claris, Claris's *Book of Time* would come to her."

Two fingers. "When Gytha severed that union, and Claris slipped out of Michael's reach, *The Book of Time* slipped out of Agnes's grasp. And then the life-ending half of *my* spirit, the deathbringer, which had been nudging Agnes toward the book, usurped Agnes's spirit and drove her to steal both of my books through treachery and murder."

Three fingers. "Now that I have bound the deathbringer's spirit to my healer's spirit, and its voice is no longer urging Agnes on, all those years of cunning and conniving are lost to her."

Four fingers—and my gut turned to lead as the whole truth dawned on me. "Hugh is seeking Agnes's motive for luring and killing those girls, but not even Agnes knows that the deathbringer—*my spirit*—had taken advantage of her desperation to cure Michael in order to seize my books and hold dominion over me."

My arm fell to my side. "Agnes is not at fault. I must not allow her to be condemned for crimes she committed while held in thrall to *my* spirit. But how can I explain this to a judge? Or worse, to a bishop? They will accuse me of heresy, witchcraft, and dealings with the devil."

But how could I remain silent and allow guards to bind Agnes in irons and lead her to the gallows?

I could not.

CHAPTER 34

AMICE

eresy, witchcraft, and dealings with the devil.
Mother and Eleanor had spoken of those things. I did not know what they were, but I knew they were grievous. They burned women for those things.

It is those priests, I thought. The priests and their fear of women.

But they did not fear all women, I reasoned. After all, many saints were women. Saint Anne. The Blessed Virgin Mary. Mother had said the priests feared powerful women. Women not of the Church.

Women like Megge.

I wondered what the priests would do were Megge to confess that her spirit had driven Mistress Gough to commit those crimes.

"They would put her to death," Anwen whispered.

CHAPTER 35

MEGGE

mice's countenance darkened, and she walked back to Ffion. Ffion offered her some cheese, and I watched her sit and eat.

Neville came to stand beside me and grinned. He held a plank of dried fish in one hand and a full cup of ale in the other. He handed me both.

Smiling at him, I shook off my thoughts of Agnes Gough and lowered myself to the deck. I set the cup on the deck beside me and leaned back against the side of the ship. Neville sat beside me. He pulled a biscuit from the pouch at his waist and held it out.

"No, thank you, Neville. But have you eaten?"

"Not yet. May I sup with you?"

I had hardly spoken the word yes when he got up and strode toward the galley. He returned a moment later, carrying planks of dried fish and a cup of ale, and sat beside me, closer this time. When he crossed his legs, his knee brushed mine, and a spark leapt through me. My breath caught—so did his—but he did not move his knee.

Nor did I move mine.

We ate companionably for a time before he stopped and looked at me, a faint frown on his face, a question in his eyes.

"You used to come to the market with your mother," he said. "I remember the first time you came into my father's shop. I was carving a headstone. Your mother watched me work, and after a moment, she said something to my father that I felt certain must have wounded you."

"'How fine that your child honors your profession,'" I said. And yes, those words had wounded me.

"That's it! That's just what she said! You were troubled even before she spoke, but when she said those words, though you were but a mite of a girl, you shrank before my eyes, and what little light was in you was suddenly quenched."

I looked into green eyes softened with memory. "You saw? How, Neville, when you were working so intently that you were covered with white dust. And we were there for but a trice."

"I felt . . . something . . . when you came in." He paused, his biscuit halfway to his lips. "I can't say what, but I felt something . . ." he searched for the word, "*quicken* within me."

"Quicken?"

He put down his biscuit and looked at me. "When my mother was with child—one of my sisters—she told me it felt like this," he fluttered his fingers over his stomach, "when the babe first stirred. That's what I felt when first I saw you. But how could I have felt a quickening? That belongs to women. And yet . . ."

The feeling of new life, Mother had called it. I once asked her what it felt like. She only shivered. "Like that," she said, "but deep inside. An awakening, you might call it. An awareness of that . . . other . . . life."

"When I saw you in the village the other day," he said, "I felt it again. As I was running to the donkey cart to subdue Tinker Penneck, I saw you in the road, your woolsack hanging over your shoulder, and I felt it again. I . . . knew . . . you. You looked so different from the girl in Father's workshop. No longer a child. But I knew you."

He stretched out his leg, shook it for a moment, then bent it once more, and there it was again—that spark as our knees touched. This time, though, it was lightning. Had he felt it?

When I had caught my breath, I lifted my eyes slowly to that sculpted face, browned by the sun—and green eyes that were fixed on mine.

"The prisoner—" I stammered, ashamed to have been caught staring. "I must see to my charge."

"He is Hugh's charge, Megge." Neville touched my hand. "Hugh's. The sheriff's."

A pair of familiar boots stopped next to us. I drew back my hand and looked up. Martyn held a large piece of dried meat and a cup of ale. He turned to go.

"Here, Martyn," I got to my feet. "Sit. Sup with Neville. I have eaten and must see to—the blacksmith."

Martyn sat down next to his friend, and they both looked up at me, Neville's gaze soft, Martyn's curious. I could find nothing more to say, so I turned and fled to the haven of my chamber.

"That child," the blacksmith said as I opened the tent flap and went inside.

"Yes?"

"Keep it away from me." He rolled onto his side so he faced the wall of the tent. "It's a girl, isn't it?"

"Yes, a girl."

"She must not come near. She must not look upon this face. She would never have another restful night. I would become the monster that pursues her in dreams. I will not have that."

This man's eyes had haunted my dreams my entire childhood. Could it be that there was hope for him?

"Would you have me believe that you fret over another's rest? And a child's at that? A girl's?"

He turned from me.

"Open this tent," he ordered. "Let the wind drive out this smell."

I opened the flap, and fresh air flowed inside. On the tent wall opposite the flap were two overlapping lengths of sailcloth. I folded one back, and fresh air rushed through. I welcomed it, as did the blacksmith. As he slowly raised himself on his elbows so he was leaning against the mast, his hood fell away, and I saw his face—not only those thick, lumpy lips, that flattened nose, those rheumy eyes, but also boils. I had not seen them in the dark of the hold.

"How long have you suffered with these boils?"

He touched one of the angry sores on his cheeks and winced.

I looked closely at them—crimson at the base with tight, domed swellings, some tipped with white. These were not leprous sores. These could be lanced and the foul matter expelled. But how had they arisen?

I folded my cloak and put it behind his back to cushion him, then handed him the small sack of cloths.

"When you cough, spit into one of these cloths. I shall take them away later." I thought for a moment, then said, "And know this, Blacksmith: it was *that child* who cut these cloths for you."

He exhaled, and I thought I saw relief come over that ravaged face.

I turned to go and saw Alf and Amice at the tent's opening, looking inside.

Amice gazed upon the blacksmith not with revulsion or fear, but with something like pity, her eyes moving from his flattened nose to his lumpy lips.

She examined that face like a healer about to choose a remedy. And the softness in her eyes was not pity, I realized, but compassion—the same empathy I had always read in Claris's. The blacksmith's monstrous face had brought forth tenderness.

Keep it away from me.

I stiffened. Would he curse at her? Lunge for her?

He only looked at her, those pale eyes never moving from her face.

Her eyes filled with tears.

Still looking at her, he shook his head, the merest movement, and pulled up his hood.

She turned away. Head bowed, she left the tent and walked toward the bow.

135

CHAPTER 36

AMICE

I could not bear to see the man who had rescued me suffering so, for I knew what awaited him. As I looked upon him, I saw what my father must have seen when looking upon his wife: someone he loved suffering unbearable torment.

Was this how Mister Gough would die? A lazar's death with no one to comfort him? No one to ease his pain? He must feel so alone.

And Megge despised him.

If only I could tell her what he had done for me, I thought, it might soften her heart.

CHAPTER 37

MEGGE

Standing outside the tent, Alf and I watched Amice go. Head down, she walked slowly to the ship's bow and settled next to Ffion. Ffion opened her cloak, drew Amice in, and pulled it snugly around them.

"She showed no fear of the blacksmith," I said with awe. "She saw that face and showed no fear."

"It seemed she knew him," Alf said.

"No, she looked upon him with the scrutiny of a healer, Alf. With compassion. And with something more." What was it? In my mind's eye, I searched her face.

"Grief," Alf said. "And he looked at her gently. Who would have believed him capable of that?" He went quiet, frowning as he thought. "He's Agnes's son. And Amice certainly knew Agnes. Could it be she knows him from that church?"

"She doesn't know him, Alf. What Amice knows is lepra," I said. "Any other child would have fled. At her age, even I, who had endured the birthing chamber, would have fled."

"Unless she knew him," Alf said under his breath.

"Stop saying that. The blacksmith is a man, and Amice is a child. Men give no heed to children."

"You may be right, Meg. She heard him coughing and cut cloth squares for him to spit into. And when she saw him, she didn't wince. Perhaps she *has* seen a healer tend a lazar."

Before I could say more, Alf said, "And if so, the lazar must have been someone close, likely someone in her family. Perhaps her father. Many of the men who went on crusades with Earl Richard were from Tintagel and Aldestowe. Some came back with lepra and spread it about. That was some time ago, but still it abounds. There are lazar houses all across Cornwall for those poor wretches. But she's too young to be a healer's apprentice."

"She is small, but she not may not be as young as she appears. And I was very young when my mother started taking me to births," I said. "I shall speak to Ffion. She'll know if there was lepra in or near her settlement and who the healers were—and if any had a young apprentice."

"Amice knows about more than lepra, Megge." He walked away, mumbling to himself. "She knows Gough."

CHAPTER 38

AMICE

Megge left her healer's tent and came to sit with Ffion and me. She began to say something, but suddenly stopped. I knew that though she had promised never to make me speak, she wanted to ask me a question.

Ffion drew an old apron from her sack and handed it to me. "The sick man may need more cloths, Amice."

I sat on the deck and cut more squares, listening as the women talked.

"Ffion," Megge said, "did many people suffer from lepra in your settlement?"

"Aye." Ffion nodded. "Men, mostly, but some women. There are lazar houses in Aldestowe. Most go there to live out their lives."

"Were there any healers who tended the ones who did not leave their homes?"

Ffion thought for a moment. "Aye. One from away. From a small farming settlement. Only a few families live there, and they keep to themselves." She lowered her voice. "I've heard it said that girls are taken from places like that—most of them orphans."

I sat very still.
I have a home and food for orphaned children—
"Taken?" Megge asked and mouthed, "By the Sisters?"
My breath came so short and harsh, I went weak.

CHAPTER 39

MEGGE

mice?" The child's face was white, and her hands had fallen into her lap. I bent down and touched her shoulder. "Amice!"

Ffion took a few of the cloths and ran to my healer's chamber. She brought them back dripping and held out a cup of ale.

I pressed the cold cloths to Amice's face and put the cup to her lips. "Drink, little one."

Amice obeyed, her eyes locked on mine.

"Amice," I said gently, "you needn't speak, but I must. I've learned a little about your past on this journey, yet much remains that I cannot know." I felt Alf was wrong, but I had to ask. "Alf believes you know Mister Gough. Do you? Have you ever seen him before?"

Amice tightened her lips.

"You needn't speak now, but once we are back at Bury Down, Hugh will ask you how Mister Gough and his mother hurt you."

CHAPTER 40

urt me? I wanted to shout. *Never would he have hurt me! He freed me!*

"Amice?" Megge held the cup to my lips again. "Drink."

I drank because she wanted me to, but I could not look at her. She wanted me to tell Hugh that Mister Gough had hurt me. He never would have—

Why, then, my mind whispered, *had he kept the blood he had taken from Megge's aunt and brought it and Megge's books back to the cliffs?*

There was a reason, I assured myself. A good reason why he had done that.

I took a quick breath and opened my mouth. I would tell her he had not hurt me.

"No, Anna." Anwen's voice so startled me that I coughed hard and almost choked.

"But Tinker is in gaol! I vowed I would not speak until he was dead, but he is in the earl's gaol, so I am safe. I must tell them what I know lest they punish Mister Gough for his mother's crimes."

Anwen's voice softened. "I understand your desire to break your vow. You spoke it to protect yourself, and now you feel you must protect Mister Gough. But for reasons I cannot yet tell you, I must ask you to remain silent. Can you trust me when I tell you that your silence will protect Megge, the goddess?"

I closed my eyes and tried to think. Mister Gough was not the only one who had saved me. Anwen, too, had saved me. By urging me to stay silent, she had kept me from harm. And I did trust her, so I would obey her now.

"Amice?" Megge bent down and looked closely at me. "Have you something to tell me?"

I tightened my lips and shook my head, then climbed onto the bench and huddled beside Ffion. She stroked my hair, but I only grew more troubled.

This was Megge, I thought, and she needs to know what only I can tell her. But I cannot.

"Amice," she began, but I looked away so I would not be tempted to speak.

Ffion looked at Megge and shook her head—no more questions.

Megge picked up the bag of cloths. "Thank you, Amice. These are what I need to help the sick man."

I slid my gaze her way.

"I believe you know about healing," she said, "and may be able to help me. Would you like that?"

I ran to her side.

"Not yet, not with this man, but soon."

I took one of the wet cloths from her to show her how else she might use it to help him. I gently dabbed my face with it, wincing as I touched what might have been sores.

Reaching down, she smiled at me and took my hand. "Thank you, Amice. Cleansing those sores will make the sick man feel better."

CHAPTER 41

MEGGE

Throughout the night, I listened for the blacksmith's breathing and tended to his weeping sores. But cleansing those sores did not make him feel better. He was quickly worsening. I needed help.

In the morning, I opened the tent flap to see Neville setting a bucket of water outside my chamber.

"How much longer?" I asked him.

"We started up the Fowey while you were inside. We're nearly at the wharf."

I looked down at the blacksmith and had to watch for his chest to rise and fall to confirm that he still lived.

"How will we ever get him off the ship?"

"Hugh asked the same question, Megge, so Martyn found two poles and a length of sailcloth and fashioned a simple litter to carry him."

When the ship had come to a stop, I walked to the side, where Neville was joining a wide wooden ramp to the wharf. His back was to me, so I could not see his face, but I knew those shoulders. They strained his tunic as he worked the unwieldy ramp into place. He took a few steps down it, bounced on it, then walked back onto the ship.

"It'll hold fast, Megge."

A boy ran down to the wharf, calling over his shoulder, "I see some carters. I'll tell 'em to make ready."

CHAPTER 42

AMICE

"Careful, there," Megge said as she entered the tent to help Hugh and Martyn lift Mister Gough onto the litter. But Hugh simply took Mister Gough's shoulders and Martyn his feet, and they laid him on it as easily as they might have moved a sack of fleece.

Mister Gough looked even more frail than he had when they brought him up from the hold. I thought he was asleep, but as they jostled him, his moans betrayed his pain.

Ffion touched Megge's elbow. In her arms, safe in that woolsack, were *The Book of Time* and *The Book of Seasons*.

"Where would you have us go, then?" she asked Megge.

"Neville's father has a cart," she said as she walked with us down the ramp to the wharf. "Perhaps Neville will take you to Bury Down."

I stayed close to Megge's side, my gaze fixed on Mister Gough as Hugh and Martyn carried his litter to the wharf, where the carters awaited goods. He was no longer a big man, and his eyes had gone dull. I ached to do something for him, so I stood very close to Megge, hoping she would take me to the lazar house so I could help her tend him.

CHAPTER 43

MEGGE

I would have taken Amice with me to the lazar house, but she was so tired, she was leaning on my leg.

I knelt beside her. "Amice, will you go for Neville? I have a favor to ask of him."

Looking anything but weary, she trotted back to the ship.

Hugh raised his chin to signal a carter, but the man looked upon the blacksmith, made the sign of the cross, and lifted both hands.

"I'll not cart a lazar," he shouted. "Not even a dead one."

The other carters also refused—until Hugh and Martyn's father drew up to the wharf in his cart.

"In here, Hugh," Mister Caerlin called. He climbed down from his seat and opened the back of the cart—the same cart that had carried Claris's body home from the copse. Though I had ridden in it several times since that awful day, nearing it with a man who was nearly a corpse—*a corpse that wants naught but the grave*—brought back the sorrow of seeing Claris covered in those blood-soaked cloaks.

"Don't you dare weep, Margaret," I heard Mother warn as Hugh and Martyn neared, carrying the blacksmith. His lips drew back, but he remained silent as the men lifted the litter into the cart and laid it atop bags of fleece—fleece which Mister Caerlin would never be able to sell after it had touched a lazar.

"It's not meant to be sold," Mother said. "It was freely given to the lazar house as alms of a sort. Brother James uses fleece whenever he can to soften the pallets of his sickest charges."

Something tugged on my tunic. I looked down to see Amice, holding Neville by the hand.

"Do you need me, Megge?" he asked.

"Do you know how far it is to the lazar house?"

"Not far. It's at the edge of the brothers' orchard, where the market road meets Priory Lane."

"How do you know where it is?" I asked.

"Everyone knows where it is." He shrugged. "And have you forgotten? I carve headstones. Even the rich die of lepra."

I looked back at the ship. The shipmen were pulling up the ramp. "Aren't you going on to Lostwithiel?"

"Nay, Megge. Hugh has Mistress Gough well in hand. He has no need of me."

"Ffion and Amice have a long walk ahead of them to Bury Down, and—"

He held up a hand. "My father has a cart. I shall fetch it and take them myself."

"You are very kind, Neville."

He held my gaze, then smiled at me and turned to Ffion. "You must be weary, Ffion. Rest here. And that sack looks heavy. May I carry it for you?" He reached for the sack that held the books, but she swung away from him.

"No, thank you, Laddie. I'll give it only to Brighida."

Megge smiled at Ffion. "I'll come home once the blacksmith is safely lodged in the lazar house with Brother James."

"We'll have a kettle of pottage bubbling on the hearth," Ffion said.

I looked down to see Amice walking hand in hand with Neville through the village to his father's masonry shop.

"Go on, Megge," Ffion said. "She'll be fine. Those two have become fast friends.

CHAPTER 44

I stared at the huts, the cottages, and the many shops that lined the market road. My settlement, my whole world, could have fit in its apron pocket.

At its heart stood a great stone church with a stained-glass window—and a tower. My heart beat so hard and fast, I feared it would burst.

Was Neville going to take me in there? Would his warm voice go icy, as Magdalene's had when she was about to imprison me?

"Amice?" Neville knelt before me and looked at me gently. "Are you ill?"

I shook my head. He took my hands.

"Your hands are sweating. You're tired, Amice. And you must be hungry. I live just over there." He pointed to a small cottage alongside a workshop with an open door large enough to admit a cart. "My mother will have prepared the midday meal. You'll be a welcome guest."

CHAPTER 45

MEGGE

I put an arm over the blacksmith to steady him as the cart dipped and heaved over furrows dug by the many carts that traveled the market road.

I called to Mister Caerlin from the back of the cart, "How did you know to come?"

"Gynneys. He saw the ship coming up the Fowey yesterday and told me it would likely be putting in at the wharf. He asked me to bring my mare for Alf and said there might be need of a cart." He looked behind him at the blacksmith. "He didn't say I'd be carting a lazar."

"He wouldn't have known. Do you know of this place?"

"Know of it? I carry the peat they use for their fires. The earl supplies their peat, gorse brush, and even wood when it's called for. I cut and carry it all. And whatever else the good brother needs."

"Does everyone know of it?"

"Oh, aye. It's been here a good long time. Keeps the poor souls warm and fed—and keeps the sickest of them off the market road."

He pointed to a grey-robed man sitting in the grass near the post that marked the crossroads with Priory Lane. The man raised a cup.

"It's here they do their begging."

Mister Caerlin slowed the cart, opened his purse, and cast a coin to the man. It struck the side of the road and rolled. The man crept to it, picked it up, and let it fall into his cup. He raised a gloved hand in blessing. Mister Caerlin bowed his head and made the sign of the cross.

We turned down a path between two orchards bare of leaves. Mister Caerlin took care to avoid the ruts. He glanced back at the blacksmith when the cart rocked as we drove over stones and branches.

"This is not the first man you've brought here," I said.

"And he'll not be the last." He crossed himself again. "I only pray I won't be carting Hugh and Martyn here one day. They've spent too much time on that ship with this one. As have you. But then, you're a healer."

We rode in silence until I saw, just ahead, a great stone building.

"Mister Caerlin! Is this—"

"Aye," he said with pride. "The lazar house is the largest house in the village, save the priory."

I could scarcely believe my eyes. It was built from the same rock as my cottage and had a slate roof just like ours. It was larger and had more windows than any house I had ever seen, and each window's shutters were open to the cool breeze. Smoke rose from chimneys that pierced the roof, as ours did.

"Look like a cottage you know?" Mister Caerlin asked.

I turned to him, unable to speak.

"Your father and Brighida's built this house."

"But they were the earl's master craftsmen."

"Aye. The earl has had lazar houses built all across Cornwall."

"Who feeds and clothes them?"

"The Church and the crown help, but the lazars do much for themselves. When they come here to live, they turn over all they own in return for being tended for their remaining days. They also pray for the souls of those who bestow alms, so don't we all give them a penny as we pass."

"Mister Caerlin, did you know that my mother . . ."

"Was their healer? Oh, aye. I've served the earl a good long time. And though your mother didn't know me until Lowenna and I came to live in the village, I had long seen her here on her rounds."

Was this, I wondered, what the earl had meant when he said our boon was given in return for our service to the village and the crown? I had thought it was for our service as midwives and counselors. No wonder it was so generous: our land and all that grew upon it; my place in the weaver's guild; and should Brighida and I ever have children, our sons escaping fealty.

Mother had rendered laudable service—the earl assumed I would do the same. And I supposed I would, for already my eye was roaming over the woods at the edge of the copse, searching for pines to make salves for boils, and birch trees to make draughts to lessen fever and ease pain.

CHAPTER 46

AMICE

eville pointed to a cottage behind his father's shop, on the other side of a muddy stream. Goats roamed freely among nearby cottages and huts.

"This is my home."

His cottage was larger than the others and much better tended. Six girls played in the tidy yard, the eldest nearly as old as Neville, and the youngest in a cradle rocked by a girl about my age. Laughing and clamoring for Neville's attention, the other three girls, wearing colorful strips of cloth in their gleaming hair, ran to him, their faces bright with excitement, their round cheeks rosy, their green eyes shining. They clasped their arms around his legs and begged him to walk with them into the house.

Such joyful girls! I had once felt such joy. And then I had been locked away and had come to believe I would never feel it again. But now, watching those girls, I believed I one day might.

"Neville!" A woman with hair the color of autumn leaves met us at the door and embraced him. "I have prayed for your safe return."

She noticed me smiling at her clean, healthy, finely clad daughters and knelt to take my hands.

"Neville," she said, still regarding me, "who is your friend?"

"This is Amice, Mother," he said. "Amice, this is my mother, Mistress Angwin."

I looked into her eyes and nodded.

"She is quiet," Neville said. "She understands every word we say, but never have I heard her speak."

Neville's mother rose, still holding my hand, and led me to the door. "You are welcome here, Amice. Come. The midday meal is ready."

"We cannot stay long, Mother. An elder woman called Ffion is waiting for us to bring Father's cart to the wharf and take her and Amice to Bury Down."

"Your father is delivering a headstone, so you will sit and eat." She looked fondly at me. There is stew, fresh bread, and cheese made from the milk of our goats. Do you like cheese?"

I could not stop nodding my head.

"Girls," she called and opened the door.

The girls ran into the house, all talking at once. Mistress Angwin picked up the swaddled babe and followed them in.

"I am Delona," said the girl who had been rocking the cradle. She pushed through the crowd of girls and stood close to me, her face bright with cheer. "*I* shall be your friend."

CHAPTER 47

MEGGE

Brother James came out of the great stone house, a leather apron over his hooded brown robe and long leather gloves dangling from his hand. As he approached, he pulled them on.

"I saw the cart," he called. "Early for the peat, yet . . ."

His words broke off when he saw me. He looked into the back of the cart.

"We have brought you someone," I said. "If you will have him."

"Is this . . ."

"Yes. Michael Gough. He told me he had once sought your counsel. Hugh thought it wise to bring him here rather than deliver him to the gaol."

His gaze still on the lazar, Brother James nodded. "We have a cell here."

"A cell?"

"A room. Although this is not the monastery, we refer to the quarters in the main house as *cells*. I shall see to him." He looked up at me, his eyes gentle. "Would you be willing to help me tend him?"

"I should count it as an honor, Brother James."

Now awake, the blacksmith wheezed, "She's a herder." He labored to catch his breath. "She'll not touch me."

"We'll have no such talk here, Michael," Brother James warned. "You are here now and under my—under *our*—care." He nodded toward me, and the blacksmith growled.

"Or," I said, "Mister Caerlin can carry you to Lostwithiel—and the earl's gaol—in the back of this cart." I awaited his response.

None came.

"It is decided," Brother James said.

Mister Caerlin released the latch, and the back of the cart fell open. "Steady now, Gough," he said as he picked up the handles at the foot of the litter.

Brother James bent over the side of the cart and grasped the handles at the blacksmith's head. "Slowly now."

The blacksmith moaned. The moan turned into a wet cough, and he spat.

Brother James looked at Mister Caerlin, then tipped his head toward the woods. "The cottage."

A small house that I had not noticed sat in a glade bordered on three sides by oaks and mistletoe. A path led from the big house to the cottage door.

"He's far too ill to be tended with the others," Brother James said to me. "He can be better tended in the cottage."

The men slid the litter back into the cart. As we neared the cottage, I saw that, like the big house, it was built in much the same way as mine. A woman wearing a hooded white robe opened the door and stepped outside.

"Megge!" She ran to me, her sleeves flapping from her outstretched arms.

"Lowenna!" I embraced her.

"Oh, Megge," she said as she held me at arm's length and looked me over. "You've made it back safely! We have all been so anxious."

As she walked me into the kitchen, I asked, "What's brought you here, Lowenna?"

"I tend the cottage." She swept her arm across the kitchen, her charge. It was much like our kitchen at Bury Down. Even the herb-drying rack hanging above the table held plants Mother and Aunt Claris might have used to season our food and make their cures. The stone floor, covered with fresh rushes, might have been the same one I had swept every day.

"You tend it?"

"Yes, I have for some time."

"And yet, you have always had time to help us."

"Your mother gave me back my life." She shrugged. "I was so ill, I believed I would die. Without her, I would have. So I will always have time for you."

"Lowenna, Mother trusted you, so tell me—what did she do for the lazars?"

Lowenna glanced around the kitchen and spoke low. "She offered them her final cure."

"Final cure? What was that?"

An eyebrow went up. "You don't know?"

I shook my head.

She glanced from side to side, then said in a low voice, "The ether. And Mentorship."

"Mentorship? But to become a Mentor, one must have shown a willingness in this life to serve, or have possessed a vital skill—or wisdom—and must vow to share these with others when summoned to return to the living world. How could she have offered Mentorship to all the lazars?"

"Some were not suited—and she knew who they were—so she did not offer it to all those who declined what Brother James offered them in their final days. But many had earned it through their work in this life, so they took that vow. As you know I did— many lives ago."

"What did Brother James offer?"

"Heaven."

"Why would some not want heaven?"

She shrugged. "Perhaps they had not completed their work here."

I looked out the door at that cart. In it lay a man who had certainly not earned heaven. Nor, though, had he earned Mentorship.

"What did Mother offer those who deserved neither heaven nor Mentorship?"

Before Lowenna could answer, Alf came in, eating a thick piece of bread.

"I stopped on my way to Bury Down," he said, his mouth full, "so I could tell Lowenna you were coming and lend a hand with Gough."

The burly Mister Caerlin was once more pulling the litter out of the cart. Thin, scholarly Brother James, on the other hand, was struggling.

"Let me help, Brother James," Alf called. Cramming the rest of the bread into his mouth, he trotted down the path and took the handles from Brother James. "This end's heavier than the feet."

With Brother James leading the way, Alf and Mister Caerlin carried the litter into the kitchen.

"In here," a young woman's voice called from the room on the other side of the great hearth, where our workroom would have been.

The men carried the litter into the room, and a grey-robed young woman motioned to the pallet lying on a raised frame. A thin linen sheet covered the bed. A fleece blanket was folded at the foot.

Mister Caerlin and Alf set the litter on the bed, then moved back as Brother James and the young woman deftly turned the blacksmith onto his side, pulled the litter from beneath him, and rolled him back. They moved with such ease, almost as one, that I knew they had done this many times. The young woman must have begun helping Brother James while she was still a child.

Lowenna brought me a white robe like her own. "Put this on while you are within doors." She helped me into it and pulled up the hood. "It keeps you clean while letting others know why you are here. Healers wear white."

Surely, Brother James's helper was a healer. But if healers wore white, why did she wear grey?

Alf drew me aside. "My father needs my help. Would you like me to take you home?"

"I have more to do here."

"But can you get home on your own, Meg?"

"It's not so far, and I shall relish the walk." *Alone. For the first time in weeks.*

Alf touched his forehead and was away.

"Walk? Nonsense," Mister Caerlin said. "It is too far to walk, and it'll be dusk before you're ready to leave. I'll finish my work in the fields and return for you and Lowenna." He stepped outside and turned to speak, but a burst of coughing came from the sickroom, and he walked swiftly to his cart.

"I've a remedy for Michael's cough," Brother James said to the grey-robed woman. "It is in the infirmary. I shall fetch it and leave you to your work, Christine."

I followed him from the room, and Christine drew a curtain across the doorway—just as Lowenna had once drawn a sheet across our workroom's entrance before tending to Claris's body.

CHAPTER 48

AMICE

I had just devoured a meal of steaming pottage, warm bread, and creamy goat cheese when Neville's father entered the kitchen sideways, his shoulders too broad to fit easily through the narrow doorway.

Neville stood. Nearly as tall as his father, but not yet as brawny, Neville took my hand and led me to the door.

"Father, meet Amice. She lives with Megge and Brighida."

He looked down at me but said nothing.

"Amice, meet my father, Mister Angwin."

I wiped my sleeve across my mouth and nodded to this giant.

He looked at Neville, a question crossing his face.

"I promised Megge I would take Amice and Ffion—one of Amice's guardians—back to Bury Down," Neville said.

"They were on the ship?" Mister Angwin's voice rumbled—so low, I believed he was angry. But when his eyes fixed on mine, I saw both wonder and concern.

"Yes, and it was a long journey." Neville smiled at me.

"What say you to that?" Mister Angwin asked me.

"She doesn't speak," piped up Delona. "She eats and eats, but says not a word!"

"That's enough, Delona." Mistress Angwin raised an eyebrow at the girl as she set a bowl of pottage, an enormous spoon, and a loaf of bread before her husband. "She is quiet, is all. Some of you girls could take a lesson from her."

"I understand," Mister Angwin said, picking up the spoon and holding it over his bowl, "that the ladies of Bury Down have taken in some other guests as well."

"Do you mean Kaatje and her daughter, Britlen, from Aldestowe?" Neville asked.

"I mean the wife and daughter of Tinker Penneck." He spat the name.

Neville laid a calming hand on my arm.

"They are nothing like him, Father. Kaatje is both learnèd and courageous. She led Hugh and Martyn to Tinker at grievous peril to herself."

"Come, girls." Mistress Angwin got up from the table. Picking up the sleeping babe and taking the next eldest girl by the hand, she led them out of the kitchen. Delona followed, keeping her eyes on me as she left the room, smiling.

Mister Angwin spoke quietly to Neville. "I have heard of the girl. Britlen. Her father blinded her, they say, though I don't see how that could be true, even of Tinker Penneck. I know he's harmed animals, but a girl? His own daughter?"

I had to hold myself back from speaking.

"Britlen herself told her mother what he did. That was why Kaatje helped Hugh find him. The girl would not lie, Father."

"Tinker will be tried soon. Haskins questioned a few people, but he got only the girl's word about this. We'll see how Hugh does. Can no one confirm her story?" Mister Angwin ate a heaping spoonful of stew, then looked at me.

Holding his gaze, I nodded.

CHAPTER 49

MEGGE

I never knew of this place," I said to Lowenna. "How is it you never spoke of it?"

"Your mother and aunt asked me not to," she said, now bent over the kettle at the hearth, stirring and tasting. She motioned to the table. I pulled out a chair and sat.

She pulled dried herbs off the rack, crumbled them, and stirred them into the bubbling stew.

"When our family came to the village from Lostwithiel," she said, "the earl charged my husband with tending the fields and keeping the peat supplied here and the gorse at the ready for the outdoor firepits. At first, he was only to haul peat and cut brush, but you've met Brother James." She chuckled.

"Before long, I was tending the cottage whenever the sickroom was being used. When I saw your mother caring for a lazar, she asked me to say nothing to you. She wanted you as her apprentice and was afraid that this," she pointed with her ladle toward the room that held the diseased blacksmith, "would frighten you."

"It would have done that," I said. But nothing would have frightened me more than Mother herself or the book she had tried in vain to force upon me.

"It was hard, caring for both this house and my own," Lowenna said as she ladled stew into bowls, "but now that Kaatje and Britlen are here, much of the burden has lifted."

A weight fell upon me as I pictured Brighida working alone in the cottage while I was gone. How had she done it all with but one hand?

"They have also helped Brighida while you've been gone and will continue to do so now that you've returned, for your work as a healer is held above all other duties."

She set a bowl before me. A week earlier, I would have had no appetite after looking upon the face of the blacksmith, but after a journey in which I had supped on dried fish after tending his weeping sores and emptying his bucket, eating in the same cottage with him caused me no unease.

And I was hungry.

"Are you to be Brother James's apprentice?" Lowenna asked.

"I believe so," I said as I savored that stew. "He's asked me to work alongside him to tend the blacksmith." Deep inside, though, I knew that soon there would be much I could teach the good brother. Knowledge was blooming within me.

Lowenna leaned forward and examined my face. "You have no need of a master . . . Lady."

She brushed my left cheek lightly, never taking her eyes from mine.

I touched my cheek. "Do you know of this mark?"

"We have waited so long, Lady."

Brother James nudged the door open and came through, carrying the bags of fleece from Mister Caerlin's cart.

"We shall speak of this later," Lowenna whispered.

"This fleece will make for a soft pallet when we replace the straw in that one," Brother James said and took them into the sickroom. He returned to the kitchen and smiled at me. "Shall we get to work?"

CHAPTER 50

AMICE

re you saying," Mister Angwin asked, "that Britlen spoke the truth?"

I silently beseeched Anwen, "I will not speak, but I must tell them. The sheriff must know what Tinker did."

I waited.

"Anwen?"

Neville turned to me. "Amice?"

I closed my eyes for a moment. Anwen remained silent.

Looking first at Neville and then at his father, I nodded.

Mister Angwin turned his chair to face me. "Are you saying that you believe her? Or that you know for certain it is true?"

Without looking away from him, I made a fist and thumped my chest.

"You know," Neville said.

Nodding, I touched my finger to my eye. *I saw.*

I had to show them what else Tinker had done.

I put out my tongue and touched my finger to it. Neville drew away, wincing, but his father leaned forward and studied it.

"It's been cut off!" He looked at Neville. "That's why she doesn't speak! Has no one ever asked her who did this to her? Not even Hugh?" He looked at me again. "Who did this to you, child?"

I could almost feel the burn of Tinker's blade.

"You can tell us, Amice." Neville knelt next to me and looked at me kindly. "It was the sick man, Michael Gough, wasn't it?"

Eyes wild, I shook my head.

Mister Angwin's breath came fast through his nose. "Tinker Penneck?"

Someone pounded on the door. "Angwin!"

Mister Angwin crossed to the door and threw it open. "Tucker. What's got you—"

A stout, ruddy-faced man grabbed Mister Angwin's arm, pulled him outside, and slammed the door. Neville and I simply looked at each other.

When Mister Angwin came back inside, his face a storm cloud, he spoke to Neville, his voice so low I could not hear what he said.

"Are you certain?" Neville asked, getting to his feet and reaching for his cloak.

"I heard it from Hugh himself," Mister Tucker called from the doorway. "He's at the wharf. He told me to find you."

"Fetch the cart, boy," Mister Angwin ordered.

CHAPTER 51

MEGGE

rother James drew a small flask from a deep pocket hidden in a fold in the side of his robe and set it on the table.

"Christine," he called into the sickroom, "I've brought the draught."

He opened the flask and waved it under my nose. The familiar aroma was pungent yet sweet.

"Thyme," I said. "With honey."

"Yes, very good. We grow thyme in the kitchen garden and have hives just behind the orchard."

Christine hurried in and poured the liquid into a cup. With a nod to Brother James, she returned to the sickroom.

Brother James accepted a steaming bowl of stew from Lowenna. He bowed his head over it and closed his eyes for a moment. Lowenna sat across from him, made the sign of the cross along with him, and they both began to eat.

"Will this be the blacksmith's cell?" I asked.

"Cell?" Brother James asked, looking up from his bowl. "Oh,

you're thinking of the house. We call the small sleeping rooms there *cells*. But we tend the gravely ill here, in the cottage, so we call his room 'the sickroom'—though, for reasons I could never guess, your mother always called it 'the workroom.'"

"Brother James?" Christine held back the curtain. "He is ready."

CHAPTER 52

AMICE

The cart lurched and bounced down the market road, and though I sat on the driver's bench between Neville and his father, every pit and bump in the road threw me into the air. Neville put his arm around my shoulders to hold me down.

"Can't have you taking flight like a seagull, now, can we?"

He laughed—to calm me, I supposed—and held me tightly as we rode over an even rougher length of road, my teeth knocking together with every jolt.

"There." Mister Angwin pointed at the ship. "It's still at anchor. Get ready, boy."

Hugh stood near the wharf, one hand shading his eyes as he searched the road. Upon seeing us, he raised an arm.

Neville did not wait for the cart to stop before jumping down.

"Father will take you and Ffion to Bury Down, Amice," he called over his shoulder as his long strides carried him swiftly to Hugh. Heads together, they spoke, and then Neville clapped Hugh on the shoulder and strode toward the ship.

"Hold." Hugh raised a hand to stay Mister Angwin.

"He'll want to speak to you, child," Mister Angwin said gently. "Don't be afraid. Show him what you showed Neville and me."

I closed my eyes and waited.

"Do as Mister Angwin tells you, Anna," Anwen said. "Hugh will not expect you to speak, but he will ask you what you know. You may make him understand the truth about Tinker."

I opened my eyes. Hugh stood beside the cart.

"Amice, Neville tells me you know something about Tinker."

I nodded.

"Can you tell me?"

I nodded my head but tightened my lips.

"I've little time, Amice." Hugh's eyes held mine. "Tell me. Did you see Tinker do something to Britlen?"

My gaze never moved from his as I nodded.

"What did he do?"

With one hand, I used my thumb and first finger to prise open my eye. With the other, I mimed touching something to it.

"He blinded Britlen," Hugh said calmly. "Are you telling me that Tinker Penneck blinded Britlen?"

I nodded.

"How do you know?"

I touched my eye and extended my finger toward him.

"You saw him."

I nodded, tears filling my eyes.

Hugh knelt beside me. "Amice, Neville tells me Tinker did something more. What else did he do?"

If he ever escapes—

I looked at Hugh, that bullock of a man, and studied his solemn eyes and serious mouth. I thought of Neville and his strong arms and gentle gaze. These men would protect me.

But they were leaving on that ship.

"Amice? Will you show Hugh what you showed me?" Mister

Angwin prompted, his voice soft and comforting. He dropped a rock-hard arm around my shoulders. Holding my gaze, he said, "Go on."

I opened my mouth.

CHAPTER 53

MEGGE

Now garbed in a grey tunic, the blacksmith rested quietly, his breath rattling in his chest, his face and hands sallow against the white sheet.

Christine had washed his hair and combed it away from his face. The thick ridge of brow over those sunken eyes, concave cheeks, and flattened nose made his whole face appear to have fallen in. Still, he was breathing.

He opened his eyes and looked around the room.

"Leave, herder," he wheezed. "Let me die in peace."

Ignoring the blacksmith, Brother James held out a cup of yellow liquid, looked at me, and tilted his head. My apprenticeship had begun.

I sniffed the cup. I knew that aroma. Musty. Spicy.

"Yellow dock tea," I said. "To feed the blood." A sweet scent, lighter than honey, rose above the earthy smell. "With coltsfoot to ease the cough."

"I said *leave*," the blacksmith rasped.

"Be still, Michael," Brother James said. He bent and picked up the blacksmith's hands.

"No nails," I said, brushing the tips of the blacksmith's fingers. "This one is shortened. This one is clubbed."

"Get your herder's hands off me."

"You were right to bring him here," Brother James said, looking up at me, "despite his apparent ill will toward you." He bowed his head beneath his hood, and I heard the pity in his voice. "I know the crimes he stands accused of."

"*Accused* of?"

I had almost begun to pity the blacksmith. During the voyage, I had buried my rage, my thirst for revenge, and my wicked thoughts beneath a thin skin of duty. I thought I had quelled them, but like the worst of the blacksmith's boils, they had festered. And that word— *accused*—had just pierced the skin. All the poison rolled out of me.

"He stands not merely accused, Brother James, but guilty. You were there, at the church, the day he arrived posing as an abbot charged with purging this village of heretics. He arrested my mother and aunt. He put them in a *cage*, Brother James. And before long, he killed them both. I needn't say more, for you know what he did."

Though horrified at my words—and at the finger I pointed at Brother James—I could not hold them back. "So do not use the word *accused* in my hearing when you speak of this murderer."

My hood had fallen back, and I could feel the weight of my hair as it tumbled over my shoulders and down my back.

"Guilty though he may be, Megge," Brother James said, his voice calm and low, "your mother would have put aside his crimes and seen to his needs."

"I have seen to his needs, Brother James." I drew up my hood and softened my voice. "He is alive today only because I took him from that cave, tended him on the ship, and brought him here."

"But not out of mercy, I'd wager."

"Out of duty. And to see justice done."

"Is it justice you seek—or revenge?" He walked to the curtain and halted. "Your mother would have done more than simply see to his sores. She would have offered him the cure that would bring him peace at the end—if he refused the peace I offered. Are you willing to do the same? Will you offer him your mother's cure?"

Mentorship? Does he believe Mother would have asked this murderer to be a Mentor?

Without awaiting an answer, he went into the kitchen, leaving me to consider his question.

I bent down and whispered into the blacksmith's ear, "I shall tend your diseased flesh, and at the time of death, I shall offer you the draughts any healer would give to soothe you. But my mother's *cure*—the peaceful transition into the ether and another span of days in the living world—is for those who ask for it. And deserve it. Are you willing to make amends for the evil you have done?"

The blacksmith was awake and listening, but he said nothing— only curled his lip.

Brother James came into the sickroom. He looked down at the wasted man and back at me. "Amends, Megge?"

"He took from this village its healers."

Brother James took my arm and led me away from the bed. He spoke in a low voice. "Making amends is a lot to ask of a dying man."

"You once denied him absolution when he refused to confess his sins and make amends. I ask only that he make amends."

"That is what God asks, Megge, for forgiveness of sin. It is not what we demand in exchange for succor."

"I have given him succor. I will continue to do so. But the deaths of my mother and aunt have left this entire village bereft of succor. Making amends is a small price to pay for—"

"For mercy?" Troubled, he walked to the doorway. He turned back to me before leaving the room. "Healers put no price on mercy, Megge. It is freely given."

I said nothing, but when he had gone, I leaned over the blacksmith.

"It is not my mercy that comes with a price, Blacksmith. I have shown you mercy at every turn."

"You took me from the sea's mercy and condemned me to—this." He looked around the room.

"You have traded in death all your life. Now you want an easy passage out of it. But the final cure I offer—to the worthy—comes with a burden you may find too weighty to bear. Service." I looked into the eyes that had long haunted my dreams, and something stirred within me—not pity, not compassion, but a sickness of spirit so deep, it made me want to weep. I had to look away to gather my wits.

"Perhaps there is more to you than I know," I said. "Perhaps you have done some good that has gone unseen. Ask me for my help, Blacksmith, and then show me one person you have ever loved, or one who cares for you—and vow to respond to my summons to serve in your next life—and I shall bring all the power of Bury Down to your deathbed."

"I see the herding wench is now a judge." He spat.

The crude words and churlish act reminded me of just who this man was. There was no unseen act of goodwill in his past, no one to whom he had ever offered kindness, no one who would weep when he died.

"And I see that you truly are a corpse that wants naught but the grave." I held his watery gaze. "Death can be fearsome, Blacksmith, or it can be serene," I said as I left his room. "Tell me when you have decided which you prefer."

CHAPTER 54

AMICE

"It's been cut," Hugh said as he inspected my tongue, "just as Britlen said. But I needed to see it for myself. You are very brave, Amice."

He looked at Mister Angwin. "I'll return once I have seen to this . . . other matter."

Hugh started toward the ship, then looked back at me. "Amice, when I return, I shall ask you what Mistress Gough did to you in that church and what her son, Michael Gough, had to do with her hurting you and the other girls." He turned and strode toward the ship.

I wanted to run after him and tell him that Mister Gough had not helped the priestess.

"Anna," Anwen said. "No."

"Why mustn't I?"

"You have taken a vow of silence. Have you forgotten? And I have told you—speaking of Mister Gough will not help him, and it may hurt Megge. Trust me, child. This is in another's hands."

"Whose hands? Hugh is the sheriff. It is in his hands."

Hugh and Neville were already boarding the ship. Somehow, I had to tell Hugh that whatever else Mister Gough had done, he had not hurt me or the other girls. My mind kept whispering Megge's words, but never would I believe that Mister Gough had taken Claris's blood and Megge's books for an evil purpose. His eyes were too gentle when he looked upon me, his countenance too sorrowful. He grieved for all the evil the priestess had done in his name.

"He rescued us, Anwen. He opened the door and saved us all. That must count for something. And who else may decide his fate?"

"Megge." Anwen's voice was calm. "His fate is in Megge's hands."

CHAPTER 55

MEGGE

I was still breathing hard when I entered the kitchen. I laid my hand over my throat to calm myself.

The kitchen smelled of sulfur and pitch as Christine poured thick, strong-smelling black salve into a small dish. The scent began to awaken memories of distant times.

As though I had not just spoken to Brother James like a peevish child—or worse, a shrew—he pulled out a chair for me. I sat, and he laid a surgeon's knife in my hand. "Do you know how to use this?"

I held the knife loosely in my right hand and drew it smoothly over the back of my left hand, not touching the skin.

"Yes," Brother James said and accepted the dish of salve from Christine. He held it before me. "We use this salve for many skin ailments—"

"Especially for boils not yet ready to burst," I finished. And though the knowledge of healing, long asleep within me, was now fully awake and surging through me, I felt I would collapse from weariness.

Brother James looked closely at me. "You learned much more at your mother's side than I realized. Yes, we shall use the salve for some of his boils and the knife for those ready to be purged. But I can see you are tired, Megge. So tired that you have gone pale. Go to Bury Down, where you can be tended. Caerlin will take you. Return to us when you've rested. We will see to Michael."

"When I return, will you forgive my harsh words and instruct me?"

"Already I've forgiven your—hasty—words. And it seems you need little instruction in healing. You've the skill to take your mother's place." He tapped his fingers on the table, thinking. When he looked at me again, his gaze was soft. "But I believe that tending this man will teach you about more than boils and salves."

Was the pity I saw in his eyes for the blacksmith, I wondered, or for me?

Drying her hands on her towel, Lowenna followed me outside. "Megge, you are weary to the bone." She helped me out of my white robe and put an arm around me to lead me back into the cottage. "Stay. Sleep here in the hut your mother used to use."

"I need time to think. I can rest at Bury Down, and the walk and the fresh air will restore me."

"Pray, wait for the cart. It is late, and you are so tired."

"I would like to walk." I kissed her cheek.

She ran a finger over the goddess mark on mine. "A true healer walks in this village once more."

A true healer, I thought with disdain as I started down the path to Priory Lane. A true healer would give those she tended whatever was in her power to give—and I had the power to ease a spirit from its tortured body.

But the first sufferer whom fate had seen fit to place in my care was not only unfit to become a Mentor—he roused in me such deep loathing that I had to struggle to speak to him without scorn.

Why, then, was I demanding that he prove himself worthy to receive Bury Down's final cure?

At the crossroads sat the grey-robed man with his begging cup.

"Lady," he rasped. He wore no gloves now, and rather than hold out the cup, he pushed it toward me with the tip of the crutch lying beside him in the dirt. "Alms for prayer?"

I opened the purse Brighida had given me as I set out on my journey to the cliffs, took out three pennies, and dropped them into his cup. I carried it to him and put it in his misshapen hand.

"What is your name?" I asked him.

"Stephen." His voice came from deep inside his wide hood. "Though that is not my given name."

"Why do they not call you by your given name?"

"Stephen is a saint's name, Lady. I took it some time ago. I pray to him, and he intercedes for those who buy indulgences."

This is no mere beggar, I thought. This is a learnèd man.

"Tell me who you . . . were. Before this sickness befell you."

"Before they took my black-and-white robes and gave me this?" That knotted hand snaked from its sleeve and shook the skirt of his long, grey robe.

"You were—" I recalled Alf telling me that the Dominicans did not like to be called Blackfriars. "You were a Dominican friar."

"*Am* a friar." He raised his hand to his hood. "May I? I would like to look upon the only one who has ever stopped to speak to me as if I were still among the living. As if I were still a man."

He pushed back his hood. The eyes that looked upon me were knowing and wise. I wanted to weep.

"Do not—" He pulled up the hood.

"Surely, you can allow me a moment of compassion for your suffering," I said.

"It's not compassion I need, Lady, but hope. Mercy. And there's none to be had in this life." He raised his head and looked at me. "If you wish, you may pray for me. Pray to Saint Stephen that my days will end as his did, in the blink of an eye."

He bowed his head beneath his hood and left me as surely as if he had picked up his crutch and walked away.

CHAPTER 56

Mister Angwin and I rode through the crowded wharf, searching for Ffion. He did not speak, but I argued silently with Anwen.

"Why does Megge hold power over Mister Gough? She hates him. She never calls him by his name, only by *Blacksmith*. She helps him, but I have seen how she regards him. She wants him to die for stealing her books."

"You do not understand—yet—what Megge feels, or why. Watch and listen."

I nodded. I would not speak. Nor, though, would I allow my vow of silence to stand in the way of Tinker facing justice for his crimes.

Anwen had not chastised me for silently "telling" Mister Angwin and Hugh what I knew about Tinker. Was that because I had not spoken or because I had not revealed what I knew about Mister Gough?

No matter. I would do as she asked. I would listen and learn. But not by eavesdropping as I had done on the ship. I would make myself useful to Megge. I knew how to tend a lazar, so I would help her in the ways I had been taught.

But she was so angry, so hard.

"Is that your Ffion?" Mister Angwin pointed to the little old woman with black hair showing beneath her coif.

I waved my arms until she saw me and bustled to the cart.

"It's been an age, child. Where have you been?"

"She had to wait for me," Mister Angwin said and nodded to her. "God give you good day, Mistress. I am Neville's father, Robert Angwin. And you must be Ffion."

"Aye, and it's a pleasure to meet Neville's father. He's a fine lad." She leaned close to me and sniffed. "What's that I smell on your breath, child? Onions? Meat?"

Mister Angwin bent close to me and quietly said, "I believe Ffion needs a bit more room up here."

"Oh, have no care for me," Ffion said.

Mister Angwin raised an eyebrow at me. I climbed into the back.

Over the thud of the horses' hooves and the clink and rattle of chains as we passed over the bumpy road, I could hear only snatches of their conversation. I watched the sky go dark, felt the wind go cold, and wished we were home.

When we arrived at the cottage, I smiled my thanks to Mister Angwin and ran inside to warm myself. The steam rising from the kettle of pottage hanging over the peat smelled so good that I felt my mouth water despite having just eaten a full meal.

"Amice!" Brighida took me in her arms and held me close. "We've missed you sorely!"

Kaatje, chopping vegetables at the sideboard, set down her knife and cried, "Ffion! Amice! You're home!"

Smiling and laughing, she and Britlen joined Brighida, and all three embraced me. Ffion waited by the door until they released me.

"Ffion!" Brighida wrapped her arm around her and pulled her close. A moment later, she looked out the door. "Where is Megge?"

"We brought Michael Gough—and your books—back from the cliffs. He's a lazar, Brighida. Hugh sent him to the priory's lazar house. Megge went with him to see him settled. He suffers from lepra, boils, and who knows what else. She'll see to him there."

Never had I heard Ffion's voice sound flat. Nor had I ever seen her face so tight.

"Ffion?" Brighida held her at arm's length, and the joy on her face faded as she looked upon the shadows darkening Ffion's countenance. Another storm cloud, I thought, just like Mister Angwin's face after talking with Mister Tucker.

"Brighida, Kaatje." Ffion twitched her head toward the door. They stayed outside for a long time. When they returned, the sound of footsteps came from the workroom, and a haggard-looking pregnant woman shuffled into the kitchen and leaned against the hearth.

Brighida went to her. "Nellie, you are meant to be resting."

"If Megge is not returning, I'll go home," she said.

Brighida closed her eyes for a moment, then opened them, looked far into the distance, and exhaled. "She is on her way and will be here soon. I know she will want to help you."

Nellie looked from Brighida to Ffion. "You must be Ffion," she said, her voice rising in what sounded like hope. "Brighida and Kaatje have told me so much about you. That you are something of a healer."

"Poultices and herbals, dear, nothing more." Ffion looked at Nellie's belly. "When is the bairn due?"

Nellie rubbed her belly, and tears glistened in her eyes. "Not for some time. But my pains have come on too early, as they did last time." Her eyes clouded with despair. "Your aunt saved both me and the child. This babe surely will die without a true healer. And we've had no true healer since your aunt passed, so we've no choice but to put our lives in the hands of these women who pass from village to village claiming to be healers. But women have died at their hands." In tears now, she beseeched Brighida, "Ask Megge to help me. Surely, now that her mother is gone and she's grown, Megge will be our midwife."

"Perhaps she will." Brighida led her back into the workroom, where a pallet covered with blankets lay between the spinning wheel and the loom. "She will be here soon, Nellie. Lie back down. Let me make you a soothing draught."

CHAPTER 57

MEGGE

ercy, I thought when I reached the spot in the copse where the blacksmith had murdered Aunt Claris. What mercy had he shown her? That memory burned like gall, and I had to fight to keep it from choking me.

I had shown the blacksmith mercy since the moment I found him in that cave, and I would continue to tend his sores and ease his fear and suffering through his last breath. Why was that not enough?

I've got demons to wrestle, I thought as I stepped from the copse into our pasture. Fields and tilled gardens spread out before me, a haven despite the violence the blacksmith and his men had visited upon it.

But not tonight. Tonight, I shall rest.

I stepped through the nearly dry creek bed, passed the barn and the pen, and crossed the shorn pasture. No sheep grazed on the slope, but the smoke rising in a great plume from the chimney spoke of home and comfort.

Brighida and Ffion would be making the evening meal, and I could almost see Amice setting cups, bowls, and spoons on the table.

I opened the cottage door, and Brighida, already wearing her warm cloak, stepped outside. She drew me to her and held me, speaking quietly, her words rushed.

"I saw all that befell you on the cliffs, Megge, and I heard you speak your vow." She held me away, looking into my eyes. "I know what you became down in that sea cave." She touched the spot beneath my left eye, then spoke slowly, her gaze unwavering. "I know who—and what—you now are. We have much to talk about, Cousin, but that will come later."

"What's wrong, Brighida?"

"Tinker Penneck has escaped."

"When?"

"Two days ago."

"How do you know?"

"Ffion just told me. Mister Angwin told her on their way here."

"How could he have escaped? He was not in some village gaol. He was in Lostwithiel, in the earl's prison."

Brighida shook her head. "Ffion said Mister Angwin knew only that Tinker was gone and that the earl had charged Hugh and Neville with finding him."

"Does Kaatje know?"

"Yes, and as Hugh is now the sheriff, he will lead the search. Already, he's looking into the murders Michael Gough and his men—including Tinker—have committed."

I thought of Amice and recalled my vision of that Samhain ceremony—all those silent girls.

Tinker Penneck's work.

And he was free.

Gone now was my quest for mercy. Tinker would get none from me. Gone, too, was my healer's spirit. In its place was the deathbringer's. I welcomed it.

Come for us now, Tinker. I dare you.

"Megge?"

I could not reply. I was planning how I would defend my family.

Brighida looked at me with concern. "There is something else, Megge."

I forced myself to swallow my rage, then looked at Brighida.

"I know how you feel about attending births—"

"Not this, Brighida. Not now."

"Nellie is here. Her last child came early and nearly died, and she's begun to have birth pains, so she fears she may lose this one. The midwives who come to the village lack your mother's skill, so she has come to ask for your help."

CHAPTER 58

AMICE

I hardly knew the woman who followed Brighida into the cottage. Megge's face was pale, her eyes hard, her lips tight. She walked around the kitchen and stood by the sideboard, picking up and setting down the knife Kaatje had been using to chop turnips. She ran a finger along the blade.

"Megge." Brighida lifted her chin toward the workroom.

Megge's breath came short. Brighida calmly took Megge's cloak from around her shoulders and laid it over a chair. She put her hand to the small of Megge's back and nudged her into the workroom.

The women spoke so quietly that I could not hear what they were saying, but I felt the despair in Nellie's voice and the strain in Megge's.

CHAPTER 59

MEGGE

ellie is in no danger," I said to Brighida after Nellie and I had spoken. "I laid my hands on her belly for some time, and it remained soft."

I had also looked at her arm, where Brother James had taken off a lump some time ago. It had not returned, nor had any new lumps appeared. *Not lepra.* I heaved out a breath. That was something to be grateful for.

"She's had no pain since she arrived," Brighida said. "I believe she had been having the same pains every woman has long before she delivers. She fears, though. She fears she will deliver too soon and lose the child."

And I feared I might collapse from weariness. But I returned to the workroom and asked Nellie, "Can you rest tonight?"

"Yes, my mother is with the children."

"Who brought you here? I saw no cart, no one waiting for you."

"Cadan had an errand. He will return for me soon."

"Brighida will give you a draught. Let your husband take you home. I shall come to you in the morning."

"Good night, Kaatje. Good night, Britlen." I kissed each of them. "Thank you for helping Brighida while I was away."

I kissed Ffion's cheek and whispered, "Tell Kaatje we shall talk about Tinker in the morning."

I lit the candle in Morwen's old lantern. Beside it lay that long, sharp knife. I slid it up my sleeve.

CHAPTER 60

egge bade us goodnight and stepped outside, an old lantern swinging from her hand.

Appearing troubled, she stopped just outside the door and raised a hand to her face. I thought she might weep, so I went to her, hoping to comfort her.

Lost in thought, she absently stroked my hair, and her hand brushed the braided cord at my neck. She pulled it from the neck of my tunic and stared hard at the stone, then at me.

"I know you." Her voice soft with wonder, she tilted her head and looked at me intently. "We have walked together—many times—in the living world."

That's just what Anwen said. But I did not remember another life.

"But I don't remember when." Megge exhaled. "So much is coming back to me, but like glass broken into shards. Healing. The blacksmith. Births. You."

She looked at me hard, and I knew she was trying to force herself to remember.

"Now I have frightened you." She knelt. "Forgive me, Amice. This has been such a long journey, and all we've been through has made me weary beyond measure." Her eyes drifted closed, and her voice went soft. "But I am loath to sleep for fear I'll not be able to face what my dreams will show me."

She looked so tired. And she must have been hungry. Unlike me, she likely had not eaten all day. She had tended to Mister Gough and then walked a great distance back to Bury Down. I took her hand and helped her to her feet. But rather than go inside with me and sup, she turned toward the lodge.

"Thank you, Amice," she said gently. "Thank you, little one."

In my dreams that night, I heard those words, *little one*, again and again—not in Megge's voice, but in a low, silken voice I could not place, and spoken in a language only the oldest part of my spirit understood.

"Like this, little one. Hold your spindle like so."

CHAPTER 61

MEGGE

The moment sleep overtook me, dreams catapulted me back in time.

The horrified face of a child of six came to me, and terror gripped me in my sleep just as it had the first time I touched *The Book of Seasons* and heard that whisper—*Murderer.*

As the fear faded, the scent of damp moss wafted over me from the forest in which, a hermit in that life, I was brewing a physick that would one day be deemed miraculous.

That whiff of loam became the scent of snow, and I was once more shivering during a short, cruel life spent begging for scraps, seeking shelter, and fleeing barefoot over stones so cold they burned my feet.

Smoke overtook me. Now an elderly seer held fast to my sacred rowan in a settlement laid low by famine, I heard my former apprentice sneer, "To hell with you, Witch," and call out for rope. I tasted the rage of the people I had long served as they bound me to that tree and lowered a torch to the straw at my feet. Though I recoiled from the lick of flames and struggled against the rope, I succumbed to the smoke and the fire.

I tried desperately to awaken, but sleep released me from that torment only to reveal countless earlier, lonelier, and even more desperate lives.

Finally, slumber swept me back to the cliffs of Kernow. Swaddled now in blessed sleep, I watched the goddess I had once been walk the seaside cliffs with her novices while gazing over calm blue water and marveling at a far-off storm that would soon churn rippling waves into rampaging surf. I relished the wisdom and serenity all my later lives would lack and basked in the richness of womanhood, the satisfaction of work, and the comfort of companionship. For in those idyllic days, the ill called me *Healer*; a peacemaker and a firebrand called me *Sister*; a bladewright called me *Wife*; and soon, our child would call me *Mother*.

Brighida's whisper woke me. "Megge—we must go to the grove."

Kaatje, Britlen, and Amice still slept soundly.

"Where is Ffion?" I whispered.

Brighida pointed toward the cottage, where Ffion would be stoking the hearth fire and beginning to make ready the morning meal.

I sheathed the carving knife in a cloth folded lengthwise, slid it into my healer's pouch, and tied the strings to the belt at my waist. Brighida followed me outside.

"There's no time to go to the grove, Brighida. If Tinker's loose, we are all at grave risk. I am sworn to protect, and that's what I intend to do."

"How? Without knowing where he is or where he's bound, how can you protect anyone? I shall cast runes, and you can summon a vision."

She looked down at the knife handle protruding from my pouch. "I know what you intend to do." She waited until I looked at her. "And women of Bury Down do not kill."

"You do not yet know all I know about Tinker, Brighida. I *will* defend us—"

Running footsteps pounded down the path to the lodge. *Tinker.* I pulled Brighida behind me, drew my knife, and waited.

Let us finish this.

The footsteps slowed, and a familiar voice called out, "Megge?"

I returned the knife to its sheath, and Brighida came out from behind me as Martyn approached.

"Hugh sent me—"

Kaatje came out of the lodge wrapping herself in a heavy cloak, her feet bare, her disheveled hair a copper-colored nimbus.

Martyn just breathed as he stared at her hair and then at her ankles and bare feet.

"How did Tinker get loose?" Kaatje asked him. "He was in the earl's gaol."

Martyn closed his eyes for a moment, then shook his head and replied, looking at Brighida rather than Kaatje.

"Not when he escaped. He was on the road to Bodmin, traveling in a caged gaol cart with other prisoners and a guard."

"And . . ." Kaatje raised her eyebrows.

Martyn finally looked back at her, his eyes traveling from her tousled hair to her brilliant eyes to the cloak she held closed at her waist.

He coughed and replied, "The driver said he heard a noise and stopped the cart. He got down and saw the guard, hands and feet bound, lying barefoot in the road in a pool of blood. He caught a glimpse of Tinker disappearing into a wooded patch, carrying the guard's boots. He followed Tinker into the woods but couldn't find him. Just ahead was a ravine nearly as steep as a cliff. It was naught but rock, so he did not venture down it."

"Why would Tinker steal the guard's boots?" Brighida asked.

"Prisoners are carted barefoot to discourage thoughts of escape," Martyn said.

"Did the other prisoners escape?" Kaatje asked.

Martyn shook his head. "The driver found the cage door open and the other prisoners still inside, hands bound, arms tied to the sides of the cart. On their faces was terror such as he had never seen. And this driver was one of the earl's men. He'd seen plenty."

"What were their crimes?" I asked.

"Theft. They were on their way to Bodmin to be tried."

"Theft? Why was Tinker among them?" Kaatje demanded.

"He was also being tried for theft. When Hugh arrested him, he was carrying a full purse. He refused to say where the money had come from, and a man from the village claimed it was his and that he could prove it. Old Sheriff Haskins never looked into all the other accusations against Tinker. He said there was no proof he had committed any other crime, so he sent him to Bodmin to await trial for theft."

"What about Britlen's eyes?" Kaatje demanded. "Aren't they evidence that Tinker blinded her?"

"Haskins said the *accusation* that Tinker blinded Britlen hadn't been proved, so he could not charge Tinker with it."

"Not proved?" Kaatje gaped at him. "Britlen herself saw him. He was her father, after all. She knew him." She glared at Martyn. "If she had been Tinker's son, her *accusation* would have stood as proof."

"That may be, Kaatje," Martyn said, "but—"

"She also could have testified that it was Tinker who cut Amice's tongue," I added. "Just before Amice, Ffion, and I left for the cliffs, she told Hugh that she had seen Tinker do it. And since Britlen saw Tinker hurt Amice, it is possible that Amice saw him blind Britlen and could have confirmed Britlen's accusation. Why did Haskins not wait for us to return?"

"I asked him to wait," Martyn said. "I told him that you and Brighida could testify to Tinker's many crimes against Bury Down. But he was so ill, he wasn't thinking clearly."

"How ill?" I asked.

"His breath came short, and he was always coughing. And he could hardly walk—his legs looked like white tree trunks." Martyn shook his head slowly. "He was trying to discharge his duties while he was still able."

Dropsy.

Shame heated my face. The poor man was not merely ill—he was dying. He had very little time left, and he had used it to complete his work as best he could.

"In the end," Martyn said, "it may be well that Tinker escaped."

"Why?" Kaatje, Brighida, and I all asked in unison.

"Because Hugh replaced Haskins. And he and Neville will find Tinker. When they do, Hugh will see to it that he's found guilty and hangs for all his crimes." He looked at me. "Now, though, you must persuade Amice to tell Hugh what befell her in that church—how many girls were imprisoned there, how Tinker harmed them, and where the other girls might be."

"I told her I would never ask her to speak about that."

"You must, Megge. What Amice knows, no one else can tell us."

Kaatje shook her head. "She may never speak, even if she is able, for I am certain Tinker threatened her." She looked at each of us. "Just like he threatened Britlen—that if she told me, he would cut out her tongue and slit my throat. What child would ever speak after that?"

"Britlen did." Martyn looked at Kaatje with admiration. "She told you."

"Only after a long time. And only because she knew I would protect her."

"Surely, Amice knows she's safe with us," I said.

Brighida, who had been lost in her own thoughts, asked, "Martyn, what did they tell him?"

With an effort, Martyn pulled his gaze from Kaatje, shook his head as if to clear his thoughts, and turned to my cousin. "Who, Brighida?"

"The prisoners. What did they tell the driver?"

"They told him that Tinker must have paid the guard to help him escape, for the guard had released Tinker and then restrained the other prisoners while Tinker tied their arms to the sides of the cart.

Once the prisoners were bound, Tinker sliced the guard's throat—one clean slash. He opened the back of the cart, rolled the guard out, took his boots, and ran."

"To have disappeared so quickly," I said, "he must have known where he was. He must have had a place to go."

"And someone waiting with horses," Martyn agreed.

"Not horses," I said slowly, for my mind's eye was showing me mules—three mules. A spare young man rode the first and pulled the second by a rope. Tinker Penneck rode the third. They were picking their way down a narrow ledge along a stone-faced ravine. "Mules."

"Megge?" Martyn touched my sleeve. "Did you say something?"

"Tinker and another young man rode down a steep ravine," I said. "On mules." Still watching, though the vision was fading, I said, "To a hut—mean, like a barn—at the foot of the ravine, nestled amongst weeds and bushes and some sort of fern nearly as tall as you."

I closed my eyes tightly, as if that would help me see more clearly.

"Both men went inside the hut. Tinker came out alone carrying a bulging sack and wiping his hands on his tunic. He mounted one of the mules and rode it out of the ravine." I strained to see more, but saw only long shadows following that mule and its rider. "From there, he rode west. Alone." I looked pointedly at Martyn.

He nodded. "I shall send word to Hugh and the Bodmin sheriff."

Something puzzled me. "If Tinker was near Bodmin, why did Hugh send you to Bury Down? Surely he could have sent a messenger to us and taken you with him."

"Because one of the prisoners said that Tinker kept on about a girl. That he'd been betrayed by 'a witch and a white-eyed girl.'"

Brighida went rigid, her eyes flat.

"He means you and Britlen," Martyn said to Kaatje.

"Of course he means Britlen," Kaatje snapped. "But are you saying I am the witch?"

"I am saying," Martyn stammered, "that you are so . . . so . . ." He exhaled hard, his gaze roaming over her face and down her lustrous hair, from her crown to her shoulders. "So . . ." A crimson stain crept up his neck.

"So . . . lovely," he finally breathed, "that Tinker must have thought you had bewitched him."

It's he who is bewitched.

Kaatje smiled kindly at him. "I know Tinker, and he sees me not as an enchantress, Martyn, but as a shrew. I have no fear of that sniveling coward. And I know how to protect my daughter."

"Hugh will find him," I said. "Amice told us just before we left the cliffs that Tinker had played the priestess during the Samhain rites in the sea cave—" I looked at Brighida "—where he bled girls to death for years at the behest of Agnes Gough."

Brighida stiffened and then looked at me hard for a long moment, wrath smoldering beneath her seer's calm. This was what she hadn't known about Tinker. She looked away—to compose herself, I believed—and when she turned back, she bore the stillness of a hunter.

"He wouldn't have done it without payment." Kaatje's words dripped disgust and rage. "That would account for the money he was carrying when Hugh arrested him."

"He lived out on the cliffs," Brighida said. "And you saw him riding west on that mule, Megge, likely returning there to hide."

"He was returning there to retrieve the rest of his money from *its* hiding place." Kaatje looked at each of us in turn. "Make no mistake—he will return to take his revenge on us. But not yet. That cowardly snake has gone back there to hire the men Michael always paid to help him with his work."

CHAPTER 62

AMICE

Britlen and I heard it all.

Kaatje had left the lodge door open, and we heard Martyn tell the women that Tinker had escaped. Britlen held her breath as she listened, but I could not stop my chest from heaving as my breath came in gasps.

Tinker will return to take his revenge on us.

I tried to listen, but could hear only *"My blade will sing . . ."*

"Will you somehow make the sheriff believe what my father did to us?" Britlen asked.

I took her hand and squeezed it.

"But what if he comes here? What if he sees you? What if he learns you told? What then?"

I reached into the pouch at my hip and withdrew Magdalene's knife. I took Britlen's hand and touched her fingers to the hilt.

My blade, too, could sing.

"You needn't stay, Martyn," Kaatje said later, as we broke our fast. "I can protect us against Tinker."

"But you said it yourself, Kaatje. It won't be Tinker alone. He will hire Gough's men to—" He stopped. "Better Alf, Gynneys, and I stay close. Hugh ordered me here because he had already thought of this."

"I have work to do," Megge said, getting up from the table. She reached beneath her cloak, felt for something at her hip, and then held out her hand to me.

"Amice, would you like to come?"

"Are you sure, Megge?" Brighida asked.

"I will not be made a prisoner by a fair-faced man with a knife."

I patted the pouch at my hip and felt my knife, then got up and took Megge's hand.

She smiled down at me. "And neither will Amice."

While the others stayed at the cottage to plan how to protect us, Megge and I walked to the village to see Nellie. Megge did not fear Tinker, so neither would I. But I patted my pouch again and again and breathed easier when I felt that knife.

As we walked through a small wood, Megge stopped and pointed to the ground beside the path.

"This is where—"

I waited.

"No. I will not put another ugly image in your mind. Nor will I think about what I have lost. I've other cares." She set off at a quick pace, her voice rising, her heels striking the path harder with each step. "For though the blacksmith has brought only suffering to others, Brother James tells me I must find it in myself to free him of his suffering in his final days by offering him my mother's final cure. I must show mercy to a man who does not know what mercy is."

She was so angry, I thought she might spit.

"I must tell her, Anwen," I silently called into the ether. "It might help her become a better healer if she knows she can show him mercy."

"Anna," Anwen warned, "Megge just said she must find it in herself. Be still."

"But first," Megge went on, "I must find it in myself to tell Nellie I will tend her and her babe, when I cannot bear—" She stopped walking. "I was younger than you when my mother began to insist that I follow her as a healer. She took me to births and tried to teach me, but even then—" She scrubbed a hand through her hair. "I do not know if I can help Nellie."

We resumed walking.

I wondered what could have made her recoil from births. Eleanor had taken me to many and had taught me how to hand her whatever she needed to help the woman and her babe. There was screaming, indeed, and blood, and that smell. But there was also a child. Eleanor would hand the wailing babe to its mother, who would weep with joy and hold it close, nestling it and letting it suckle.

"That silence," Megge said, still brooding. Her eyes filled, and she stopped walking again. "That terrible silence when a child does not take a breath. Who could be expected to attend another birth after seeing a silent, blue child whisked away from its shrieking, grieving mother?" Her eyes brimmed with tears. "Not I, Amice. The death of a child—"

Though the tears had begun to spill, she resumed walking. "I could not."

CHAPTER 63

MEGGE

"Tell me about these women who call themselves midwives, Nellie."

Seated on a low stool in her husband's market stall, Nellie settled her youngest child on her lap. "They know nothing, Megge. They are not healers. They are wicked."

"Have they harmed any of the women?"

"Harmed them?" Nellie's voice rose. "They have killed them. And their babes. Only weeks ago, Dora's niece was struggling to give birth, and this *woman*—I cannot call her a midwife—gave her a draught of nightshade—deadly nightshade—believing it was a red raspberry draught, to hasten the birth. She died, and the babe along with her."

Sorrow struck me like a fist. "The poor thing. And Dora—how she must be suffering. I didn't know, Nellie."

"You have been away. How could you have known?"

"Did anyone tell Sheriff Haskins?"

"Oh, aye, and he says he searched for her, but she has never been seen again. Others have taken her place. None as bad as her, but none with proper skills."

"How long have they been coming here?"

"Ever since we lost your mother. We have all prayed you would take up her calling." She opened her hands and raised them, a plea. "Will you, Megge?"

Even if I had Mother's skills, I could not assure Nellie that I could ever be a midwife.

"Will you?" Her eyes begged me to say yes.

"I want to help you, Nelle." My skin felt cold and damp. My heart was pounding. "Let me think. I shall return soon with my answer."

"Oh, Megge, hurry."

Why, I wondered as I left Nellie, was I able to tend a lazar who hated me, but unable to tend a pregnant friend? My healer's skills had returned while I tended the blacksmith, I reminded myself, so surely the midwife's skills would return when I tended Nellie—

And it would not matter, I finally admitted. For the difference between tending the lazar and tending the pregnant woman was not a lack of skill—it was fear.

I needed to speak with someone who could help me.

CHAPTER 64

AMICE

As we left Nellie's pottery stall, I watched Megge's countenance change from daunted to resolute. She took my hand and nearly dragged me up the market road.
"We're going to the lazar house, Amice."

CHAPTER 65

MEGGE

I heard Amice panting and realized I was pulling the poor child through the village, so I slowed my steps. As we neared Gus and Dora Tucker's cottage, I saw Dora sitting outside mending, so I waved and called to her.

"Megge." She tucked the needle into the fabric and set it aside.

"Dora, I am so grieved to hear—"

"I heard Tinker got away," Dora said, cutting off my words. "Where do you suppose he is? Are you safe? Oh, my dear, this is a dreadful, evil thing." She stopped suddenly and looked at Amice. "Is this the little girl that Tinker—"

"This is Amice, Dora." I turned to Amice. "Amice, this is Mistress Tucker, a dear friend and the wife of the man who buys our fleece."

Dora clasped Amice's hands in both of hers and drew her close. She kissed Amice on the forehead and released her. "You've got naught to fear, dear. The men are watching for Tinker Penneck, that snake, to show his face. And when he does, our new sheriff will show him no mercy."

"Thank you, Dora. You have set our minds at ease." I knelt next to her. "Nellie told me what befell your niece and her child. I cannot find the words to tell you how I grieve for you."

"I try to put it aside when I can." Dora's nose reddened, and her eyes filled with tears. She wiped them on her sleeve and nodded to me. "But I pray you, Megge, take care of our Nellie."

As we passed the village green and neared Priory Lane, I asked Amice, "Are you afraid Tinker will come here? Would you like me to take you back to the others? Martyn, Alf, and Mister Gynneys will keep you safe."

Amice shook her head slowly and laid her hand on the pouch at her hip.

"What is it you're carrying?" I asked her.

After a moment, she withdrew a knife with a short wooden handle and a blade as long as her hand.

A laugh rose from my gut to my lips. I reached beneath my cloak and drew the carving knife from my healer's pouch.

Smiling, Amice returned her weapon to its hiding place and took my hand.

"I'll make a sheath for that so it doesn't cut you, and we shall sharpen both our knives."

Amice nodded solemnly.

She had been brandishing that knife the first time I saw her in the grove, I now recalled, but I had forgotten. I wondered now where she had found it and if she had ever used it.

We came to the crossroads, and I looked for Friar Stephen. Not seeing him, I wondered if he had duties at the lazar house. Or perhaps he had taken ill. Brother James or Christine would surely know.

"On the other side of those trees," I said, pointing to the woods as we neared the lazar house, "is the cottage with the room they call the sickroom."

The cottage door was closed, but the shutters were open, and I could see someone moving about in the kitchen. I knocked, and Christine opened the door.

"Lady." She inclined her head for us to enter. As we did, she set two cups and a vial on the table.

"Christine, please call me Megge. And tell me, is Brother James here?"

"He is at the priory but will be back soon." She looked down at Amice. "Who is your friend?"

"This is Amice."

Christine took me aside. "Lady, children do not belong—"

"She belongs here," I said. "You'll see. She belongs."

Christine opened a wooden crate, withdrew a white robe, and handed it to me. "Put this on over your clothes and draw the hood up before you enter his room." She looked down at Amice. "We have no robe small enough to fit you."

Lowenna came inside carrying a basket of clean linens.

"Amice!" She kissed Amice on both cheeks, then raised an eyebrow to me. "You have an apprentice?"

I finished putting on my robe. "Yes, and she needs a robe. Have you something that will do?"

CHAPTER 66

AMICE

owenna drew a small sheet from her basket and shook it out so it fluttered over me. She laid it over my shoulders so it covered my arms and tunic, then tied the ends at my throat.

"There." She stood back and looked at me. "She has no hood, but her coif will suffice for today, I think."

Christine picked up the cups from the table, dipped them into a kettle of steaming water, and set them on a clean cloth. "Come."

Megge pulled up her hood, and we followed Christine.

"We are going to the sickroom," Megge told me.

Christine drew aside a sheet that covered the doorway, and there on a clean bed, covered in soft linens, lay Mister Gough, a wet cloth over his brow and eyes.

"My gaoler has come," he croaked. "That I can smell you with this worthless nose should tell you something, herding wench."

Christine's eyes blazed. "*Herding wench?*"

Megge shook her head subtly to calm her, then merely raised her arm to her nose and sniffed. "I smell nothing, Blacksmith."

"Give him no heed, Lady," Christine said gently. "You've no smell of sheep. He heard your voice, and though he is at your mercy, still he would goad you."

"I know what that grey robe you wear means, Christine," Mister Gough said. "You're another lazar. I doubt you've smelled a thing for years."

Christine turned her face away, but not before her cheeks flamed scarlet.

"She cured you of your putrid smell, *Blacksmith*, and that was no easy task," Megge said. "And I can see she has done you a great deal of good in the time I have been gone. Whether you like it or not, I have come to learn how she performed such a miracle."

Christine's serious face lit from within.

"How *did* you, Christine?" Megge asked her.

I sniffed the air. I could have told her what Christine had used to stop his sores from stinking. Lavender.

Christine bowed her head. "He has sores, Lady—great, festering sores. I cleaned and covered them as your mother taught me."

I had no doubt she had applied a balm of lavender and walnut oil to those sores. Eleanor had taught me this and had urged me to rub the oil into Mother's joints and skin to ease the pain. This scent alone told me that, like Eleanor, Christine was a good healer. I hoped she would allow me to stay and learn from her.

CHAPTER 67

MEGGE

As Christine spoke about remedies, I saw in my mind's eye the many women who had come to me in my cave, their hands or arms burned. I saw children wailing from welts caused by harvesting stinging nettle. I saw fishermen with hooks caught in their hands or cheeks. I had tended them all.

"Megge?" Christine touched my arm.

I startled.

"There is something you should see."

"That herding wench will not touch me."

"If only you were as pleasant as my sheep," I said. "Or as worthy of breath as the least of them."

I turned to Christine. "What is it you would have me see?"

Christine motioned with her head toward Amice.

I put up a hand and shook my head to tell her that nothing Amice saw would trouble her.

She drew back the sheet. A line of sweat ran down the blacksmith's grey tunic from neck to belly. Christine loosened the neck of the tunic, drew it down, and bade me look.

Small lumps dotted his chest.

"Boils." Christine pointed to one. "Not the usual sores of lepra."

She turned him on his side. A thick poultice covered his right hip. "There is a troubling sore beneath this. Hold him on his side. I shall go for water, then we shall remove the poultice and cleanse the skin."

"Allow me to go for it, Christine," I said.

"Nay, Lady. Stay with him."

Amice followed her out. Kindred spirits, I thought.

Unable to bear looking upon the blacksmith's hip, I drew the sheet over him.

"This pallet is full of straw," he grumbled. "It makes my skin itch. I saw those sacks of fleece—"

"You are in a place of comfort and are being tended. You could be dying on a stone floor in a gaol cell, so I'll hear naught of your complaints."

Christine returned carrying clean towels and a basin of fragrant water. Amice followed with a bulky sack.

Christine set down the basin, laid the towels beside it, and emptied the sack of squares of soft linen to cover a wound, several rolls of sturdy linen to bind the cloth to an arm or leg, and a small knife.

She drew back the sheet, and the blacksmith moaned.

"Have I ever hurt you?" she asked.

He grunted.

"We must remove this poultice." Christine ran a finger over the thick cloth stuck to the blacksmith's skin. Amice moved in closer to see. I moved aside to give her room.

"I won't hurt you, Michael," Christine said and gently teased the poultice free. Amice held out her hand, and Christine laid the sodden cloths in it. Amice carefully rolled them and dropped them into the empty sack.

The top layer of skin was gone, and the raw, fiery skin beneath looked so painful that I nearly cried out. But though the wound was raw, it was clean.

"The basin, Amice. And a towel and a cup." Christine held out a hand to Amice, her gaze still on that wound.

Amice gathered them and solemnly handed them to her, so proud to be her helper.

Christine rolled the towel and slid it under the blacksmith's hip. "To hold him fast," she said to Amice. She filled the cup from the basin and poured a light stream of the draught over the raw flesh. The blacksmith panted through clenched teeth. The flesh glistened when she was through. She took a small, lidded pot from her sack, opened it, and rubbed salve on the wound.

"Lavender and honey," she said. "And we are finished, Michael."

The blacksmith pulled the wet cloth from his eyes.

"What is this girl-child doing in here?" He coughed until his eyes filled with tears. "Brother James would never allow this. Get her out. And for God's sake, cover me."

"She is Megge's apprentice," Christine said. "She stays."

I was helping Christine draw the sheet over him when I heard a man's voice from the doorway.

"Let us have a look, shall we?"

CHAPTER 68

brown-robed priest came into the room. I shrank back and pressed close to Megge, watching him but praying he would not notice me.

He was very tall, and his thin wrists extended well beyond the ends of his sleeves. His fingers were long and thin, as was his nose. His wide lips were set in a gentle line. His long-lidded brown eyes warmed his serious face, which brightened when he saw me.

As Christine had done, he knelt before me. "I am called Brother James," he said. "And who are you?"

"This is Amice," Megge said. "She is an apprentice healer."

"Apprentice, you say?" he asked me.

"She doesn't speak. Her tongue was . . . injured. But though she is quite young, I believe she has learned a great deal at the side of a good healer." She lowered her voice. "She knows lepra, Brother James."

I felt certain that when they were alone, she would tell him what had been done to me, but I was grateful she said nothing now. For too long, I had been the orphan, the tortured child, so it was good to be simply an apprentice, a quiet girl who learned at the side of skilled healers.

Without raising an eyebrow or asking to see my tongue, Brother James got up, went to the other side of the bed, and bent to examine Mister Gough's wound. When he looked up and asked me to hand him the clean cloth, I knew he was not the kind of priest my mother had known.

He placed the cloth on the skin that Christine had just covered with salve and picked up the knife.

He rolled Mister Gough further onto his side and pointed to a sore on the back of his leg. "It's larger today, and the flesh is dead. Do you see?" He pointed with the knife at the black crater. "It must be removed so there is naught but good flesh."

He touched the tip of the knife to the sore. "This shall not pain him, for—"

"For these sores feel no pain," Megge said.

"To feel so little is the blessing—and the curse—of lepra," Brother James said to me. "A blessing because—at least at first—there is no pain. A curse because feeling no pain allows the lazar to damage the skin, which then festers and dies." He prodded the black crater. "Cutting away spots like this keeps deadly humors from fouling the blood. Black skin heralds black blood, which brings naught but death."

Brother James swept the knife in a circle and handed the black skin to Christine.

We watched as blood began to seep from the flesh at the crater's edge. "This is how we know we have removed all the dead tissue." Brother James pointed to the blood. "Only healthy skin bleeds." He looked up at Megge. "Shall we close the wound?" he asked, the tilt of his head and his inquiring gaze telling me he was testing her, just as Eleanor had tested me.

"Better to leave it open and apply a honey salve. Honey helps the raw flesh heal."

Eleanor had said the same words to me.

"We use a rose-and-honey salve," Christine said, opening a small crock and dipping her finger into the sweet-smelling salve. She dabbed it on the circle of raw flesh and laid a clean cloth over it.

With Brother James's help, Christine rolled the blacksmith onto his back and covered him with the sheet.

Brother James nodded to Megge and tipped his head toward the kitchen.

CHAPTER 69

MEGGE

mice stayed at Christine's side, helping her gather her basins and cloths. I followed Brother James to the table. He poured ale into two small cups.

"There is little I can teach you—I see that already."

"There is much I can learn from you, Brother James, and not only about lepra." I took a deep breath. "I would like to ask your counsel."

He sat forward, hands clasped before him. "How can I help you?"

"It seems the village needs a midwife."

He leaned forward, head tipped, eyes interested. "Are you skilled in midwifery?"

I could not tell him that I had practiced midwifery before it had a name. My hands gripped each other as I fought to steady them. "My mother tried to make me her apprentice, and I learned a great deal at her side, but she released me when it became clear that I could not bear to witness another birth.

"I believe that what I learned will return to me if only I can find the courage to enter the dwelling of a woman about to give birth."

"Why can you not bear to witness a birth?"

Will he judge me harshly? I studied his calm, pleasant countenance and took comfort in the compassion in his soft, brown eyes.

"Because so many result in a blue, lifeless babe."

There. I blew out my breath and sat back. I had admitted it. I had said it aloud.

He laid a hand on mine. "Sometimes, Megge, the worst simply comes to pass. No one can prevent it. Having a child is the most perilous thing a woman can do. Not even your mother could save every child."

"That is why I am loath to tend Nellie. Suppose, despite all I do, her child enters the world blue? Suppose it is born still? Suppose—"

"Those are not the questions I would ask, Megge." He tapped his finger on the table as he thought. Finally, he looked at me. "I would ask where these fears came from."

CHAPTER 70

AMICE

I see you are undaunted by Mister Gough, the sickest man we have had here in some time," Brother James said when I joined him and Megge in the kitchen. He pulled out a chair for me and poured me a cup of ale. "You, Amice, may be that rare thing—a born healer. How do I know this? I cannot say." He laughed. "But I believe that, like Megge, you have spent time at a healer's side. Also, like her, you have the innate qualities of a healer. I only wish all my acolytes possessed these strengths."

He turned to Megge. "But I feel I must warn you both about something before you take this work upon yourselves. Terrible harm may befall you should you choose to work amongst us."

"*Us?*" Megge sat forward.

Slowly, Brother James drew a sandaled foot from beneath the table. His second toe was white at the tip, and the next toe had no nail.

"Oh, Brother James." Megge sounded as if she might weep.

"It can take many years for the disease to show itself. I have worked amongst lazars since I took my vows as a monk, long before the abbot selected me for ordination so that I might meet all the spiritual needs of the lazars I attended. Over time, never seeing the stigma of disease on my own skin, I came to believe myself blessed, a man apart." He shrugged and lowered his voice. "But alas, I was wrong and shall suffer the same fate as this wretched man." He raised his chin toward the sickroom.

"I shall see to it that you do not," Megge vowed.

"There is nothing you can do to stop it. It has begun, and that is that. You, though, have spent but a few days with Michael. Likely, you have not yet fallen ill with the disease. And what of your young apprentice? Though it appears she has helped a healer tend lazars, her skin is unblemished. Would you risk her further?"

"Are you advising us to leave? To abandon you and Michael Gough and all the others you tend?"

"Mister Kendall, the surgeon at Lostwithiel, will continue to help us. We can bear it if you feel you must protect yourself."

"We shall never abandon you to save ourselves," Megge said. She looked to me, and I nodded. Then she simply took a sip of her ale and smiled at Brother James. "I know Mister Kendall. He is a kind man. A skilled surgeon."

"He comes here when someone needs—" Brother James hesitated.

To have a limb removed, I thought.

Looking down at me and wincing, Megge said, "I understand."

"It is often necessary," Brother James said, "when it is not merely a lump or a spot that goes black, but a toe, a foot."

His countenance clouded, and I felt a surge of pity for him, for I could tell that in his mind's eye, he was seeing this Mister Kendall approach his own bedside.

CHAPTER 71

MEGGE

Christine called Amice to the sickroom to help her set out clean basins and cloths. Brother James rose from the table and already had his hand on the door when I remembered something.

"Before you go," I said, "tell me—is Friar Stephen well? He was not sitting at the crossroads today."

He offered me a weak smile. "You knew him?"

"*Knew?*"

"He passed away last night. He battled that disease valiantly, but it defeated him in the end."

Grief threatened to overwhelm me. I had to cover my face so Brother James would not see me weep. "Did he suffer terribly?"

"No, Megge. He slipped away peacefully."

I dropped my hands. "Peacefully?"

He nodded. "Christine and I gave him the sleeping draught of boar's gall, vinegar, hemlock, henbane, and poppyseed that Mister Kendall gives before setting to work. It greatly eased his pain, and his faith carried him back to God. That is all he ever wanted."

"He told me he wanted death to take him with all haste, as it had done for Saint Stephen."

Brother James gaped. "Do you know how Saint Stephen died?"

I shook my head.

"He was stoned to death."

Poor Friar Stephen, I thought. He would have preferred a quick death in fear and agony to the ever-present torment of the slow death that, for him, was life.

"Why did you not call for me before he passed away?"

"Because he received the sacraments. The draught eased his pain and brought him sleep, but it was his faith—and the sacraments— that ensured his peaceful passage."

He folded his arms on the tabletop, leaned toward me, and spoke so only I could hear.

"I just offered Michael those same sacraments and assured him that I am empowered to forgive him of even mortal sin and that he could rest in peace in heaven if he were to but ask for absolution. He refused." He shook his head slowly. "He said he did not deserve 'God and His heaven.'"

He watched me.

I had no reply. I agreed with the blacksmith. Perhaps now, Brother James would stop insisting that I make that murderer a Mentor.

"There is little I can do now for Michael's soul but pray," he said. "His final spiritual choices are his own. And his suffering at the end is now for you to assuage. Are you still unwilling to offer him the final cure your mother would have offered?"

If he believes the Blacksmith merits our 'cure,' I thought, then he clearly does not understand what it is. He must believe it is some remedy or incantation that Mother would not reveal.

"I am willing to offer him whatever will ease his suffering—"

"Bless you!" Brother James leaned back. "Bless you, Megge."

I put up a hand. "But I am not certain you understand what it was that my mother offered. Did she ever tell you what her 'cure' was?"

"She would neither speak of it nor allow anyone to be present as she gave it. And when I asked Morwen, she offered to tell me but warned me that if I knew, I would be breaking my vows as a priest if I allowed your mother to offer it here. She said that I might be excommunicated—or worse—for heresy."

He raised his eyebrows and tightened his lips. "But you have seen how the lazars suffer. I would withhold nothing that would give them the ease I witnessed when your mother had left them. So I chose to believe that it was some rare herb whose name she could not share that eased their passing. And when a sufferer refused the sacraments and I could do no more for him, I left the decision regarding his final days to him and the Healer of Bury Down."

"What if he refused Mother's cure?"

"Then he would receive the best we could give—Mister Kendall's draught and a comforting hand."

"And when she chose not to offer it, Brother James? Did you press her, as you have pressed me, to act against her own counsel?"

He tapped his finger on the table as he so often did when he was deep in thought or about to render an opinion that I might oppose.

"I am beginning to see there is more to this *cure* than I realized . . ."

I nodded along with him as he completed his thought.

He stopped tapping and looked at me. "And I can now see why my insistence that you offer it to Michael has troubled you. You must weigh what you can give him as a healer against what you are reluctant to offer him as the Healer of Bury Down. My demands have brought you to a grievous choice."

"Yes, Brother James." I heaved a sigh and rose to leave, grateful that he understood.

"Megge?" There was that tapping finger again. "Have you ever considered that simply forgiving Michael might clear your vision where his suffering, your duty, and his final days are concerned?"

CHAPTER 72

"Forgive the blacksmith," Megge muttered as we walked back to Bury Down. "How can I forgive what I cannot understand?" Railing now, she threw her arms in the air. "I cannot. Next, he will want me to forgive Tinker!" She shook her head, disgusted.

"'A white-eyed girl,' Tinker called little Britlen," she spat. "How dare he?" Her hand went to the bulge at her hip, and as she walked, her contempt for Tinker narrowed her eyes and drew down the corners of her mouth. "Poor, kind little Britlen, blinded at the hands of a beast—and now, threatened by him. And you, silenced by his knife." She heaved out a breath, then looked at me. "Well, he's not the only one who can cut."

Her pace and her breathing slowed. "I grew up with one rule." She looked me in the eye. "Women of Bury Down do not kill."

Her mouth a grim line, her voice dangerously low, she spoke as if to herself. "It is time to leave that rule behind."

CHAPTER 73

MEGGE

lf and Ffion were speaking quietly at the table when we arrived, a glowing candle and two cups of wine before them. I heard Ffion ask Alf what more they could do to protect us.

"Meg! Amice!" Alf stood when he saw us. "Come, sit." He pulled out two chairs and filled two more cups.

"Not now, Alf." I kept my cloak on and motioned for Amice to sit. "Where is Brighida?"

"In there." He pointed into the workroom.

I looked inside, and Brighida glanced up from her spinning wheel. "The grove, Brighida."

Brighida studied my face for a moment, then got up and whispered something to Britlen. Britlen laid down her drop spindle and sat at the spinning wheel. In an instant, white fleece became yarn as soft as a breath.

For the first time since my return, I studied the workroom. The many fleece-filled bags that had lined the walls before Kaatje and Britlen had joined us were now filled with balls of yarn and thread—black, smoke, and brilliant white.

"You have done all this?"

"Brighida and I have. She taught me," Britlen said without stopping the wheel.

"They have worked tirelessly," Kaatje said from her seat at the loom. Martyn stood behind her, struggling, it seemed, to keep from laying his hand on her shoulder. Kaatje subtly evaded his hovering hand by bending forward to show me the snow-white altar cloth Dora Tucker had commissioned for the priory and that I had begun to weave. Kaatje's beautiful work rendered me speechless—much as her beauty, I thought, had rendered Martyn bewitched.

I watched him until, flushing, he went to the kitchen and poured himself a cup of ale.

"Kaatje?" I asked quietly, tilting my head toward the kitchen and smiling.

"He is a lad," she whispered, her countenance tender. "And soon, he will be my brother. This . . . fondness . . . he feels for me will pass—as it has for a score of men." She shrugged and smiled. "Until it does, I shall not give him false hope; nor, though, will I wound him. He has behaved like this since first we met. Hugh finds it amusing—I find it heartbreaking." She looked at Martyn, who was guzzling his ale, and shook her head kindly. "Once Hugh and I are wed, Martyn's yearning will come to an end." She turned back to her weaving.

"Brighida's waiting," she reminded me, tipping her head toward my cousin, who stood at the door. "When you return, you can inspect my work and tell me if it meets the guild's standards."

"I can see from here that it far exceeds them," I said, taking Morwen's lantern from the sideboard and following Brighida out the door. The brilliant blue seer's cloak slung over her shoulders, and all that golden hair hanging in waves to her waist, told me she was prepared to cast her runes.

"You already know what I intend to do," I said as we crossed the pasture toward the slope.

"'*A white-eyed girl*,'" she spat—her face a mask of loathing. "Yes, I know what you must do."

"Then you know why I have asked you to come with me to the grove."

"Because death is sacred," she said, her countenance now as solemn as a vow. "It merits ritual."

I nodded, sealing our oath.

She started up the slope to the grove. "Let us find him so you can finish this."

Once in the grove, surrounded by ancient oaks, Brighida spread her cloak on the warm soil that marked the resting place of our great-grandmother, Gytha. I found a stick and began to scratch a wide circle in the ground.

Brighida took a green candle from one of her cloak's inner pockets and fitted it into a small rowan holder. She struck her flint, lit the candle, and set it in the center of the circle. We knelt across from each other, one on each side of the candlelit ring, eyes closed, breathing quietly. Brighida cast her stones, and the ether came alive, filling the grove with power such as I had never before felt.

Show me Tinker.

Garbed in a tattered cloak and boots so large they slapped the ground with each step, Tinker Penneck trudged along a riverbank, heedless of the morning mist and the low, grey sky that spat upon him. Lifting his gaze for a moment, he looked ahead—and caught his breath. On the horizon was a high, round hill, and beyond that, the sea.

He exhaled softly. I could almost feel his relief.

On the other side of the hill, nearly at the edge of the cliff, a strapping man and a gangling girl lay on their bellies in the tall grass, hardly breathing. Listening, listening.

"There," the man whispered.

Leaves crunched and rocks skittered as the sound of leather slapping dirt grew louder with each step.

The man held out a hand to stay the girl and crept on his belly around the foot of the hill toward the sound of footfalls. I felt his breath quicken and his heart begin to tap, faster and faster, at his breastbone. Mine did the same until he quieted his breathing and drew a dagger from the sheath at his hip. Both edges of the two-sided blade glinted all the way from its brass hilt to its needle tip. I felt a stillness come over him as he awaited his prey.

A shadow appeared at the foot of the hill. Every muscle in me tightened as the man moved into a crouch. The toe of Tinker's boot appeared, and the man sprang. He took Tinker to the ground and straddled him, his blade at Tinker's throat.

Tinker flung him off and seized the dagger. He was nearly on his feet when the girl, blue eyes blazing, rushed at him.

"My blade will sing," she bellowed, her voice thick, her words nearly garbled, as she drove a knife into his mouth.

A quick twist of her wrist freed a small slab of meat. It flew into the air and drew a crimson arc as it fell to the ground.

Howling, Tinker ran blindly, one hand clutching the dagger and the other searching his bloody mouth for what was left of his tongue. A boot fell off, and he stumbled toward the cliff. The girl ran toward him.

"Daughter!" the man hollered. Too late. Fueled by rage, the bellowing girl flung herself against Tinker, pulling herself back from the brink in time to watch him tumble over the edge, thrash through the air, and land, lifeless and broken, on the rocks.

Wiping her knife on her tunic, she turned and met the man's gaze.

"Emma," he said on a rough breath and bent forward, hands on knees.

The girl pointed to the path that I had once walked with my novices. She raised her hands before her and traced the shape of an arc—the mouth of the cave. After a moment, her father nodded and put an arm around her, and they descended the path to the sea.

The candle was nearly spent when Brighida and I finally opened our eyes. Panting, our hands pressed to our chests, we tried to slow our breathing.

"That girl was a Sister," Brighida said.

I simply nodded.

"Does Amice carry that same rage in her heart?" Brighida wondered aloud.

"No," I began to say, thinking of Amice's kindness toward a lazar and his mad mother. But then I remembered her knife and the calm, simple way she had shown it to me—and how she had smiled when I showed her mine.

"Amice, I think, carries fear—fear gone cold, which may be more deadly than rage."

"Shall we tell the others what we just saw?" Brighida asked as we walked back to the cottage.

"It might ease their minds," I said. "But consider this—we don't know when what we just saw happened, so Hugh and Neville might already have found Tinker's body. They might well be on their way home."

"If so, they will have looked into his death," Brighida said.

"And if they haven't learned who killed him?"

Brighida looked at me, her lips tight.

"And if *we* ever learn who they were?"

Brighida touched a finger to her lips.

CHAPTER 74

AMICE

Megge and I set out for the priory the next day at dawn, but she said little as we walked. A frown came and went, her countenance changing from troubled to peaceful and back again by turns. I bumped into her hip as we walked and did not feel the bulge of her knife. She had forgotten it! I patted my hip to assure myself that mine was still close at hand.

She spoke briefly with Lowenna in the kitchen while I helped Christine clean the basins and instruments at the well. I followed Christine back into the sickroom.

Mister Gough silently writhed on his pallet, sweat matting his hair, his hands clawing at the sheet. His eyes clamped on mine as if he would suck the breath from me, for he was not merely in pain—he was suffocating.

"This is how a lazar dies," Eleanor had once whispered to me at the bedside of an old soldier. "Death comes not through the skin but through the breath."

Christine and I tried to raise Mister Gough's head and shoulders, but he fought us in his struggle to take a breath.

"Megge," Christine called. "Come quickly."

CHAPTER 75

MEGGE

At Christine's shout, I took her place behind the blacksmith's back and lifted him higher. Amice raised his head while Christine stuffed a blanket beneath his shoulders.

He coughed, and his lips took on a bluish hue, his skin a grey one.

Listening to him wheeze and gurgle, I saw in my mind's eye the smelters who had fallen victim to such a cough and had come to me, weak as babes, for a cure.

I touched the blacksmith's shoulder to wake him. His bleary eyes tried to settle on mine.

"Where have you been these past months?"

He rolled his head from side to side, coughing and spitting.

"Have you been hiding in those sea caves?"

The dank cave I had found him in had smelled only of rotten fish. But what of the others? He could not have stayed only in that one, for the tide filled it daily.

He looked away.

"Would you suffocate rather than answer my question? I may be able to relieve your cough and restore your breath. Now, which will it be? A simple answer? Or death by drowning in your own phlegm?"

He coughed until his face was nearly purple. "I worked as a smelter."

Lowenna came in just as the blacksmith took a long, rattling breath. "Oh, Megge."

"He may have the smelter's malady," I said. "From breathing the dust and smoke."

"But he is a blacksmith, not a smelter."

"He hid amongst them."

"In that foul, smoky air," Lowenna said. "He needs clean, fresh air, as your mother ordered for me when I could not breathe after burning gorse in our hearth."

"And a coltsfoot draught," I reminded her. "It had calmed your cough even before the fresh air could help."

"What do you need, Megge? I shall send for Timothy. He will fetch whatever you need from the infirmary."

"Coltsfoot." I touched the blacksmith's brow. It was on fire. "And birch or willow bark for this fever. Comfrey for a poultice. Poppyseed to calm him."

I filled Lowenna's kettle with clean water and swung it over the heat. The water was nearly boiling when I heard Lowenna speaking quietly with someone just outside the door.

"Thank you, Timothy," she said and came inside.

She handed Amice four small cloth bundles closed at their tops with drawstrings.

"Who is Timothy?" I asked as I poured boiling water into four cups.

Amice dropped a pouch into each cup. As the draughts steeped, Lowenna tore cloth into long strips, and Amice and I folded them to make poultices.

"He's an acolyte under Brother James's tutelage in the infirmary." Lowenna lowered her voice and smiled gently as she spoke. "He is something of a favorite of Brother James, but we all believe he will find his true vocation in the library—or, with his love of honey, at the hives—rather than at the bedside."

"The library?" I looked up from the cloth I was folding. "Perhaps he will one day want to share what he learns with others."

"Perhaps he will," Lowenna said as she tore the last cloth in two, "The priory has a great many books, and I hear he has read nearly every one of them. Brother James hoped he would put his knowledge to work at the bedside, but I have seen him attend the ill and, well, let's just say he is a fine scholar. I can see him one day teaching healers." She stacked the cloths and walked to the door. "I've some tasks to see to," she said as she went outside.

Feeling someone's gaze upon me, I looked up and saw Christine looking at me.

"Are you ready for the draughts, Christine?"

She went to the other side of the table, where the cups sat cooling. "Listening to you two talk called to mind my days with your mother. She and Lowenna often mused as they worked."

"Mused? What did they muse about?"

"Your mother often mused about having a true apprentice." She touched the cups and nodded. "One who would one day take her place."

"But she had one. She had you!"

"I was not the one she wanted."

I wondered if Christine had felt the same pain I had felt when Mother's sharp tongue had made clear to me that she did not consider me her true apprentice.

She leaned forward and sniffed each of the cups. When she found the comfrey draught, she poured it over one of the folded cloths and took it to the sickroom.

"Lay it over his chest, Christine," I called. "Just below his collarbones."

She pulled back the curtain and glowered at me. I raised my hands in apology. Without comment, she carried the poultice into the sickroom.

Amice and I followed her with the poppyseed, coltsfoot, and willow-bark draughts.

Christine took them from us. "Allow me to do this, Lady. He will sleep now. It may be best for you and Amice to rest, for I believe it will be a long night."

Lowenna came into the sickroom, took my arm, and drew me away. "There is nothing more you can do here. I shall see you to your hut."

She walked us out to a small cottage just beyond a tilled garden plot. She opened the door and held it for us. A small table stood beneath the single window between two raised pallets covered with thick blankets. I looked for the hearth but saw only the wattle-and-daub walls. Recalling Ffion's hut, I looked up, and there it was: the hole in the center of the roof that would let out the smoke from a fire pit.

"I'll ask the men to cover that hole. That will keep you warm at night until—"

"Yes," I said. *Until the blacksmith dies.*

CHAPTER 76

AMICE

I felt certain Lowenna was about to say, "Until Mister Gough dies." I knew his death was near, but I could not bear the thought.

Megge drew back the heavy fleece blanket on one of the pallets, and though it was little past midday, I sank into it and fell into a deep sleep.

When she woke me, the room was dark but for the candle glowing on the table.

"We have work to do, Amice," she whispered. "You needed your sleep, but a good healer sees those she tends often when they are as sick as the blacksmith."

As we approached the drawn curtain, we overheard Mister Gough ask Christine, "Is this how I am to die? In torment?"

Megge and I looked at each other.

"Hush," Christine said. "Drink." A moment passed in silence. "Until we lost our healer, most who succumbed here passed in blessed peace."

Megge put out a hand to stop me from entering and opened the curtain just far enough for us to see inside. Christine took the cup from Mister Gough and set it on the table. Hard.

Her voice, though a whisper, was brusque. "Why do you think we have a sickroom just for those nearing their end? Why do you believe Brother James is here for but a trice each day since you refused the sacraments, while I tend you night and day alongside the new Healer of Bury Down?"

She gave him a moment. He made no reply.

"It is because the Church would punish him for allowing the healer to give her final cure to those who denied themselves the sacraments and the promise of heaven. Megge's mother had ways no other healer ever had of sparing those sufferers the misery of their final days." Her voice went so low I had to strain to hear. "Alone with a dying man, she somehow parted his spirit from his failing body. Brother James could have no part in that. But for years, I did. Once a lazar took his final cure, I tended his body—still alive, but at peace in that space between life and death— until it had breathed its last.

"You put an end to that when you burned her alive." She took a ragged breath. "Finally, we have a new healer, one whose power surpasses even her mother's, yet you refuse her care. Worse, you demean her. For centuries, women across Cornwall have given their lives to bring her back. Now she is here, and you dismiss her as a . . . a herding wench." She turned her back on him until her breathing had slowed. When she turned to face him, her gaze steady, her voice was serious. "And when you revile her, Mister Gough, you revile me, for I know her worth."

The blacksmith's breathing was suddenly so quiet I wondered if he had fallen asleep. Or died.

"So, yes," Christine said quietly as she gathered the cups. "Without the Church's sacraments or the Bury Down cure, this is how a lazar dies."

CHAPTER 77

MEGGE

The night wore on as Christine and I dribbled coltsfoot draught into the blacksmith's mouth, and the hue of his ghastly lips slowly changed from bluish-grey to merely pale.

By dawn, his fever had abated. Over the next few days, as his cough lessened, we opened the shutters when the breeze was not too cool and let him breathe fresh air. On the fourth day, I felt his eyes upon me as I cleansed the sores on his hand.

"You've eased my breathing," he wheezed.

Saying nothing, I dropped his hand, gathered the soiled cloths, and turned toward the kitchen.

"I would say you're more than a herding wench," he called to my back.

I turned, a score of retorts on my tongue, but his look of bewilderment—and gratitude—quelled them.

"I am your healer," I said, and wished I could have said those words to Nellie.

CHAPTER 78

AMICE

Now that the danger had passed and Mister Gough was once more able to breathe, Megge went to the priory to visit with Brother James. When she returned to the cottage, her countenance was thoughtful, and her arms were laden with food from the refectory.

Her breath caught when she saw who was sitting with me at the table.

"Hugh! Neville!" She set two loaves of bread and a big crock of honey on the table and smiled at them.

Seeing the grim set of their mouths, she sat, no longer smiling. "Tell me."

Hugh glanced at me and motioned with his head toward the door. I knew he was suggesting to Megge that I leave the room.

"If it's about Tinker, she deserves to know," Megge said.

Hugh folded his hands on the table. "Martyn sent word to me and the Bodmin sheriff that you suspected that Tinker and another man had gone down that ravine on mules."

Megge nodded.

"The Bodmin men found tracks and followed them. They found a young mule-keeper alone in his hut—dead, his throat slit. They saw no sign of Tinker. Neville thought he might have returned to the cliffs and hidden in the cave where we found Gough, so we rode there with all haste."

Hugh looked at Neville and nodded.

Neville leaned forward and spoke quietly. "We found Tinker's body deep inside a narrow passage at the very rear of the cave."

I gasped. Megge moved closer to me and laid her hand on my arm.

"He had so many broken bones," Neville went on, "that he must have gone over the cliff. Either he fell or was pushed." He glanced at me and then looked at Megge. There was more. Something he did not want me to hear.

Megge nodded. "Go on."

"I cannot guess how anyone would have thought to hide his body way back there. I only found him by following the rats."

I recalled the rat that had scuttled into that hidden passage while Tinker carried out his grisly rite. If I had seen that passage, then the other girls must have seen it, too.

Mister Gough's words came back to me. *Run! Go to your homes. Tell your fathers what has befallen you here.*

And then I heard Anwen's. *Five were orphans, but Sister Two yet had a father.*

Had Sister Two, the new Sister One, found her father and been courageous enough to tell him who had cut out her tongue?

"He was not long dead," Neville was saying. "And he was caked in blood." Neville gagged. "His mouth was open, as if he had died screaming."

"Go on," Megge said when Neville had caught his breath.

He closed his eyes. "His tongue was gone." He winced—and then retched. Megge quickly got up and poured him some ale.

I, though, did not retch. I had to struggle to keep from smiling.

"Do you know who did this?" Megge asked Hugh.

He shook his head. "No one we asked had seen any strangers nearby, so we left his carcass where it belonged—amongst the rats—and reported our findings to the earl. So that's finished."

I could still see Sister One's rage as she struggled to pull open that huge door to the courtyard, and I could still feel her fervor as she kissed me. I would never forget that breathy *H'ank you*.

And then I remembered Anwen's words: *You are not to harm Sister One. She has a charge.*

This was her work.

Your secret is safe with me, Sister One.

Megge filled four cups with ale and handed each of us a cup and a slice of bread slathered with honey. When we had refreshed ourselves, Hugh scrubbed a hand over his beard and coughed.

"We found something else," he said. "In the church tower."

Megge raised an eyebrow. I stopped breathing.

"Another corpse. This one, a woman."

Megge gasped. My insides froze.

"Who was she?" Megge asked.

Hugh tightened his lips and shrugged. "The most I can say is that she was slender and had long, fair hair."

Magdalene. My mouth fell open. *I killed Magdalene.*

Megge asked another question, and Hugh replied, but I could barely hear him for the roaring in my ears and my great, gulping sobs.

Hugh is going to take me to gaol.

"Amice." Megge knelt beside my chair and took my face in her hands. She studied my eyes for a moment, then drew me to her. "Let me take you outside. You need fresh air."

"Neville," she said quietly, "would you fetch a cup of ale for Amice?"

I buried my face in Megge's hair, unable to stop weeping.

Do they hang girls?

Megge took the cup of ale from Neville and held it to my lips. "Was this woman someone you knew? One of the Sisters, perhaps?"

I took a sip, unable to meet her gaze.

"We don't know who she was," Neville said quietly to Megge. "But a woman two settlements away said she once saw a woman who looked like that—lean, with fair hair—selling remedies."

"How long ago did she die?" Megge asked. "Could you tell?"

Shaking his head, Neville looked to Hugh.

"Her body was not decayed, so—a week?" Hugh shrugged. "Two?"

"How did she die?" Megge asked.

I opened my eyes in time to see Neville twist his hands as if breaking something.

"Someone broke her neck?" Megge whispered.

"Aye," Hugh said.

Someone broke her neck! This brought more tears, a flood of relief. I hadn't killed her!

But I thought I knew who might have.

I could still see Mister Gough's fury as he stalked into the church after freeing us. I could still hear his boots ringing on the stones as he charged down that aisle.

Would I tell Hugh what I suspected?

Never.

CHAPTER 79

MEGGE

aving delivered his grisly news, Hugh sat back and sipped his ale.

"Can Brother James spare you for a day or two?" he asked.

"What do you need, Hugh?" He had not yet mentioned Agnes Gough. I hoped my voice had not betrayed my fear.

"It's not what *I* need. The earl requests your help. He's in Cornwall for only a few more days and wishes to speak to you."

My gut tightened. "Is it about Agnes?"

I feared Hugh could see my heart pounding against my breastbone, so I took a long, deep breath to calm myself.

"Agnes?" He shook his head.

"About her trial."

"No, Megge. Agnes won't be tried."

"She won't—" Relief swept through me.

I cleared my throat. "Why not?"

"She's mad. And the mad are not brought to judgment. Not even for murder."

"But—"

"Megge," Hugh interrupted, sitting back and looking at me. "You saw her on the ship. She thought you were your mother. And she thought Gough was betrothed to your aunt Claris. She picked her nose and stared into her hands. No judge would ever condemn her. Most would never even try her. The earl has ordered her to a convent, where she'll spend her remaining days."

"That sounds just." I sighed. "Now, what of the blacksmith?"

"When he's able to make the journey, Neville and I will take him to a lazar house in Launceston, where he can be held until his trial."

"Launceston? He's not able to make so long a journey—he cannot even leave his bed." I leaned forward. "And you said it would take months for him to be tried. He needs proper care if he is to live another week."

"It won't take that long." Hugh spread honey on another slice of bread and took a bite. "The bishop means to visit Launceston for Twelfth Night."

"Why Launceston?"

"It's on the Tamar, so it would be an easy journey for him." He brushed crumbs from his tunic. "Normally, trials wait until the Lent assizes, but the earl and the bishop agree that this one can't wait that long. Learn what you must quickly, Megge, for you shan't have Gough to hone your skills on for long."

Amice finished her ale and looked at me. I thought she might finally say something, but she merely pressed her cheek to mine, then motioned with her head toward the door.

She's going to the well, I thought, to wash her tear-streaked face. I hugged her. "You're safe now, little one."

Hugh stood and prepared to leave. "What would you have me tell the earl?"

"It is not for me to tell him—"

"Megge, the earl has requested your counsel."

My counsel, I thought. As a woman of Bury Down . . .

I could not let the blacksmith leave.

I pushed back from the table and rose. "I propose that the trial be held here, at the priory, if the prior consents. Surely the bishop will not object, since the blacksmith is accused of crimes against the Church. And he committed those crimes here, in this village, so it's only fair that we be allowed to witness the trial. Ask the earl to hold the trial here."

"But why should a bishop and a judge be burdened in this way?"

"Because they need Michael Gough alive."

"But in a lazar house? We can't expect them to come here. They'll refuse."

"I did not say the trial should be held at the lazar house, Hugh. I said at the priory."

I finished my bread and wiped my hands on a clean towel. "That is my proposal. If you take Michael Gough from here, he will be dead in days. But if you allow Brother James and me to see to him, he may live until Twelfth Night."

As Hugh and Neville left the cottage, he looked back at me. "You're no longer the girl I saw off at the quay with an old woman and a child." He lifted his chin toward Amice, sitting beside the well, her countenance now calm. "And she's no longer a child."

Neville went to the well and sat beside Amice. "I'm sorry you heard what I had to tell Megge about Tinker and the lady. But after all you've endured, perhaps you'll rest easily now, knowing you've naught to fear from them."

Amice leaned on him, and he put an arm around her for a moment, then rose and came to me.

"And what of you, Megge?" His voice was soft.

I could not look away from that face, chiseled and now bearded. Thanks to him, Amice was free of her dread that Tinker would return. And judging from Amice's weeping—with relief, I suspected—that woman must have been one of her gaolers. Another nightmare put to rest.

I took his face in my hands and kissed him.

CHAPTER 80

AMICE

ell one person—Sister—and my blade will sing over your throat.
I no longer had to fear that Tinker would find me—but how long would it take to silence that hissing voice?

Megge came to me at the well and sat beside me.

"It's over, little one. For you, me, Kaatje, and Britlen." She laid an arm over my shoulders and pulled me close. "Perhaps one day you'll tell me who that fair-haired woman was."

"Anwen," I silently called. "Tinker is dead. May I tell her?"

"Hold your silence a little longer. When I give you leave, you may tell her whatever you wish."

CHAPTER 81

MEGGE

*T*inker is dead.

I repeated the words in my mind like an incantation as I readied myself for sleep.

Agnes Gough is in a convent, and her son shall remain in the sickroom.

As relief lulled me into slumber, I glanced at the sleeping Amice, arms flung wide, mouth agape, a child at peace in her world.

I woke before Amice and walked to the sickroom, my proposal to Hugh still on my mind. I did not need the blacksmith's illness to teach me to heal, and he was not fit to become a Mentor. Why, then, did it matter to me if he died now or later, here or in Launceston?

Why could I not let Hugh take him? Why is it so vital that he stay here—with me?

Unable to answer, I went inside and looked into the sickroom. Christine had turned the blacksmith on his side and was washing his back.

"Megge, come look at his neck."

At the nape of his neck was a crimson boil the size of a small egg, with a white dot at its peak. It would burst on its own, but until it did, fiery pain would seize him every time he moved his head.

"Hold him there." I pulled on my white robe and took the knife from the basin on the bedside table. I laid clean cloths around the boil.

"Lie still, Blacksmith."

I touched the blade to the point of the boil and opened it. Pus flowed onto the cloth, followed by rancid blood. Laying my hands alongside the base of the boil, as Mother had done to the festering wound on Dora Tucker's leg, I pressed until more foul matter burst from deep within the skin. The blacksmith heaved a long sigh of relief.

Christine held out a vial filled with an aromatic liquid. I sniffed—witch hazel. Holding the wound open, I poured a scant few drops into it.

He pushed my hand away. "You're burning me, you herding wench—"

Christine pressed a clean cloth into my hand. I held it to the wound, and she rolled him back so the cloth was held in place between the back of his neck and the thick pillow.

"He does not mean it, Lady," she whispered as we left the sickroom.

"He does mean it." I went to the kitchen table and sat. "Already, he was suffering, and I inflicted yet more pain upon him. Have we any more poppyseed draught?"

"In here."

I followed her back into the sickroom. She handed me a small flask, and I carried it to the blacksmith.

"This will ease your pain."

"Give me something that will end this life," he growled.

"I've told you I won't, and I've also told you what my final cure requires."

"Then, to hell with you, Witch."

CHAPTER 82

We returned to the hut, and Megge paced. Across the room she walked, heel to toe, back and forth, from window to door, mumbling to herself.

"Why do you cling to the hope that he will repent?"

She was not speaking to me, so I lay back on my pallet and watched. And, as Anwen had ordered, listened.

"*Herding wench.* He detests you and all you could offer him." She stopped, turned, and resumed pacing, her voice rising in frustration. "Never will he make amends. Never will he ask to serve. Never *has* he served." She stopped. "And why should I care? Why *do* I care?" She threw up her hands. "What is he to me?"

She stopped pacing. "That's it."

Nodding her head slowly, she finally looked at me. "That's the question."

CHAPTER 83

MEGGE

A knock at the door silenced me. I lowered my arms and looked at Amice.

The door opened, and my cousin stepped inside.

"Brighida!"

"Take me to him."

I forgot my raving and went to her. "Do you mean it? Are you ready to face him?"

"You forget that I've faced him once. I have no fear of him. I have remedies."

She handed me a cloth-covered basket. I looked inside. Flasks of draughts and crocks of herbs.

"Come with us, child," she said to Amice. "You are learning to be a healer, and you shall have no better master than Megge."

Softening, she reached out and touched my cheek. "You have aged, Cousin."

"No longer 'little Megge,'" I said, "though I almost wish I were."

"What has you so weary?"

"A decision."

"About the blacksmith?"

"About how I shall ease his pain as the end nears. Already he has suffered so—"

Her raised eyebrow silenced me.

"Where is this sickroom?" she asked, taking my arm. "Alf told me of it. Is it a hut of sorts?"

"There." I pointed to the cottage in the glade. "It's for those nearing their end. Are you saying you have never been here?"

"Never. My mother did not come here, and yours never brought me. She must have feared I would speak to you of it."

As we neared the cottage, her face brightened. "Why, that looks like *our* cottage!"

"Wait until you see, Brighida." I quickened my pace.

Clapping her hand over her mouth, she pointed to the shutters. "My father carved those. Do you see the leaves, Amice? The vines? The sparrows? That was my father's work!"

That was Gregory Carver's work, I thought as I opened the door. Not your father's.

I wondered if she had had the same thought as she stepped inside and moved toward the curtain, beyond which lay her true father.

CHAPTER 84

AMICE

Christine looked up from the table when we entered the kitchen. Before her was a cup of wine, and on a plate were thin slices of bread and a lump of cheese she was chopping into fine bits. She stood and moved to the curtain, placing herself between Brighida and the sickroom.

She looked at Brighida for a moment, but she spoke to Megge. "He is feeling better and has asked for food."

"Christine," Megge said, "this is my cousin, Brighida."

"It is an honor to meet you, Christine," Brighida said warmly.

"Lady," Christine said, nodding to her.

"Mother taught Christine how to tend to the needs of those afflicted with lepra, and she is teaching me."

Brighida looked at me in surprise. "Not Brother James?"

"Brother James has taught me some of the surgeon's skills, but the real work—the tending, the soothing, the feeding—is done by Christine."

Christine picked up the cup and plate. Carrying them into the sickroom, she said over her shoulder, "I shall ask if he will see you."

After quite a long time, she opened the curtain. "You may come in."

She had combed Mister Gough's wet hair back from his face. Though his sores no longer oozed, the smell of rot now lingered despite her diligent care. Megge and I were accustomed to the odor, but I could tell by Brighida's forceful swallowing that she was struggling not to retch.

"Will you leave us for a moment, Christine?" Not taking her eyes from Mister Gough's, Brighida motioned with her head toward the kitchen.

"Lady?" Christine looked to Megge.

"My cousin would like to speak with him alone, if she may." Megge waited a moment, and when Christine did not move, she added, "Amice and I will remain here should they need anything."

Christine moved the plate and cup about on the small bedside table. "I shall return to feed him," she said. The curtain fluttered behind her when she departed.

Brighida stared at Mister Gough's face, her eyes narrowed, her mouth drawn into a short, pale line. I could not tell if she was angry, fearful, or sorrowful.

Some of his sores had healed, but below that monstrous brow and above that sunken nose, his rheumy eyes stared at her.

His thick, split lips barely moved. "Have you come to gloat, Daughter?"

Daughter? Mister Gough is Brighida's father?

I looked afresh at the shutters that Brighida said her father had made.

And also a carpenter?

"I have come to help you." Brighida picked up the bread from the table, tore off a piece, dipped it in the wine, and put it to his lips. "Christine said you asked for food. This will nourish you."

He tightened his lips and turned his head, but she touched the bread to his mouth. The wine leaked from the bread and trickled over his lower lip. Brighida lifted a corner of her apron and touched it to the drops. "Go on, take the bread. It is soft."

He opened his mouth just wide enough for Brighida to slip a tiny piece of the bread past his gourd-like lips. As he chewed, he winced.

"Does your mouth pain you?"

The look he gave her rivaled the priestess's sneer.

"Let me see."

He swallowed and opened his mouth. The reek of decay made me turn away to hide my grimace, but Brighida's countenance revealed no distaste as she leaned closer and pulled down his lower lip. Raw, flame-red sores abutted thick white patches. His lower teeth, the few that remained, were black at the base.

"Christine," Brighida called.

Christine came to the doorway and looked inside. "Yes, Lady?"

"Come, look." Brighida held down Mister Gough's lip. "Do you truly believe he could have eaten bread and cheese with these sores?"

Megge drew in her breath, and her gaze shifted from Brighida to Christine.

Christine replied not to Brighida but to Megge. "His mouth is much better today, Lady."

"Better?" Brighida gaped at her.

Christine walked to a table in the corner of the room that held a cloth-covered bowl, an empty bowl, two lidded crocks, a cup of water, a single candle, a piece of flint, and a roughened rod. She removed the cloth. The bowl held a pestle, a spoon, and a small pyramid of greyish powder.

Once more addressing only Megge, Christine pointed to the powder. "This is salt mixed with ground coal of hartshorn." She lifted the lid on one of the crocks. "Honey." She removed the lid from the second, which was empty. She spooned some of the powder into it, drizzled honey over the powder, and lit the candle. She stirred three drops of melted tallow into the honeyed powder, carried the crock to the bed, and blew on it. Touched it. Blew on it again. Touched it.

Satisfied, she said to Mister Gough, "Your lip."

Obediently, he pushed out his lower lip. She dipped a finger into the thick paste and rubbed it on the sores. "Now, your tongue."

He put out his tongue, and she dipped her finger into the honey and gently rubbed it over its tip.

"I saw no sores on his tongue," Brighida said.

"The honey is a reward, Lady. For obedience. And for not biting me."

She picked up the cup of water. "From St. Mary Magdalene's Holy Well."

I shrank from her.

"Amice?" Megge touched my shoulder.

I tried to smile to tell her all was well.

Mister Gough reached for the cup.

"Patience," Christine told him. "Let the plasters do their work." She looked at me. "The plasters make the mouth water, which helps it heal. Little else does now."

When saliva leaked from Mister Gough's mouth, Christine put the cup to his lips and held the empty bowl beneath his chin. "A sip now, to cleanse the mouth. Then, spit."

He sat forward, took a sip, rolled it through his mouth, and spat into the bowl. He exhaled, closed his eyes, and lay back.

One by one, Christine set the cup, bowl, crocks, pestle, and spoon on a small tray.

"Now, Brighida, you may give him that bread." Her back rigid, she left the sickroom, snatching the curtain across the doorway as she passed.

A smile tugged at Megge's lips, but Brighida looked aghast.

"Christine," she called, but there was no response from the kitchen. She looked at Megge. "She is furious."

"She was Mother's pupil," Megge said. "She appears humble and demure, but she knows her work." She laughed. "I, too, have felt her wrath."

"You might have warned me."

"I never thought to do so. No one has ever taken offense at your words. But the next time you come, we shall ask her before we approach him."

"There will be no next time." Brighida looked down at Mister Gough. He was asleep, his mouth agape.

"I don't believe she told us all she had put in that remedy," Brighida muttered.

She took Megge aside and handed her a vial. "This, too, will bring on sleep. It is a draught of birch bark, ironweed, and steeped seeds of the horned poppy—the *horned* poppy, Megge, not the common poppy—and mandrake. Put—"

"A few drops in a cup of red wine," Megge finished for her.

Brighida tilted her head.

"Memories from my days on the cliffs," Megge explained. "The remedies I used at the dawn of time are still bringing healing and rest."

"This one will bring more." Brighida picked up her basket and cloak and moved toward the cottage door. "I shan't be back." As she stepped outside, she turned back to Megge. "I can see that some part of you pities him and wants to help him, but also that something haunts you. You want from him something that he cannot give. Perhaps the answer to a question?"

Before closing the door, she said, "You've a task to complete here. Give my father a few drops of the draught, then take a sip yourself."

"Me?" Megge asked.

"You. So you will share his dream—and perhaps you shall have your answer."

CHAPTER 85

MEGGE

When I returned to the sickroom, I found the blacksmith sweating and moaning. Amice wiped his face with a wet cloth. A fever flush once more colored his glistening face and neck. He tore off his shirt and hurled it across the room, then tossed from side to side, his lips drawn back in a feral grimace.

That rasping cough was back. This was not the smelter's malady.

Amice and Christine turned him onto his side, and I put my ear to his back. Each inhalation gurgled, and each exhalation whistled as he forced the breath out.

"How had he sounded so well but a moment ago?" Christine asked.

"He had calmed. Seeing Brighida gave him a moment of peace."

Amice watched closely as I poured a few drops of Brighida's draught into the blacksmith's wine. I turned him on his back, raised his head, and poured drops of the liquid over his lips. He swallowed. After a moment, he took more and then lay back and dropped into slumber. His scarlet hue faded, and he began to breathe easily once more.

Christine looked from him to me. "That was no mere wine."

"Brighida left a draught of ironweed to cleanse the blood, birch bark to lessen fever, and essence of horned poppy to bring forth sleep."

And dreams, I thought. Dreams that will reveal to him—and to me—all that has been. All *he* has been. And perhaps, what he once was to me.

He stirred, his head moving slowly. His breath quickened. His hands picked at the blanket.

I did not need a sip of the draught to share his dream.

Show me, I ordered the ether.

Astride a galloping mount, I flew along a cliff's edge as a storm churned the sea, blowing spray nearly to the brink. I pulled up the collar of my cloak, brushing my knuckles over several days' growth of heavy beard.

Where is she? I searched the cliff, distress settling over me. *Surely they lied. I took her to wife; we conceived a child. Surely she did not—*

Whispers rose from the cliffs.

The babe is no more.

'Twas a girl, but she cast it out.

The storm was nearly upon me when the healer—the goddess, my wife—glided along the cliff's edge like a wraith, her skin taut over brow and cheeks, her full lips pale, and her flat belly showing me what I had refused to believe. Distress gave way to anguish as the gale carried away the words I could read on her lips, "I did not kill her."

I pulled down my hat so the brim hid my face.

"She forsook me," my lady cried as I spurred my mount, my face awash in tears.

The blacksmith and I awoke at the same moment, gasping.

He rubbed his eyes and strained to see me.

"What was that dream?" He put a hand to his brow and rubbed it.

"It was another life, Michael. In another time."

He shook his head and tried to sit up. "You—you were there. But not a herder."

No, I thought. Not a herder. Not in that life.

"You were my *wife*." Bewildered, he tried to sit up but fell back onto the pillow. "But you looked nothing like—" He waved his hands over his head to indicate my hair. "You carried my child."

A knife twisted inside me as the memories I had banished came rushing back. My lovely but lifeless daughter. My grief. My guilt. My loving husband.

My fault.

Then all the lonely, childless lives that followed. A spinster. A hermit. A fleeing child. And finally, in this life, a midwife's daughter who could not bear the sight of another child born blue.

"The child was not meant to be, Michael," I said gently. "She was born still."

"They told me you had killed her." His voice was ragged, his eyes narrowed with suspicion.

Sometimes, Megge, the worst simply comes to pass. No one can prevent it . . . Not even your mother could save every child.

"Sometimes, Michael, for reasons we cannot know, babies are not born alive."

"No—I remember." He pushed himself up on one elbow, stared at me, and wheezed, "You told me she had forsaken you because of what you were—a deathbringer. Then you took your own life." He nodded to himself. "I was there. In that cave."

"You were there? You witnessed that rite?"

"Aye." He stared at me. "You could not bear the guilt."

I had to see it again. The vision that had come to me on Samhain Eve had shown me only a portion of it—perhaps because that was all I was prepared to see.

But now I was ready to see it all. And I owed it to Michael—and to Amice—to share what I was about to learn.

"Close your eyes," I said to them, "and watch."

Show me, I commanded.

Robed in brilliant white, I stood in my cave before my font, my black braids gleaming in the candlelight. At my side stood a white-gowned young woman and five white-gowned girls, heads bowed beneath their hoods, hands clasped behind their backs. Four of the girls stood as straight and still as tallow tapers, but the young woman reached behind the back of the small girl beside her, and they struggled over something the girl held in her hand.

I had just opened my mouth to reprove them when my husband, Mihalis, his tunic bearing the soot and char of the swordsmith, arrived breathless at the mouth of the cave no man was allowed to enter.

"Atropos—" His countenance showed both confusion and fear.

"Our child was born still, Mihalis," I called to him. "She forsook me."

"Forsook?"

"I carry within me an evil seed. The child sensed it and could not allow her spirit to be bound to it as mine was, so she forsook me."

"No—they say you killed her."

"I would have given my life for her. And now I *shall* give it. For her." I stretched my left arm over my font and held out my right hand to the young woman at my side. She laid a knife on my palm.

"What are you doing there?" Mihalis shouted. "What is this rite?"

"I am returning to the ether, where I shall banish the death-bringer. One day I shall return to the living world a healer—a mortal woman unencumbered by the charge to kill."

With one last look at the loving man who had fathered my daughter, I drew the blade across my wrist.

My novices closed around me, and as my blood spilled, a terrible sadness rose within me, born of love lost, of hopes dashed.

"This will not be our last life together, Atropos," my husband vowed, his voice ragged, his gaze hard on mine. "I take my oath on it."

And there it was, the answer to my question.

"You have followed me through all my lives, Michael," I said once we all had recovered, "protecting me from that evil seed—the death-bringer's spirit. Only in this life—and only because of this dread dis-ease—did you fail."

I could not help but compare the blacksmith's frightful face with the bronzed, sculpted face of the husband whose eyes had held mine as he vowed that our first life together would not be our last.

"Though your acts have been grievous—and cruel—I understand now that you wished only to free me from the deathbringer, whose spirit I had gone to my death to banish. So I forgive you for your misguided devotion. But your crimes against this child—" I looked at Amice, "and all the girls condemned to death so that you might live—are not for me to forgive. Only Amice can grant—"

"He told us to run!" Amice cried.

CHAPTER 86

AMICE

mice?" Megge stared at me for a moment, then took me in her arms. "Amice!"

"He opened the door," I said, amazed to hear my grating voice and glad that Megge finally knew the truth. "He told us to run!"

"Willful child!" Anwen scolded. "Say no more, I beg you."

I stopped listening to her.

My voice had sounded like rocks being crushed, and the shards had scraped my throat, so I coughed. Then I coughed again. Megge released me and waited.

"He did not ask the priestess for the blood cure. He refused our blood. And he freed me. He freed us all."

"Amice . . ." Drawing her gaze from mine with difficulty, Megge returned to Mister Gough's bedside. "Is this so?"

He turned away from her.

She moved to the other side of the bed and knelt to look into his eyes. "Brother James told me that you refused the sacraments because you believed you did not deserve 'God and His heaven.'"

"Leave me." His voice, already thin, was fading.

Why did he say he did not deserve heaven?

I searched his tormented face, and the same questions came to me that had burdened me ever since I overheard Megge tell Hugh that Mister Gough had taken her books and her aunt's blood back to the cliffs: Had he planned to ask his mother to use them after all? Had Magdalene found another maiden? Had *he?* Was that why he felt he did not deserve heaven?

No—I could not believe it. There must have been another reason.

"There is something more . . ." Megge said, a frown creasing her brow as she stared at him. He would never tell her, I knew, so she would soon summon a vision.

"May I share your vision?" I asked.

Show us, she ordered.

I saw Mister Gough lying in the sea cave as the tide crept in. Megge stood over him, the point of her herder's stick at his throat, demanding that he tell her what his mother had meant to do with her aunt Claris's blood.

". . . blend it with a virgin's," he rasped. "And with water from this font. While speaking an incantation. One she believes she'll find in your books." He coughed to clear his throat. "Already she has the water. She lacks only the blood and the books." He barked out a laugh. "And a virgin."

"The blood," she ordered. "Give it to me."

He reached into a pocket and withdrew a vial.

"Take it." He handed it to her. "The tide'll soon be in. That'll be my cure." He revealed the books hidden beneath his legs, and as Megge took them, Hugh arrived at the mouth of the cave.

The vision dispersed, and I said nothing, for my gut was sending me a very bad feeling about Mister Gough. I tried once more to make sense of all I knew.

After arguing with Magdalene and the priestess, Mister Gough left the church, promising to return with the blood and the books. He went to Bury Down late in the summer, killed Megge's aunt Claris, took her blood, and then returned to the cliffs in the fall—likely, I thought, to bring the priestess the *whore's blood* she had demanded. But when he discovered us in the church, he set us free.

Why, then, did he return to Bury Down, steal Megge's books, and carry them—and her aunt's blood—all the way back to the cliffs when they would serve no purpose—and he knew it?

Or, would they have?

"Amice," Megge said. "You appear unsettled."

"May I ask Mister Gough a question?"

"Quickly."

"Mister Gough, why did you steal Megge's books and bring them back to the cliffs after you had set us free? The priestess had no virgins to give her their blood, so even had you given her the blood you had taken from Megge's aunt, she could not have made the potion that she promised would cure you, unless—

"To destroy the damnable things," he whispered. "To take them with me into the sea, so my mother would never take another maiden—as she had taken you, Amice—for her blood." He struggled for breath. "And to put an end to that accursed *Sisterhood*."

I had little time, and I felt like a traitor asking, but I had to know. "Why, then, did you keep Claris's blood? Did you intend to take another maiden?"

"No. Never." He turned away. His voice was choked when, finally, he replied. "I kept it because it was Claris's."

So, he *had* loved someone. And she had loved him. Claris had been Brighida's mother and Mister Gough her father—they had to have loved each other at one time. Now, I knew, he loved her still. It was that disease—the suffering brought on by that evil, godless disease—that had made him take her life. And I believed him: He never would have taken another girl.

"Michael—" Megge turned his head so he could see her. "After what you did for Amice and the other girls by freeing them and destroying the Sisterhood, why did you tell Brother James's you did not deserve forgiveness and eternal peace?"

How can she not see?

Looking at his tortured countenance, I knew why. It was because his desperate suffering had made him do that terrible, unforgivable thing to the woman he loved.

He did not reply.

Megge pressed. "Was it your hope that for rescuing Amice and putting an end to the Sisterhood, I would offer you a time of rest in the ether and another span of days in the living world in which to serve others?"

Silence.

"Help him, Megge," I pleaded. "He is in such agony, he cannot speak."

She looked gently upon Mister Gough. "What did you hope for, Michael?"

"Another span of days," he breathed, looking upon me as he had in his tent the first time our eyes had met—with sorrow.

"To atone." Megge exhaled. "Is that your wish? To take your vow as a Mentor and use your next life to make amends?"

He pulled his gaze from mine and turned slowly to her, his countenance revealing first bafflement and then wrath.

"Amends?" His voice, though scarcely a whisper, carried venom. "To the witch who killed my daughter?"

CHAPTER 87

MEGGE

mice's hands flew to her face as she fled the sickroom. I followed her, but she put up a hand and shook her head.

Though she sank into grief, I embraced newfound peace. I understood at last who Michael Gough was and why his spirit, in its many guises, had put me to so many brutal deaths—and I forgave him for all of them.

I called out, "Why are you fleeing, Amice?"

She stopped and turned, her voice despairing, "He refused God and His heaven, and now you will refuse him the Bury Down cure."

I followed her to the hut and sat beside her on her pallet.

"Do you understand what 'the cure' is?"

"It parts the spirit from the failing body so the body remains at peace in the space between life and death until it breathes its last," she recited without taking a breath. "I believe it is a remedy—an herb or seeds—a cure that your mother kept to herself. And now, because of Mister Gough's harsh words, you would keep it from him."

I took her hand, still scarcely able to believe I was hearing her voice, her thoughts, her words.

"Amice, though Mister Gough has brought only suffering to Bury Down, have I withheld any remedy that might have brought him ease?"

Amice's eyes searched mine. For the truth, I felt. She shook her head.

"The cure is not an herb. Nor is it a seed. It is a path. A path to another life. It is a promise made at the end of life to those who have freely offered their skills, their knowledge, or their wisdom to others in the living world. It is my promise to them that I shall protect them as their spirit makes its way into the ether—and theirs to me that they will return to the living world when I summon them to serve. When they take this vow, their spirit enters the ether, leaving their suffering body behind.

"I cannot force anyone to take that vow. Nor can I offer Mentorship to one who does not wish it—or merit it. And I see I was wrong about Michael Gough. He did love someone. He loved you. And you will surely weep when he dies. And he has done at least two good deeds in this life. He freed you, and he ended the Sisterhood—"

"And he loved your aunt. He regretted what he did to her. Why, then, will you not make him a Mentor?"

"Even if I willed it, Amice, I could not, for his spirit has chosen a different path. Though Michael the man did some good in this life, his spirit still believes that in that long-ago life, I killed our child. Though she was not yet born, she was Mihalis's daughter, and he loved her. He vowed to avenge her death—or, as his spirit still sees it, her murder."

"So, you will allow Mister Gough to suffer."

"No." I shook my head slowly. "I cannot offer his spirit the ether, nor would it allow Michael to accept were I to do so. But I shall give Michael the draughts that will ease his breathing and help him rest, and you may comfort him in any way you know. We shall ask Brother James to come, and together we shall all give Mister Gough the peaceful passage he craves—and, perhaps, deserves.

"Christine," I said as Amice and I entered the sickroom, "will you send for Brother James? Ask him to bring some of Mister Kendell's sleeping draught."

While we waited, I applied drops of poppyseed draught to Michael's lips while Amice cooled his face and neck with wet cloths. He slept fitfully, so I was relieved when Brother James arrived. With him was a tall young man, fair and mild, his blond hair tonsured, his pale blue eyes glancing from Amice to me. He lowered his gaze and followed Brother James to the bedside.

"Megge," Brother James said, "this is my acolyte, Timothy. He studies Medicine. Has done so since he was a boy."

"Lowenna has spoken of you, Timothy. She says you're a scholar. Thank you for bringing us the herbs we needed."

He shrugged, his face going red.

Brother James took me aside. "Did you give Michael your final cure?"

"Nearly," I said. "I nearly did. But—"

"He refused."

"He would have."

Brother James nodded, his eyes warm on mine.

"Timothy," he said, looking up at the young man whose hands now trembled. "Give Mister Gough three drops of the draught."

Amice and I stayed with Brother James and Timothy, watching through the night as the acolyte gave Michael drops of the sleeping draught until his body had gone still—and then dusky. At dawn, when it was over, Lowenna saw us out, and Christine brought in the basins, water, cloths, lavender oil, and sheets they would use to tend Michael's body.

"Go back to your hut now and rest," Lowenna said, "We shall see to things here."

As Amice wept for the man who had set her free, her hand went to the neck of her tunic, and she withdrew the braided string she always wore, gripping the stone that hung from it in her fist.

When finally she stopped weeping, she opened her fist and kissed the stone—and all at once, I felt as though a gust of wind had torn off the roof and knocked the sky askew. Tilting and tumbling, I feared I would lose my grip on this life.

When the earth stilled, I saw myself in the company of two girls garbed in white, one a child and the other nearly a woman. Seated side by side upon pillows, they worked silently, the little one spinning silvery thread, the elder measuring out lengths. I, the eldest, stood poised to divide it.

I cut the thread, and a tiny, golden flame leapt, vanishing into the air.

"Another life gone." I stared at the broken thread.

My sisters, Lachesis and little Clotho, took no heed of me, for this was simply our charge.

"That was the last." I laid down my shears.

Lachesis did not look up. "You've said that before, Atropos."

"That was unkind, Lachesis," Clotho scolded.

"Unkind? Who stood by her when she defied Father? Who echoed her demand that he release us from the curse under which we were all born?" Lachesis stood now, feet spread, shoulders squared, eyes ablaze. "It was I. And it was I who vowed to follow Atropos through fire and a thousand lives if that's what it takes to free her to become a healer."

"I, too, take that vow," Clotho declared.

"It is time," I said. "I am leaving."

"Not alone." Clotho leapt to her feet.

"You are too young." Lachesis waved her away. "Stay here with Father."

"She needs me." Clotho faced Lachesis. "Atropos taught me to spin, and she shall teach me to heal. I shall be her apprentice." She bent to lay down her spindle, and a fine chain bearing a silver stone slid out of the neck of her gown. She took the stone in her hand and looked at me—and then, reluctantly, at Lachesis—and pressed it to her lips.

Lachesis withdrew hers and did the same, though she could not hide her smile or the shake of her head as she looked at Clotho.

"Willful child," she muttered.

I looked down. Disappearing into the neck of my gown was a silver cord. I reached inside and drew out a stone much like theirs—a gift from our mother, a woman of courage and wisdom who, in her final act as our mother in that life, had blessed her daughters with the gift of sight.

"Heed your dreams," she had said. "For what are dreams but moments in spirit?"

Looking first at Lachesis and then at Clotho, I kissed my stone, and our vow was sealed.

I opened my eyes and saw Amice watching me as I fingered the stone at my throat. Our eyes met, and I saw not the silent, brown-haired little girl I had come to love, but my black-haired, headstrong little sister, Clotho.

CHAPTER 88

AMICE

I awoke from the dream of the sisters to see Megge touching the stone at her throat, her gaze resting upon me with tenderness. I had seen that stone every day since I arrived at Bury Down; but looking at it now, I knew its wearer not only as Megge, the woman who had given me a home, but as my eldest sister, the goddess reborn, Atropos.

And though I had never seen a stone at Anwen's throat, I knew her as my valiant elder sister, Lachesis.

CHAPTER 89

MEGGE

Tell me, Amice," I said when she had released me from her embrace, "what name did your mother give you?"

"I was baptized *Anna*—only the women knew my shadow name."

"Your shadow name?"

"*Anwen.* For the Huntress. But that name was spoken 'only in shadow,' my mother told me. 'Only when it is just we women.'"

So, I thought, her mother, too, was one of us.

"Shall we call you *Anwen*? Would you like that? Or, perhaps, *Anna*?"

She smiled and shook her head. "I am Amice now."

"Have you family to return to?"

"I had only my mother and father, and they both died."

"Why did your mother name you for the huntress?"

"Because when I was being born, long before I should have been, Anwen's voice told her to name me for her and promised that she would protect me." She frowned as she thought. "I know now that Anwen was once Lachesis—that they are the same spirit. I saw that in our vision. But—"

She frowned. It appeared she was trying to understand something beyond her ken.

"What is it?" I asked.

"Why did Lachesis tell my mother to name me *Anwen*? Why not *Clotho*? That is my true name." She spoke faster as she became ever more vexed. "And why was she called *Anwen*? Why is she not always called *Lachesis*? And why do our memories return to us so slowly?"

I had to smile at her impatience. "They return slowly because when we return to the living world, it is always to a new place, a new time. A new family. With a new charge. As Mentors, we must become fully a part of that world before we regain our memory of our former lives, lest we fail to learn what we must in order to carry out our new charge."

"But our names!"

"Yes," I said. "Our names. Lachesis was called *Anwen* in that long-ago life because *Lachesis* is not a Cornish name. In her most recent life, she was known as *Aleydis*, for her family were Dutch, as were my grandfather Arjen and my great-grandfather Adaem. I was born in Cornwall, so I was named for Lady Margaret, the Countess of Cornwall."

"Do all spirits return to the living world with a new name?"

I shook my head. "Not all. Some suffer so deeply in the living world that something within them breaks. Unwilling to forgive those who harmed them or make amends to those they harmed, they wander from life to life clinging to a familiar name, skill, trade, or habit— anything that once comforted them—all the while bearing the same scars and seeking to right a wrong they cannot name."

Megge. Margaret. Murga—

Realization struck me silent. I sat open-mouthed for a long while.

"There is something you deserve to know, Amice."

Can I admit it?

I must.

"I have done much the same thing in all my lives. In my first life, steeped in grief over the loss of my daughter, I took my own life and never again became a mother. Though I had vowed to return as a healer, I shunned midwifery. And bound to the belief that my husband had loved me, I tried in vain—in every life—to make him the Mentor I believed he was meant to be.

"Why, in my life as the seer Murga, I took him as my apprentice! When I learned he was unfit and cast him out, he became a blacksmith, stole my writings, and turned those I served against me. They burned me at the stake.

"In this life, he murdered my mother and stole the books that hold my power. Yet, even as he raged against me—on the ship and in the sickroom—I tried to make him say the words my spirit longed to hear Mihalis's say: 'Let me walk with you—once again and forevermore.' So I am no wiser than any other spirit."

Amice tipped her head. "You lost your daughter, and that made you so heavy of heart that you could not bear to lose another—or to see another child die. And your love for Mihalis made you so trust him that, in every life, you wished to give him what you believed he deserved. Where is the shame in that?"

Who is this child?

Her brow furrowed. "Lachesis told me that Tinker's spirit, too, was damaged in a long-ago life." She looked at me, thinking. "But his wound made him cruel." She thought for another moment, and her voice rose. "When he returns, will he still be damaged? Might he be more damaged? Even more cruel?"

"I do not know, Amice," I said truthfully and drew her close.

She pulled away, eyes wide, looking not like the thoughtful, ancient spirit she truly was, but like the terrified child I had found in Bury Down grove. "Will he cut me again? Will he hurt Britlen and kill Kaatje? Will he kill us all?"

I shook my head and tried to calm her. "I cannot know what he will do. But you are safe with me. You know this. And perhaps whoever killed him taught him something in his final moments—something of worth that he can carry into his next life."

"I hope she did." The words were hardly out when Amice drew in her breath and held it.

She knows, I thought. Somehow, she knows who killed him.

"I hope she did, too," I said and smiled at her.

We quieted for a time, each deep in thought, Amice with her eyes closed and her head cocked. After a time, she shook her head and cocked it again. "I can no longer hear her voice."

"Whose voice?"

"Anwen's."

"Anwen's? You've heard Anwen's voice?"

Amice nodded. "All my life, a woman's voice has spoken to me in my sleep and taught me how to heal. When my mother was dying, the woman came to me in spirit and told me she was Anwen the Huntress. While I was in the tower, Anwen taught me about you, the goddess. We spoke silently, night after night, so words would not be lost to me, and so that when finally I spoke, I would speak not as a child but as a woman.

"I vowed never to speak aloud while Tinker lived. And even after he died, I remained silent, for Anwen had forbidden me to speak aloud until she gave me leave to do so.

"When I began to tell you that Mister Gough had freed me, she tried to silence me. But I disobeyed her, and she called me a willful child and never spoke to me again. Then I saw Lachesis in our vision and knew that she and Anwen were one. But still I cannot see or hear her." She lowered her head, and tears fell onto her lap. "Where has she gone?"

"Let us find her." I put an arm around her shoulders, closed my eyes, and called out to the ether, *Show us Lachesis.*

The vision took us not to the ether but back to my cave, where Lachesis and Clotho stood beside me at the font as I told my husband that our unborn child had died.

Unlike the other novices, so silent and still, Lachesis and Clotho were struggling over something Clotho held behind her back. Finally, Lachesis wrested from Clotho's grip a long, slim knife.

I reached for it, and Clotho began to weep. Lachesis laid it in my hand, and when I swept the blade across my wrist, Clotho shrieked and Mihalis shouted that this would not be our last life together.

But the last thing I heard in that life was Lachesis whispering, "I shall protect you from him."

And she had tried. In every life, she had tried to protect me from him.

"Thank you, Lachesis," I whispered as the vision faded. "And thank you, Mother, for giving your daughters the gift of sight through dreams."

"What are dreams," I heard a familiar voice ask, "but moments in spirit?"

My eyes flew open. "Morwen!"

"Megge." Before me, in spirit, stood an elderly woman wrapped in a ratty brown cloak. She offered me a wry smile, and a single dimple appeared in her cheek.

"And Clotho." She smiled tenderly at Amice. "It is lovely to see my daughters together again after so long a time."

"I have missed you so." Tears blurred my vision. "I always believed you were my mother."

"I wish I could have been your mother in this life as well." Her eyes went misty. "Your own mother made your childhood so hard. But now, seeing why she so desperately wanted you to become a woman of Bury Down and her true apprentice—so you could continue her work serving the suffering lazars—perhaps you understand her demand that you take up her book."

I finally did. Grief and remorse swept through me as I recalled the night she urged me to accept and protect her book. Though she had explained that its power sustained the Mentors, I had not understood what would befall our village were it to be usurped.

"And you, my dear Clotho," Morwen said, her eyes filling with tears. "All you have endured—" She wiped her face and spoke briskly. "But now, you are seeking your sister."

"She was with me in the tower," Amice said, her words rushed, her tone urgent. "She told me a hundred times to keep silent, but I disobeyed her today, and I can no longer hear her voice. Is she with you?"

"Aye, she's having a moment's rest in the ether. She has shadowed Mihalis throughout time, protecting Atropos from him as she vowed to do, and these perilous months with you, my dear Clotho, have been wearying, even for Lachesis." She chuckled. "You always did wear her to the bone!"

After a moment, Morwen turned serious. "You could not know this, Clotho, but it was Lachesis who was meant to return as the child *Anna*. Lachesis is fearless, resilient, *patient*, and has vanquished both Tinker and the blacksmith a thousand times. But you—" Shaking her head and smiling again, Morwen clucked her tongue at Amice. "You insisted on doing your part for Atropos. 'I have been kept in the shadows long enough,' you said as your spirit left the ether and entered that tiny babe that was so like you: impetuous and eager to be born. Lachesis could not but watch your birth and then teach you, comfort you in that tower, and then lead you to Atropos." She smiled at me. "To Megge."

"Lachesis tried to keep her from speaking," I told Morwen. "She forbade her to do so."

"Always the wrong thing to do with Clotho." Morwen chuckled again.

"She must have feared that Clotho would tell me Michael had saved her—and that for his kindness, I would have made him a Mentor." I shook my head. "I nearly made that terrible mistake, Morwen."

"Only because the blacksmith spoke with such humility, denying himself God's forgiveness, that you believed he wanted another span of days to make amends for his many wrongs. How could you have known that his spirit had already ordained its return?"

"And it will return—"

"Aye, most like his do," Morwen said with a shrug. "Driven by a wish never granted, a task yet to by fulfilled, or a gnawing hunger."

"Revenge."

"Aye," Morwen said slowly. "A powerful hunger."

A weight dropped in my gut. "In the dream Michael and I shared just before his death, he tasted that bitterness and learned its source."

"Aye," Morwen said. "And his fury will only hasten his spirit's return."

"But isn't it possible," Amice asked, "that Mister Gough learned something in this life that will temper his spirit's rage in the next?"

"Aye, child," Morwen said. "There's always that hope."

"Morwen," I said, still hearing the blacksmith's last words and unable to cling to that hope, "you said Lachesis was having a moment's rest in the ether. For you, a moment can be eternity or the blink of an eye. Which shall it be?"

Someone pounded on the door, and Morwen's spirit vanished.

Amice ran to the door just as it flew open. Lowenna rushed in, her coif hanging off her hair, her breath coming fast. She pressed a fist into her side and bent over, breathing hard.

"Cadan Trelawney is here." She huffed, struggling to catch her breath. "Nellie needs you. The babe's coming, and that awful woman is with her. She told Nellie that if the child were born now, it would not live." Finally breathing normally, she straightened. "So she is steaming Nellie's nether parts to keep the child from leaving the womb. Nellie is begging you to come."

CHAPTER 90

AMICE

Christine bustled into the hut carrying a full sack.

"Basins, clean cloths, string, shears, a knife, and a threaded needle. You must be off." She thrust the bundle into my arms, hurried us onto the potter's cart, and stepped back.

"Christine," Megge shouted as the cart began to move. "You must come with us."

"I cannot." Christine swept an arm down the length of her tunic. *Grey.*

"I cannot do this without you. Come with us, Christine, I pray you."

Christine looked to Lowenna, who nodded. Christine climbed into the back of the cart, Mister Trelawney whipped the horse, and we were away.

Nellie's cottage was crowded with a dozen women deep in prayer.

Sitting on a three-legged stool like the one Eleanor had used for births, Nellie swayed, panting and groaning. Beneath the stool's center hole sat a pot of steaming water and a pile of bloody rags. On the low stool before Nellie hunkered a woman whose unkempt hair had escaped from her soiled coif and fallen in tangles to the shoulders of her torn and dirty tunic.

"Be silent!" She wiped her hands on her blood-smeared leather apron. "Your screams will kill the child. And stop bearing down."

"The child is coming!" Nellie grunted.

"Make way." Christine pushed through the praying women to the fire pit in the center of the floor and touched the water in the kettle hanging over the peat.

"You." She picked up the bellows lying beside the hearth and handed them to Dora Tucker. "Tend the fire." She turned to the others. "The rest of you—" She pointed to the door.

Megge touched Nellie's shoulder and whispered something that made Nellie lay her head on Megge's hand and sigh.

"Amice," Megge called. "Come, stay with Nellie. You know what to do."

"All is well, Nellie." I touched the lock of hair clinging to her brow and smoothed it under her coif. "You have a new midwife, you know."

Megge looked down at the false midwife. The woman glanced up, sweating and cursing. Without a word, Megge took her by the elbow and raised her to her feet. The woman planted a hammy fist on an ample hip and spat on the floor. "You'll not tell me—"

Megge leaned forward, her eyes still on the woman's, but said not a word. The woman shoved her tools into a sack and backed to the door.

Christine ushered her out and closed the door behind her, but the woman's face soon appeared at the window, sputtering and cursing, demanding payment and respect.

Megge closed the shutters, removed the steaming pot from beneath the stool, and took her place on the stool opposite Nellie. She slid her hand into Nellie's birth canal and looked up at Nellie.

"You've done all you could to forestall this birth, but the child is about to be born. Bear down now."

Groaning, Nellie squeezed her eyes shut and bore down with all her might. I looked beneath the stool and saw the babe's thick, black hair appear.

I moved quickly to the window and threw open the shutters, that the child's spirit might come.

CHAPTER 91

MEGGE

Stop bearing down, Nellie. The head is out, but the child is not yet born. I must clean its nose and mouth."

As I wiped away the mucus, I looked upon that still face, those closed eyes, and dread rushed through me. *Let it be alive.*

Nellie began to groan.

"Again, Nellie. Bear down."

The shoulders and chest appeared, and the child took a gasping breath and squalled. I nearly fainted with relief.

"Megge, you've gone pale." Christine took hold of the half-born child, nudged me off the stool, and slid onto it to finish the birth.

I stepped outside and exhaled. *The child is alive!*

My breath caught. *Let it not be Mihalis.*

I watched from the doorway as Christine cut the cord, swaddled the babe, and motioned to Amice to come. Amice laid the howling bundle in Nellie's arms.

Speaking quietly with Nellie while Christine awaited the afterbirth, Amice caught my eye. We looked at each other, distressed rather than joyful, and I knew we shared the same fear—that this birth marked the return of a foe.

When the afterbirth had come and the bleeding had nearly ceased, Amice helped Nellie onto her pallet and put the babe to Nellie's breast. I stepped back into the cottage. It was as hot as a bakehouse.

Though Dora's face glistened and her tunic was stained with sweat, she continued to pump the bellows as Christine had ordered, and the peat glowed.

"Dora." I touched her shoulder. "Pray, take your rest. The peat is hot enough, as is the room." Smiling, I reached down to help her up. "I fear you'll melt!"

She sat back on her haunches and struggled to rise.

It's that hip. I grimaced, recalling the gaping, bleeding hole the boar's tusk had torn in it years before.

Sliding a hand under her arm, I helped her to her feet. She gazed upon me with both tenderness and relief. "We've long awaited this day, Lady."

"Dora—"

"No," she said. "You'll not gainsay me. You are no longer 'young Megge.' You are the Lady—the *Healer*—of Bury Down. Didn't we all see you cast out the false midwife and take her place, just as you have taken your own?" She withdrew a small cloth from her apron pocket and blew her nose. "If only you had been here when my niece—"

"I know, Dora." I held her. "But I am here now, and I am not alone. Christine and Amice are healers as well, and we shall see to it that there is no place in this village for false healers."

From outside the window came the ring of joyful voices—Nellie's friends talking, laughing, and rejoicing, for their prayers had been answered.

The voices rose to a clamor as the women strained to see inside the cottage through the tiny window.

"Would you like your friends to come in, Nellie?"

"Oh, yes. Their prayers saw us safely through." She tried to tuck her tousled hair under her coif. "As did you, Megge."

I opened the door, and the women surged in. One pulled the blankets up to Nellie's chin and tucked them snugly around the babe at her breast. Another put a pillow beneath Nellie's head. A third led Nellie's daughter into the room, while a fourth carried in Nellie's little boy, laughing and cooing at him.

A little girl I did not know came inside. She approached a woman whose russet hair and deep green eyes matched her own and whispered, "Mother, may I see?"

Her mother pulled her close and whispered to her while pointing to the newborn babe. Then the girl's gaze fell upon Amice. With a squeal of delight, she freed herself from her mother's arms and ran to her.

"Amice! My friend!"

"Delona!"

The girl's eyes flew open. "You can speak! Neville said you could not, but you can! Now we can truly be friends!"

CHAPTER 92

AMICE

My joy at seeing Delona was marred only by the dark thought I could not banish—that I would once more face Tinker Penneck. After so vicious a life and so violent a death, he would no doubt make his way back to the living world long before the memory of the evil he had wrought had begun to fade.

While Nellie rested, Megge and Christine took the instruments outside to the well, and I cleaned the floor. As I scattered fresh rushes, I prayed, *Don't let this child be Tinker.*

"You've gone pale," Mistress Tucker cried when she came inside. She laid a hand on my brow. "What is it, my dear? Are you ill?"

I shook my head. "No, Mistress Tucker."

Her mouth fell open, and she stared at me. It took her a moment to compose herself.

"Forgive me, Amice! I never dreamed you would speak! It cheers me more than I can say to hear your voice, for I was told that Tinker . . ."

Tinker, I thought as she prattled on. What sort of name is *Tinker*? Who would want to journey through countless lives burdened with that name?

"Mistress Tucker," I broke in, "was his name truly *Tinker?*"

"Nay, child," she laughed, waving a hand. "His father called him that because he never stayed put. Even as a child, he wandered hither and yon—like a tinker! His real name came down from his mother's line, may God rest her soul. She was a Dane and nearly as comely as Tinker grew to be." She sighed. "So fair of face." She sighed again. "But she died so young."

"What, pray, did she name him?"

"She named him for his grandfather and great-grandfather across the sea. *Mikkel.*"

One of Nellie's friends drew Mistress Tucker away, and I practiced saying that name so I would never forget it. "*MEE-kel. MEE-kel.*"

I noticed Delona looking shyly at Nellie, so I took her hand and led her to the bed.

"Ohhh," she breathed, gazing at the infant nestled in swaddling. "It's so small!"

"Would you like to see?" Nellie invited.

Delona nodded, unable to take her eyes from the bundle at Nellie's breast. Nellie drew back the blanket and turned the sleeping child so Delona could see.

After but a glance, Delona turned and ran out of the cottage. Moments later, she threw open the door and rushed back inside. Face flushed, breathing hard, she ran to Nellie and held out her fist.

"What's this?" Nellie asked.

"A gift for the babe," Delona panted, opening her hand.

On her palm was a pile of fine, white thread.

"Thank you, Delona," Nellie said, smiling at her uncertainly.

Delona untangled the thread and held it up. Hanging from it was a small, grey stone.

My hand flew to the stone beneath my tunic.

"It's charming, Delona," Nellie said.

Megge came inside and set the clean basins beside the sack of instruments Christine had left by the door. She approached the bed as Delona was carefully placing the string with its grey stone atop the swaddling blanket.

"May I see it?" Megge asked her.

Delona nodded, and Megge drew a sharp breath when she saw the stone. She picked up the thread and rubbed it between her thumb and forefinger.

"As fine as a spider's thread," she said as if speaking to herself, then pulled the white thread taut. "But strong as wire." She looked at me. "Goddess thread."

"Yes! Brighida gave it to me," Delona said with pride. "She didn't tell me what I was meant to do with it, but that night, I dreamed of this." She touched the stone. "In the dream, I saw myself give it to a newborn babe who looked just like Mistress Trelawney's. I told my father about the dream, and he gave me a bit of granite, just the right color. Neville carved it and burnished it. I was there. I watched."

"May I, Nellie?" Megge held the string and the stone above the child's neck.

Smiling, Nellie nodded.

Megge gently laid the thread over the child's neck and tied it loosely in the back.

Delona pointed to the stone visible just above the neck of Megge's tunic. "Why, it looks just like yours!"

Megge touched the stone at her throat. She looked from the babe to me and then down at my stone, which Delona was now comparing to the one she had given to the child.

"All three are just the same!" Delona proclaimed.

Megge's eyes met mine, and my heart swelled with love as we both looked down at our sister.

CHAPTER 93

MEGGE

I am sorry, Lachesis," I murmured, "that your rest in the ether was so brief. But I am thankful you did not tarry. The spirits of Tinker and the blacksmith will be swift to return, their memories fresh and their rage kindled anew. It will take all three of us to put it out."

CHAPTER 94

AMICE

"Thank you, Lachesis, for returning to us," I said in our silent language, my heart now light as I gazed at the newborn babe. "Megge and I shall protect you as you grow, just as you have protected Megge and watched over me."

CHAPTER 95

hat will you call the bairn, Nellie?" Dora called out over the din of a dozen women speaking at once.

A rush of emotion snatched my breath. I leaned closer to hear.

"The name came to me the moment I knew I was with child," Nellie said. She lifted the babe so the cooing women, already enchanted with the child, could see its face. "I shall call him *Lucas*."

Lucas! Amice and I shared smiles of relief and joy, then glanced back at the babe, who had begun to fret.

Nellie patted him and kissed his head, but he shrieked and writhed until an arm had escaped from the swaddling blanket. As he shook his fist furiously in the air, his tiny hand clutched the stone and tore it off. I watched in horror as it flew through the air, fell to the floor, and rolled to a stop at my feet.

Amice's smile froze. My gut heaved.

"There, there," Nellie whispered as she tucked his arm beneath the blanket. Smiling and nodding to herself, she said, "Now I know what I must call you!" She smiled into his face as he howled. "Your name can only be *Myghal*."

CHAPTER 96

AMICE

inker's name was *Mikkel*!" I called to Megge as I struggled to keep pace with her long strides through the copse.

"The sun is about to set, Amice. We must hasten our step if we are to get home before dark." Despite her haste, her voice was light, her eyes soft.

I rushed to add, "And Nellie named her baby *Myghal*." I was running now to keep with her. "That sounds very much like *Mikkel*." My rising voice trembled. "Do you think this child might be Tinker?"

"I do not know, Amice. But my heart is lighter now that Nellie's child was born alive and wailing. I am grateful beyond measure for that."

"But Mister Gough's name was *Michael*. Before that, it was *Mihalis*. Those names sound like *Myghal*, too!"

"Calm yourself, Amice." Megge stopped and knelt before me, her hands warm on my arms. She looked into my wild eyes and brushed my hair back from my face, tucking it under my coif.

"Yes, damaged spirits often return bearing the same name. And *Myghal* does sound very much like *Michael*." Her voice was quiet and assured. "But do you see me quaking?" She shook her head, her eyes steady on mine. "It does not frighten me. His spirit does not frighten me—nor does Tinker Penneck's. And do you know why?" She watched my face closely, her countenance calm, until I shook my head.

"Because we know they are returning. We shall make ready so that if what they learned in this life has not changed them, we are never again their prey."

"But how will we know who they are? Many boys have those names."

"Skills and habits can be more telling than a name, Amice. In every life, no matter his name, Mihalis has always been a smith—a swordsmith, an ironsmith, a blacksmith. And in every life since first we came to the cliffs, whether a huntress or a scribe, a man or a woman, Lachesis has been a protector, a defender. A reckoner. Will this child be a smith? A sheriff? Perhaps he will one day be a potter—like his father. Only time will tell."

Perhaps he will one day be a knife-man.

Her arm came around me and drew me close, and I knew I had naught to fear.

But that night, I trembled from guilt.

I felt certain that Lachesis had inspired Brighida to give Delona the goddess thread and had sent Delona the dream of the stone. Then, when Nellie learned she was with child, Lachesis whispered *Lucas* into her ear, so Megge and I would know by the child's name that Nellie's son was, indeed, our sister, Lachesis.

But he cast off the stone! Never would Lachesis have done that!

This baby is not Lachesis, I concluded, and it is all my fault. I opened those shutters, and a spirit desperate to return to the living world swept in and claimed that child—just as my spirit had swept in and claimed Anna. Now, Lachesis was trapped in the ether, and we were all at the mercy of the spirit I had let in through that window.

CHAPTER 97

MEGGE

We passed the weeks after the blacksmith's death and Myghal's birth in rest and quiet work—spinning thread, weaving cloth, and tending the sheep.

Amice finally told us of the horrors she had endured in the tower at the hands of Agnes Gough, Tinker Penneck, and Magdalene, her gaoler. But something else haunted her. She tossed and cried out in her sleep, never able to recall in the daylight what had troubled her in the dark.

One night, she awoke with a shout. "My fault!"

Ffion, Brighida, and I ran to her.

"... let him in!" she cried. "I let him in!" Her eyes, wild with fear, fastened on our faces.

"Who, Amice?" Brighida coaxed, her arm drawing Amice close. "Who did you let in?"

"My fault." She hung her head. "All my fault."

"What do you mean, Amice?" I asked. "What is your fault?"

"That Lachesis is wandering alone in the ether while Tinker Penneck basks in the warmth of his mother's arms—and grows stronger day by day."

"Tinker?" Brighida stared at her, open-mouthed.

Amice looked from Brighida to me, her torment raw. "I opened the window, Megge! I opened it so that Lachesis might come. But instead, Tinker's spirit claimed the child Lachesis was meant to be."

"Megge?" Holding Amice tight, her hand stroking the child's back, Brighida looked at me, aghast. "Opened a window? Tinker came in? What does she mean?"

I cast my mind back to Myghal's birth. Nellie was bearing down. I sat before her, waiting to receive the child. And Amice—

Where was Amice? I closed my eyes.

Show me.

Amice stood at Nellie's side until the child's head appeared—then she ran to the window and flung open the shutters.

"She opened the window as the child was being born," I told Brighida. "It seems she believes that by doing so, she invited Tinker's spirit in—and that Tinker's spirit claimed the child Lachesis was meant to be."

I spoke quietly to Amice. "You had no say in that child's birth. Nor in what he would be named or in what he will become."

Brighida looked at me, not understanding.

"Nellie had meant to call the baby *Lucas.*" I raised an eyebrow, and Brighida nodded. "But she suddenly named him *Myghal* instead."

"But all mothers struggle when choosing a child's name."

"Yes, but Tinker's real name was *Mikkel.* And the blacksmith's name was—"

"Ahhh." Brighida nodded slowly.

"Amice?" Ffion waited for her to lift her head from Brighida's shoulder and look at her. "Mark me well, child—you had no part in the return of any spirit. Do you hear me?"

Amice nodded slowly, but broke again into sobs before finally wiping her eyes and nose on Brighida's shoulder. When she had settled, I sat back. "Sleep now. We shall go to the village once we've broken our fast and look in on Nellie—and Myghal."

"No!"

"Yes. Women of Bury Down face their fears, so you shall face yours by looking upon Myghal. Together, we shall watch him as he grows. That is the only way we will know who he truly is."

Amice approached Nellie the next day as if the swaddled babe in her arms were a viper about to strike.

"Amice—" I frowned at her, shook my head, and touched her shoulder to coax her through the market stall.

"Megge! Amice!" Nellie left the woman who was looking at a bowl and came to us. She lowered the blanket to show us the baby's face.

"Three weeks have gone by, and thanks to your care we are both well.

I touched the child's rosy cheek. "You're a comely lad, aren't you, Myghal!"

Nellie blushed. "That was a fancy, Megge."

"What was a fancy?"

"Calling him *Myghal*. I named him for my father, who had died but a short time before I gave birth."

"Naming a child for his grandfather is not a fancy. Many children are named for a beloved grandparent. And you were grieving."

"Yes, Megge, I was grieving. But Cadan was not. And he did *not* love my father. The man roared, cursed, and fought with every man he believed had crossed him." Her voice softened. "And he believed poor Cadan had done just that. But he was my father, and he had just died. And here was his grandson, bellowing and shaking his fist just like him."

Amice and I smiled at the memory of that enraged child.

"When Cadan learned that I had called our son *Myghal*, he told me he wanted to give him the name that had come to him the moment I told him I was with child." She lifted the babe to her shoulder and smiled at me. "We baptized him yesterday. *Lucas*."

CHAPTER 98

*L*ucas!" Megge said, a smile on her face.

Nellie dipped her hand into a small pouch tied to her apron string. She took out the stone and the thread Delona had given her and held it out to me.

"I have kept this for you," she said. "I've put it on him many times, but those little fingers always tear it off, and he either throws it or puts it in his mouth. I fear one day he will swallow it. You and Megge kept me safe. Pray, keep this safe for Lucas, will you, Amice?"

I took the stone and assured her I would—for I prayed that Lucas would one day keep me safe.

But as we walked back to Bury Down, I recalled Megge telling me that names mattered less than skill or habits. Though the child was now named *Lucas*, how could I be certain he was truly Lachesis?

CHAPTER 99

MEGGE

As spring approached, ghostly dreams began to haunt my sleep—glimmers of tasks and troubles to come. Shadows of the Mentors I would one day summon.

Amice finally slept soundly, but each morning as we broke our fast, she would tell me that her sleep had been filled with dreams of Nellie's babe fighting with swords.

Then came the questions.

"How will we know if he is truly Lachesis? How will we know?"

"We will watch—and one day, we will see."

"But how will we be certain?"

CHAPTER 100

No response Megge could have given me would have dispelled my fears, so she proposed that we visit Lucas every few days "to come to know him." But spring came, and still I saw nothing that assured me that the child was Lachesis.

Just after May Day, we visited Nellie in her shop and found her setting out cups while Lucas, content in his cradle, gummed the shaft of an untipped arrow.

"Megge." I tugged her sleeve and pointed. "Look!"

Nellie came to us, smiling when she saw me point at Lucas.

"This child." She picked him up, laughing. "Never can he draw his eyes from Cadan's quiver—he reaches for the arrows the moment he sees them. So Cadan made him this." She eased the arrow from the child's fist and held it up so we could see.

"It's a willow branch covered in leather and decorated with feathers," she said, "a plaything his father made so Lucas would have an 'arrow' of his own. Now it soothes him as he teethes. Cadan calls him *Lucas the Hunter*."

CHAPTER 101

The sweet, breezy days of May brought long hours in the sheep pen, where I was teaching Amice to shear.

"Hold the shears like so," I said, guiding her hands. "Keep the tips up so as not to cut the tender skin."

"I once said the same thing to you, Megge." Morwen stood before me in spirit, smiling at Amice's first attempt to shear a ewe. "You always have preferred cutting fleece to cutting the thread I once gave you."

"I would prefer cutting off my own ear to cutting that thread!"

"This life has long suited you. Seems it suits our Clotho as well."

"Like this, little one." Taking Amice's hand once more, I tilted it up and guided it as she sheared.

"Lachesis has revealed herself to you, I see." Morwen smiled, her eyes bright, that dimple showing in her cheek. "Poor Cadan likely hoped his son would become a potter."

I brushed away some fleece, laughing. "He calls the boy *Lucas the Hunter*, so I doubt he will force him to throw pots."

But Morwen was no longer listening. Her eyes had lost their shine, her cheek its dimple. She watched me closely, her eyes soft on mine. After a moment, she looked down at my hand. "Do you wear it always?"

I held up my hand and splayed my fingers. There, on the long finger of my right hand, was the ring she had given me so long ago—the Guardian's ring. Four intertwining silver circles—life, death, transition, and rebirth.

"Always."

"Never take it off, Megge." Her gaze roamed over my face as if committing it to memory. "My work as Guardian is done—and I hear in your voice and see in your bearing that you know it is so. The wisdom, knowledge, and power that I have long guarded and wielded have returned to you, and you wear them with dignity."

She waited for me to respond, but I had no words. What was she saying?

"I've a favor to repay in the living world," she said.

"A favor? I shall gladly repay it for you."

"You cannot. I must do it. And I shall."

Understanding dawned. Morwen was returning to the living world. Her spirit was leaving me. Sorrow fell over me like a shroud. Grief, such as I had only ever felt when she passed from the living world, engulfed me. I wished I could wrap her in my arms and hold her fast.

"I won't know you when I return," she said, "so on the eve of my sixth natal day, take me to the grove. At midnight, show me your ring. For on that night, in Bury Down grove, seeing that ring will awaken me, and I will know you. Then you must show me my stone."

"Your stone?" I thought for a moment. "Your *head*stone? The cross in the grove?"

"Aye. When I see it, I will know my next path."

"Your next path . . ." I closed my eyes but saw only brown-robed men. I heard church bells toll matins and lauds. I smelled coltsfoot and thyme, tasted honey and mead.

Morwen's gaze drifted from the sheep pen to the creek, then from the creek to the cottage, and finally settled far in the distance on Bury Down grove.

"After you have shown me your ring and my cross," she said, her gaze returning to me, "take me for a walk down Priory Lane."

There it was. "You mean to serve Brother James."

"Aye. I owe him a great debt of gratitude." And there was that wry smile. "Already I've sent him an acolyte—a scholar who will one day teach healers."

"Timothy! The shy young man with the trembling hands!"

"Aye. Brother James's disease will take him slowly, but he shall never want for care, for Timothy and I—and Amice and you—shall tend him for his remaining years."

Knowing she would once more be at my side, I felt my sorrow at losing her turn to joy.

I searched the future for the child I was fated to lead to the grove as Morwen had once led me, but I could not see her face—nor her mother's—nor where she might be born. My heart, so light but a moment ago, now turned to lead.

Morwen's spirit began to fade.

"Morwen, wait! How shall I know you?"

"Megge . . ." That dimple appeared in her cheek. "Can't you guess?"

The rumble and clatter of a cart making its way across the pasture drew my eye. High on the driver's bench, smiling and waving, was Neville.

"Megge!" he shouted.

I looked back at Morwen.

Still smiling, she winked and was gone.

The Bury Down Chronicles

CHARACTERS

Books 1, 2, and 3: The Goddess Trilogy
Not every character occurs in every book
Listed by first name

Adaem: (*Ah-dehm´*): Captain of *The Navigator*. From Aldestowe.
> Husband of Gytha of Bury Down
> Father of Natalje
> Grandfather of Claris and "Mother"
> Great-grandfather of Megge and Brighida

Agnes Gough: (Agnes *Goff*): Conjurer
> Mother of Michael and Jenifer
> Grandmother of Harold, Vivienne, and Gwyneth Penneck
> Priestess of the Sisterhood (Book 3)

Aleydis: (*Ah-lee´-dis):* huntress. From Aldestowe.
> Daughter of Beatrix Couper. Sister of Arjen
> Aunt of Claris and "Mother"
> Great-aunt of Brighida and Megge

Alf: Shepherd and shearer
> Earl's man

Amice: Orphan from the North Coast

Anna: Daughter of lazar and farmer
> Orphan from the North Coast

Anwen: Huntress of Tintagel
> Scribe and protector of the writings of Murga

Arjen: Stonemason, builder, artist. From Aldestowe
> Former holder of *The Book of Seasons*
> Son of Beatrix Couper. Brother of Aleydis
> Husband of Natalje
> Father of Claris and "Mother"
> Grandfather of Megge and Brighida

Atropos: (At´-row-pose) Sister of Clotho and Lachesis
    One of the three Fates
    Clips the thread of life
    The Lady of the Cliffs (healer at the dawn of time)
Beatrix Couper: Midwife and conjurer
    Mother of Arjen and Aleydis
    Grandmother of Megge and Brighida
    Sister of Egbert Couper ("Roon")
Brighida: (*Bri-gee´-dah*): *Apprentice seer*
    Heir to The Book of Time
    Daughter of Claris, cousin of Megge
Britlen: Daughter of Kaatje and Tinker
Brother James: Benedictine monk, ordained priest
    Physician/surgeon trained by Megge's mother
Bryluen: (*Bree-loo´-en*)
    Apprentice to Murga
Christine: Assistant to Brother James
    Former apprentice of Megge's mother
Claris: Seer of Bury Down, Holder of *The Book of Time*
    Mother of Brighida
    Twin sister of "Mother"
    Aunt of Megge
    Widow of Gregory Carver
Clotho: Sister of Atropos and Lachesis
    One of the three Fates
    Spins the thread of life
Colluen: (*Cah-loo´-en*): Blacksmith.
    Rejected apprentice to Murga, the Seer of Bury Down
Delona Angwin: Sister of Neville,
    Daughter of Robert Angwin and Mistress Angwin
    Friend of Amice
Derwa: mother of Gytha
    A Mentor.
    Former holder of *The Book of Time*
    (Lowenna, in a former life)

Dora Tucker: Shopkeeper
    Wife of Gus
Edmund: Second Earl of Cornwall (reign: 1272-1300)
    Husband of Margaret de Clare, Countess of Cornwall
Egbert Couper ("Rudh"): Brother of Beatrix
    Uncle of Arjen and Aleydis
Eleanor the Healer: Healer in North Coast settlement
    Teacher of Anna
Elizabeth: Lady-in-waiting to Lady Margaret
Ffion (Fee-on): Former "Nursemaid" to Kaatje
    Sister of Morwen
Francis Penneck: Carter
    Husband of Jenifer Gough
    Father of Tinker, Harold, and Gwyneth
    George Gynneys (Mister Gynneys): Herder, shearer
    Father of Alf

Gregory Carver: Master carpenter
    Deceased husband of Claris
Gus Tucker: Weaver, tucker, wool merchant
    Husband of Dora
Gwyneth Penneck: Daughter of Francis and Jenifer Penneck
    Sister of Harold and Vivienne
    Half-sister of Tinker
Gytha: former Seer of Bury Down
    former holder of *The Book of Time*
    Wife of Adaem
    Mother of Natalje
    Grandmother of Claris and "Mother"
    Great-grandmother of Megge and Brighida
Harold Penneck: Assistant carter
    Son of Francis and Jenifer Gough Penneck
    Brother of Vivienne and Gwyneth
    Half-brother of Tinker

Hugh Caerlin: Herder
      Son of Lowenna
      Brother of Martyn
Irene: Wife of Odo
      Holder of *The Book of Time* in eleventh century
      A Mentor
      (Lowenna, in a former life)
Jago: Field hand
      Patient of Brother James
Jenifer Gough Penneck: Daughter of Agnes Gough,
      Sister of Michael Gough
      Second wife of Francis Penneck
      Mother of Harold, Vivienne, and Gwyneth Penneck
      Step-mother of Tinker Penneck
Kaatje: Wife of Tinker Penneck
      Mother of Britlen
      Daughter of Agnes Gough
      Sister of Michael Gough
Mihalis: Husband of Atropos
Mister Kendall: Surgeon at Restormel Castle
Lachesis: Sister of Atropos and Clotho
      One of the three Fates
      Measures the length of life.
Lady of the Cliffs: Atropos
      Goddess
      Deathbringer-turned-healer
Lowenna Caerlin: Homemaker
      Mother of Hugh and Martyn
      Assistant to Brother James (housekeeper)
Lucas Trelawney: son of Nellie and Cadan Trelawney
Magdalene: Gaoler for the Sisterhood
Margaret, Countess of Cornwall: Wife of Edmund,
      Second Earl of Cornwall

Martyn Caerlin: Weaver, Earl's man
      Son of Lowenna and Mister Caerlin
      Brother of Hugh

Megge: (*Meggie):* herder, shearer, apprentice weaver
      Heir to The Book of Seasons
      Daughter of "Mother"
      Niece of Claris, Cousin of Brighida

Michael Gough: (Michael *Goff):* Blacksmith
      Son of Agnes and Robert Gough
      Brother of Jenifer Gough Penneck and Kaatje

Morwen: Bard and shearer
      Companion of Megge
      Guardian of the Books

"Mother": Healer of Bury Down, Holder of *The Book of Seasons*
      Mother of Megge
      Sister of Claris, aunt of Brighida
      No first name. Called Mistress, Mother, Sister, Aunt, Niece
      Widow of stone mason

Murga: First Seer of Bury Down

Natalje: (*Nă-tal´ -ee)* Former holder of *The Book of Time*
      Wife of Arjen
      Mother of Claris and her unnamed twin sister ("Mother")
      Grandmother of Megge and Brighida

Nellie Trelawney: shopkeeper, wife of the village potter

Neville Angwin: Stonemason's apprentice, Earl's man
      Son of Robert Angwin

Odo: Manor lord of Bury Down in mid-eleventh century, at the
      time of the Norman conquest
      Husband of Irene

Polly Pounfrect: Governess at Restormel Castle
      Richard, First Earl of Cornwall (reign: 1257-1272)
      Son of John, King of England
      Father of Edmund, Second Earl of Cornwall
      Led crusades to the Holy Land

Robert Angwin: Stone mason
>Father of Neville

Robert Gough (Goff): Blacksmith
>Deceased husband of Agnes Gough
>Father of Michael Gough

Timothy: acolyte of Brother James
>Studies Medicine

Tinker Penneck: Real name :Mikkel
>Son of Francis Penneck and Francis's first wife (deceased)
>Half-brother of Harold and Gwyneth Penneck
>Husband of Kaatje
>Father of Britlen

Vivienne Penneck:
>Daughter of Jenifer Penneck and Gregory Carver

Vitale Magor: artist (deceased). Former holder of *The Book of Seasons*
>Father of Arjen
>Husband of Beatrix Couper

About the Author

Rebecca Kightlinger holds an MFA in creative writing from the University of Southern Maine's Stonecoast MFA program. The full-time writer of the *Bury Down Chronicles* series, she studies medieval medicine, Anglo Saxon wortcraft, the arts and manuscripts of the mystical healers, and the history of Cornwall.

About the Editor

Vinnie Kinsella is an editor and book publishing specialist from the Pacific Northwest. His work with books began when he and his second-grade classmates wrote and illustrated a story about the adventures of an ice-cream-loving giraffe. Years later, he earned his master's degree in writing and publishing from Portland State University. He has since helped hundreds of authors and publishers release quality books into the world. For more information about Vinnie's work, visit vinniekinsella.com.

About the Poet

Sappho (Born c. 610 BC- Died c. 570 BCE) was a musician and lyric poet who resided for most of her life in Mytilene on the island of Lesbos, Greece. Much of her work was found in quotations from other authors or discovered on fragments of papyrus in Oxyrhynchus, Egypt.

About the Designer

Tamian Wood, born near Oxford, England, is currently living and working in her cozy lake front office in North Florida. She works with several publishers and a growing number of indie authors. Her most famous client to date is Pope Francis, whose Encyclical Letter, won first place for cover design. She holds degrees in Computer Science and Graphic Design Technology, and is a proud member of Phi Theta Kappa National Honour Society. She can be reached at Tamian@BeyondDesignBooks.com, www.BeyondDesignBooks.com

About the Audiobook Narrator

Jan Cramer is a London born actress trained at The Central School of Speech and Drama and has worked in Theatre, TV, Film, and Radio. Now a very busy voice over artist and award winning Audiobook Narrator, Jan is proud to have narrated over 100 audiobooks. She has enjoyed every single one of them. Find her online at:
www.voiceannouncements.com

About the Translator

Canadian Anne Carson, translator of Sappho's Fragment 147, is an acclaimed poet, translator, and professor of Classics. Her body of work has earned her the Pushcart Prize, the Griffin Trust Award for Excellence in Poetry, and fellowships from the Mac Arthur and the Guggenheim Foundations. Her lovely translation of Sappho's Fragment 147 was published in If Not, Winter, Fragments of Sappho, in 2002.